Could it be something of Kent's they were after? Something he'd kept hidden? He was good at keeping secrets. In fact, he'd been a master at it. After his death, I'd packed the few possessions he hadn't moved out of the apartment and sent them to his parents. I'd kept nothing except the gold wedding band he'd thrown at me from across the room and his cell phone.

Kent's death.

Hard to even think those words, much less say them out loud. It was all still so surreal.

Maybe everything that had happened in Bitter Ridge was karma. Maybe the Universe was finally giving me exactly what I deserved. Kent's death had been my fault. And no matter how much he had deceived me, or betrayed me, or reduced my sad little trusting heart to shrapnel, I could never forgive myself.

I laid my head on my knees and closed my eyes. I rocked my body back and forth, like a child trying to soothe itself when sleep will not come. Then at last, in the cool dark shadows of the night, I began to cry.

Oh, God, I am so sorry.

I hadn't loved Kent for a long time. At the end of our marriage, I hadn't even liked him. But I had never wished him dead.

The House on Crow Mountain

by

Rebecca Lee Smith

This is a work of fiction. Names, characters, places, and incidents are either the product of the author's imagination or are used fictitiously, and any resemblance to actual persons living or dead, business establishments, events, or locales, is entirely coincidental.

The House on Crow Mountain

Contact Information: info@thewildrosepress.com

Cover Art by *Kim Mendoza*

The Wild Rose Press, Inc.
PO Box 708
Adams Basin, NY 14410-0708
Visit us at www.thewildrosepress.com

Publishing History
First Edition, 2021
Trade Paperback ISBN 978-1-5092-3591-9
Digital ISBN 978-1-5092-3592-6

Published in the United States of America

Dedication

For Amy.
Friend, daughter-in-law, beautiful inside and out.
And one of the strongest, bravest women I know.

Other Wild Rose Press Titles by Rebecca Lee Smith:

A Shadow on the Ground
A Dance to Die For

Chapter One

Never drive faster than your guardian angel can fly.

"Fat chance of that." I glanced up from the tiny sticker someone had stuck to the dashboard of my rental car and focused on the narrow winding road. I'd kept the little Ford Fiesta ten miles under the speed limit all the way in from the airport, and the drive through the Blue Ridge Mountains had still been one mini-adrenaline rush after another.

I pulled into a foggy scenic overlook, bemoaning the fact there was zero cell service, and grabbed the map I'd picked up at the North Carolina Welcome Center. I reached for the bag of candy I used to keep myself calm and selected a dark chocolate square, perilously warm from sitting too near the heating vent. With two miles and six switchbacks to go, I risked the inevitable mess it would cause and tore the foil open with my teeth.

One single drop of dark raspberry chocolate dripped onto the center of the map. One tiny dark red dot. Just like the one that had been sitting in the middle of Kent's forehead when the coroner rolled him over on his back.

I shoved the memory out of my head—something I had gotten decidedly better at in the last two months—and tossed the map on the seat.

It had been a long day.

And it was about to get longer.

I hadn't driven a car in years, even though I'd kept my license up-to-date living in New York City, hoping that one day I'd come back to the mountains I loved so much. I had returned two months ago with that same hope in my heart but didn't stay. I was only destined to live in Asheville, North Carolina, for exactly one week and one day. Long enough to unpack eighteen boxes of household goods, lose a husband twice, and see my rent-controlled apartment with the sweeping mountain views turned into a crime scene.

I pulled into the nursing home parking lot, taking a few seconds to admire the three shiny black crows going at it over what looked like the end of a discarded bean burrito, and found a space behind a towering privet hedge. As soon as I switched off the engine, the rented Fiesta, which had not lived up to its party name, discharged a death rattle that shook me to the core. The lights from Laurel Haven Assisted Living and Senior Care Center shone through the rain, turning the wide expanse of grass into a glittering green carpet. I snapped my collapsible umbrella open and made my way along a lighted path to the front entrance. It was the first time since jumping in the Uber outside my friend Esther's Manhattan apartment that I hadn't felt like someone was watching me.

The brick nursing home appeared larger than the photos on its website, but the fancy landscaping and the cleverly placed floodlights couldn't hide the fact that it looked like a maximum-security prison.

A man in his early forties or mid-thirties, if he'd had a rough life, leaned against the brick wall beside the front door. His hands were shoved into the pockets of a ratty safari jacket and a rain-soaked Carolina Panthers baseball cap covered his head. He smiled as I approached, slashing a long dimple on the left side of his cheek.

"I heard your engine sputter," he said in that vowel slurring North Carolina accent that used to make me weak in the knees. "You having car trouble, ma'am?"

"Probably, but I'm fine. Thanks. It's a rental. I'll get them to check it out later."

His brown eyes studied me closely, and his smile faded. His gaze cut away from my face then lasered back to it with a rush of recognition. The very thing I'd hoped to avoid. He could have seen my picture splashed across the front page of the *Asheville Citizen-Times*. The tiny town of Bitter Ridge was slammed into a valley between five mountains, some in the Blue Ridge and some in the Smokies, less than thirty miles from Asheville. The residents were bound to get the Asheville paper.

A squall of rain suddenly let loose and pounded the pavement.

"Good night for ducks," he drawled, staring down at me from the landing, sizing me up.

"Not this duck." I turned away and pulled my jacket closer around me, quickly moving past him. The last thing I needed was some local good old boy—or any boy—trying to pick me up. If he'd recognized my face from the news, he only wanted to satisfy his morbid curiosity.

Laurel Haven's electric doors slid open with a *whoosh*, sounding like the *Starship Enterprise*, then closed behind me with a reassuring clank. I blew out a ragged breath. *Stop it,* I told myself. I was just being paranoid. Everything was fine.

I brushed the rain off my short cotton jacket and crossed the foyer to the information desk, trying to ignore the knot hardening in my empty stomach. A gray-haired lady in a Pepto-Bismol pink smock glanced up and smiled.

"I'm Emory Chandler," I said, my mouth dry as dirt. "I'm here to see Priscilla Austen. I talked to her nurse this morning. She's expecting me."

The smock lady nodded and pushed a black button on the edge of her desk, setting off some secret silent alarm in the distance. A few minutes later, a young nurse's aide with blue streaked hair, black nail polish, and a gold nose ring appeared as my guide. I followed her down a maze of corridors, past stacks of empty dinner trays waiting for transport back to the kitchen, and tiny rooms where elderly residents watched *Wheel of Fortune* or slept. In the hall, a rail-thin woman in a wheelchair crooned to a baby doll cradled in her arms.

I tried not to peer into the resident's rooms as we power-walked down the hall—it felt rude to invade what little privacy they had left—but I couldn't help it. The side of aging no one ever believes will happen to them flashed at me like a slideshow. Was this where you ended up when you had no place else to go? When your body broke down and clogged up like an old carburetor? When your mind, once so sharp and clever, couldn't quite latch on to someone else's version of reality?

Whoever said getting old ain't for sissies must have spent time in a nursing home. I missed my parents more than anything, but I was grateful they had been spared these final indignities.

As we turned the corner and entered the hospital wing, the noise faded from a friendly dull roar to deathly quiet. The odor that hung in the air like a breath had also changed, from the faint, sharp tang of urine to the woodsy scent of pine oil disinfectant, a scent no self-respecting pine forest would ever try to duplicate.

The aide slowed her pace and waited for me to catch up. “You're the portrait artist from New York,” she said between chomps of grape-flavored gum.

“That's right.”

“Miss Priscilla showed me that picture you painted of your dad. It was awesome.”

“Thanks.”

“I want to go to art school someday. I’m just volunteering here so it’ll look good on my college application.” She stretched a ribbon of purple elastic across her tongue and popped it. “I Googled you. The article I read said you moved from New York to Asheville with your husband, then moved back to New York again after he died.”

“Gotta love Google.”

“One of the nurses said your husband moved in with his new boyfriend, then stopped by your place to pick up something and got shot by a burglar. Right between the eyes. Just like on *The Walking Dead.*”

“Just like it,” I whispered.

The memory I could usually hold at bay slammed into my brain: A policeman gripping my arm saying, “*Don’t worry, ma’am. He didn’t feel a thing.*” Me, opening my mouth to thank him, but instead, turning and vomiting into the brass umbrella stand.

“Did they ever find out who killed him?” *Snap-*

pop-chomp.

"No," I said, fighting the urge to shove her aside and run.

The image of Kent's dead body lying on our white alpaca rug with his leather backpack still grasped tightly in his hand blazed across my mind. The back of my eyes began to ache. I pulled my purse strap higher on my shoulder.

The girl stopped at the nurse's station. An older nurse wearing lime green scrubs and a sour expression on her weary face looked up from her computer screen. "Are you Mrs. Chandler?"

"Yes. I'm Emory Chandler."

"You can go, Tracy," she said to the girl, then regarded me coolly as if she dealt with outsiders a hundred times a day. Every day. "They explained about your aunt's stroke on the phone? That she still hasn't regained consciousness?" She didn't wait for a reply. "For the moment, she's stabilized, but the longer she remains in a coma, the less hopeful her situation will become. She has a living will and a DNR on file, but since you have POA, I thought I should—"

"Whoa," I said. "DNR? POA?"

The nurse sighed. "Do Not Resuscitate. Power of Attorney."

"I have power of attorney?"

"You are listed as next of kin, Mrs. Chandler, with full medical and financial power of attorney. Miss Austen's account here at Laurel Haven is paid through July, which is the end of our fiscal year, and—"

"How is she?" I said around the stone in my throat.

"I can't say what her prognosis is at her age—"

"Eighty-three."

"Right. She's one of our long-term residents and she's deteriorated quite a bit since her sister died."

"But that was two years ago."

"Didn't her brother—your father—die recently?"

"Four months ago." A steel band tightened around my chest.

Her expression softened. "It's hard losing so many loved ones in such a short time."

"Tell me about it."

She peered over her rimless glasses. "We're all rooting for Miss Austen to bounce back. Bitter Ridge is a small town. Most of us have known her since we were children." She motioned for me to follow her. "You're the niece from New York, aren't you?"

"I'm the only niece."

She nodded. "Well, it's good she has family with her now."

If the nurse had been surprised I hadn't visited my aunt in the two years Pris had lived at the home, she had the good grace not to show it. She held the privacy curtain open while I went in. "Let me know if I can get you anything. We're right outside if you need us."

Need them? Need them for what?

I waited for her to leave then walked to the end of the bed.

Aunt Pris lay on her back hooked up to a tangle of wires and tubes connected to a vital sign monitor with colorful flashing lights. I watched her jagged heartbeat scroll across the screen then curled my fingers around the cold metal railing. Finally, I looked down at her face.

The Aunt Pris I remembered had been round and robust, bursting with life and a wicked sense of humor.

This woman—the one wearing Pris' name on a plastic ID bracelet—was tiny and shrunken and still. The sharp ridge of her collar bone pushed against the thin hospital gown. Her braided hair, almost as long and curly as mine, draped over her knobby shoulder like a frayed gray rope. Beneath the plastic oxygen tube taped to her nose, loose skin pooled into her neck.

The resemblance to my father caught me off-guard. I had inherited the Austen height, the clear blue-gray eyes, and the ungodly natural curls, but the wide mouth and high, proud forehead were traits the three Austen siblings shared alone. Tears stung my eyes. I hated seeing her lying there like a corpse. As if she had already passed.

I studied her face. There were no more Austens on the planet to remind me of my father. This was it.

"Do you remember the first time I came to Crow Mountain?" I said softly. "Aunt Portia was away on one of her trips, and we had the whole place to ourselves for the summer. Just you and me. I remember that house so clearly. I don't think I'll ever forget living there."

I had been a skinny sassy thirteen-year-old starved for the kind of home life it had never occurred to my jet-setting parents to give me. At school, I had been obsessed with old TV shows, and to me, life on Crow Mountain was like *Little House on the Prairie* and *The Andy Griffith Show* all wrapped up into one comforting homespun fantasy. Those glorious sun-drenched days I'd spent with Pris on Crow Mountain still haunted my dreams with such vivid yearning, I was sure I could smell the scent of honeysuckle long after I shook myself awake.

I leaned over the bed railing and touched her arm

beneath the white crisscross of IV tape. The blotchy bruised skin felt like warm tissue paper.

"It's just you and me now," I said. "Mother, Father, Portia, Edward, Kent—they're all gone. They're all dead." My heart caught hard in my throat.

Pris turned her head. Just a fraction of an inch, but I saw it move. Her eyes, always so blue and bright, twitched beneath the delicate folds of skin covering her lids.

"I'm back, Aunt Pris. I've come back home."

I was deep in the mountains of western North Carolina. Again.

But this time I was there as an orphan and a widow, of sorts, for what was probably the last time.

Whether my last living relative wanted me there or not.

Chapter Two

As I left Laurel Haven, the rain that had been hammering the Blue Ridge for the past two hours had finally downgraded to an annoying drizzle. I tucked my umbrella beneath my arm. My hair already resembled a mop that had seen one too many kitchen floors, so covering it with a flimsy travel umbrella wasn't going to change anything. I glanced to my left, curious to see if the man I'd spoken to was still standing beside the front door.

He was.

My eyes flicked from his face to the toes of his scuffed Timberland boots and back to his face in record time. It was a nice face. A face a girl might think she could trust. But my days of trusting anybody, especially a good-looking guy with an irresistible southern accent, were over.

I pulled my chin into the snug of my collar and started for the parking lot, hoping I could disappear into the sea of cars before he noticed me.

"Emory?" the man said.

I stopped and turned around. He had the name right, although I doubted if he could spell it. I hadn't expected anyone to recognize me at a nursing home in the middle of nowhere, much less two people in less than an hour.

"You're Emory Austen Chandler, right? Miss

Austen's niece?"

A shadow from the chipped light sconce fell across his jawline. One of those tiny clefts that looked like it had been karate chopped at birth split the middle of his chin. His thick brows shielded a pair of liquid brown eyes that could have given Bambi a run for his money and at the moment, didn't seem all that thrilled to be looking at me.

"I'm Emory Chandler." I could feel my hackles go up for no apparent reason other than the fact he knew my name. "And you are?"

"James St. Clair. I'm a—my family is old friends of your aunt's. I've seen the photograph of you that she keeps in her room. When I saw you tonight, I thought I recognized your—"

"—curly hair?"

"Well, yeah. And it's blonde, but it's pretty wild. Hair like that is hard to miss."

"Then I guess I'd better start investing in some hats." I reached up and smoothed the curls I'd corralled into a ponytail that morning. As if it would make a difference. I had always despised my bushy hair. Kent used to call me Miss Frizzle.

"Nice to meet you." I forced myself to smile and hold out my hand.

"Nice of you to finally visit your aunt."

My hand floated in the air like some strange appendage I hadn't noticed before and didn't know how to use. Once I realized he wasn't going to shake it, I let it drop. "I live in New York," I said as if that were the only explanation he needed. But if he were friends with Pris, he probably already knew where I lived. He probably knew a lot of things.

"Yes, you live in New York," he said. "Except for the weeks you lived in Asheville."

"Except for that."

"Then let me ask you something."

"Go ahead."

He started down the front steps. "Exactly what kind of person abandons her eighty-three-year-old aunt, lets her pine away in a nursing home for two years, then shows up the minute she has a stroke and the inheritance looks like a sure thing?"

"What?"

"You heard me."

"I—" And the hackles were back up. "You…you don't know what you're talking about."

"A couple of months ago, you moved to Asheville, less than an hour away. But you never came to see her. Never even called. She kept waiting and waiting for you to show up, but you couldn't be bothered to find the time."

Blood crept up the column of my neck like a heat-seeking missile. "This is—none of this—is any of your business." I turned to leave.

"Not so fast." James caught my elbow and spun me back around. "Look at your face. Guilt is plastered all over it."

"That's not guilt. That's the expression I use when I'm two seconds away from calling the cops." I jerked my elbow out of his grasp. "Who do you think you are?" We stood glaring at each other under the streetlamp, my words crackling between us. "You may know what my hair looks like from a photograph, but you don't know me. Or my life. Or my intentions. I don't give a flying flip what you think about my relationship with my aunt, so you can take your judgmental—"

"Everything okay, miss?" A heavyset man holding a small black umbrella over his head stepped off the portico and walked toward us. "Is this man bothering you?"

"No," I said. "He's…we were just having a disagreement."

"Because if he's bothering you—"

"He's not," I said firmly. "Everything is fine."

"The lady says she's fine, Melvin," James said. "So you can leave us alone and continue trolling the parking lot with your cute little Mary Poppins umbrella."

"Melvin Owens, ma'am." He held out his stubby hand. "Don't think I've had the pleasure. Are you a friend of this man?" He smiled broadly, mashing his jowls into the collar of his green windbreaker, looking like Toad of Toad Hall's great uncle. "Because if you are, I'd call that a miracle. I didn't think James St. Clair had any friends left in this town."

"Thanks, Melvin," James said.

Melvin sucked in a wheezy gulp of air and shrugged. "I just thought if she *wasn't* friends with you, I'd give her a heads up and let her know what kind of an ass wipe she's dealing with."

"She's Priscilla Austen's niece," James said.

So much for moving around town anonymously.

"Well, I'll be damned." Melvin's little piggy eyes squinted at me. "I shoulda known that. She sure looks like an Austen, don't she?"

"I need to be going." I fumbled in my pocket for my keys and backed away. "Nice meeting you, Melvin. Nice meeting you, James. Wish I could stay and chat—

because it's been so very much fun—but I really have to go."

"I'll hang around until I know your car's going to start," James said.

"Are you having car trouble?" Melvin said. "Because I'll be glad to call the garage for you." He lowered his voice. "You don't want James St. Clair helping you, miss. Ask anybody around here and they'll tell you not to trust him as far as you can throw him." He grinned. "Which ain't very far."

"Goodnight." I gave Melvin the sincerest smile I could manage, ignored James, turned on my heel, and didn't slow down until I'd unlocked my rental car and slid beneath the steering wheel. It took me a few tries to get it started, but once I did, I sailed past James and Melvin with my head held high. Melvin had said the people of Bitter Ridge distrusted James. If that were true, then how on earth did Aunt Pris come to be such good friends with him?

I shook off that disturbing thought and forced myself to concentrate on my driving. Getting to the hotel in one piece had catapulted me to the top of my priority list.

Traveling through the narrow valley on the winding road toward town, I felt like I was moving through a dream. Wispy gray clouds clung to the mountains, floating across the face of Old Baldy like tufts of cotton. The setting sun made a brief visit, spilling unexpected shards of amber light across the pavement. I lowered the car window and let the cool air caress my face. Everything, as Aunt Pris used to say, smelled green.

I drove past small but well-kept tobacco farms, an

abandoned gas station, a couple of diners with names like Carla's Country Cookin' and the Wild Thyme Café. I passed country churches with white pointed steeples that reached to the sky, grassy rolling fields spotted with brown cattle, an empty wooden produce stand waiting to be filled with homegrown tomatoes and sweet corn and okra. The tension in my shoulders and neck began to melt away. I thought of the Austen house on Crow Mountain and all the things I loved most about it: The wide brick fireplace with its carved wooden mantel, the warm cozy kitchen, my white iron bed with painted forget-me-nots on the headboard, the cold rushing water in Stoney Creek, the inherent sense of belonging I'd felt.

I'd never known that kind of domestic security with my parents. I loved them dearly, but growing up, I rarely saw them. They traveled ten months out of the year, and except for holidays and the odd visit to my boarding school, I was left to manage on my own. Something I got really good at it over the years. But the more I excelled at becoming self-sufficient, the more I longed for a normal family like the ones I saw in Disney movies and on TV. Why didn't I just go back and live there if it meant so much to me? Good question. And one I asked myself over and over. Pride, I guessed. And getting my adolescent feelings hurt when I begged to go back the following summer, and the summer after that, but was never allowed to return. Aunt Pris always had some reason why I couldn't visit that year. And the older I became, the flimsier her excuses seemed to me.

Maybe I could finally get a straight answer about that, too, while I was here.

I parked the car beside the McAlister Inn. I'd chosen to stay there the first night because as a teen, I'd been obsessed with its gray stone façade towering over the center of town like the left wing of Hogwarts Castle. I'd always wanted to see the inside of it and was sure it would be the perfect place to get my bearings before I moved into my aunt's empty house on Crow Mountain.

I rolled my bag to the edge of the stone veranda and looked through the arched opening. The Blue Ridge Mountains curled around the northern end of Bitter Ridge like a sleeping dragon then trailed off, one hazy layer at a time, into the distance. I gazed down Main Street toward the town square. Twenty-two years had changed the little town. But not by much.

The old brick and stone buildings that had been the hub of Bitter Ridge's artists' community housed quaint specialty shops patronized by tourists from the nearby ski resorts, a major part of the town's winter economic support. Several art galleries were still prominently featured, so it looked like the downtown art scene, which had always seemed so magical to me, was still thriving. The huge elms on either side of the street were gone. I remembered them reaching into the sky like green guardian angels to form an arc of shade. The fancy wrought iron light posts were still there, spruced up now with glossy black paint and swinging baskets of red geraniums. The streetlamps flashed on. In the gathering dusk, the cobblestone sidewalks beneath them glowed like shiny brown jewels.

A chill danced across my shoulders and down my spine. There it was again. The feeling that someone, somewhere was watching me.

I glanced behind me, half-expecting to see a shadowy figure hunkered down in the rhododendron with a pair of binoculars, but there was nothing. I scanned the upper windows of the four-story hotel. Again, nothing. If someone had been spying on me, they were gone now.

Since Kent's death, my imagination had clocked too many hours churning out chilling scenarios and expecting my brain to deal with them. It was a game it played. And I hated it. My best friend Esther had been right. Instead of retreating to her New York apartment after Kent died, I should have slapped on those big girl panties and thrown myself into the world again.

I pushed open the door to the McAlister Inn and gasped with delight. High ceilings with amber and gold stained-glass panels, Art Deco light fixtures, an intricately carved front desk. It was gorgeous. A little rundown if you looked closely, but still impressive.

"I have a reservation." The girl behind the desk didn't look old enough to vote, much less take a sip out of the beer bottle she stashed hurriedly under the counter.

"Hey, I'm Maddie," she said cheerfully. "You must be Mrs. Chandler." Her smile deepened a vertical dimple on the left side of her angular face.

"That would be me."

"Welcome to the McAlister." She swiveled the huge reservation book around facing me. "I know, right?" She rolled her dark eyes. "But we're kind of old-school here. I've got your credit card on file, so all you need to do is sign in. You're in Room 309." She handed me a key and laughed. "People freak out because it's a real key, but Mr. Spencer says converting to those little plastic cards is just good money down the drain."

"And he's right," a man's voice echoed beneath the counter.

"Jeez, Gordon," Maddie cried. "I thought you'd already left."

"Sorry, kid." The man raised up from behind the massive desk and gave me a little salute. "Gordon Spencer. I took your reservation this morning. Sorry you had to phone. The website's down again. Thought you were going to work on that for me today, Maddie."

"You said I could do it tomorrow."

Gordon laughed. "She's right. I did. You're only booked for one night, Mrs. Chandler, but if you decide to stay longer, we're never full this time of year. We're doing repairs on the second floor, so I put you on the third. Hope that's okay. We have an elevator."

"That's fine."

I smiled back at him and mentally took stock. Sandy blond hair, pale blue eyes, shoulders that didn't want to quit. He reminded me of Kent. A more masculine Kent, as it turned out. He was shorter than Kent, and a bit stockier, but handsome. Both men had been on the front row when the good looks had been handed out.

"I have to run, but Maddie's going to take good care of you. Aren't you, Maddie?"

"Yes, sir," Maddie said.

"And not talk her ear off."

"No, sir."

Gordon tucked a brown cardboard folder under his arm. "If you need anything, just call the front desk."

"I will," I said. "Thanks."

Maddie waited until her boss had disappeared inside the adjoining restaurant to roll her dark brown eyes again, this time accompanied by a head shake. "Gordon is pretty hands-on. Drives the staff crazy. But I guess it's better than working at Gene's Burger Bar, which is the only other job I could get for the summer." The soft cadence of her Western Carolina accent slid over each vowel like melted butter.

The entrance bell tinkled. Maddie's gaze shot past me to the double front doors. She pushed her dark bangs back from her face and sighed softly. A gangly boy in his early twenties shuffled across the creaky floor toward us. Dark blond hair framed his narrow face in long unwashed strings. A denim jacket, tied low on his narrow hips, encircled his baggy jeans like a holster. The picture on the front of his snug black T-shirt showed a vampire biting a girl's neck with the phrase *Love Sucks* printed beneath it in white.

"I'm *so* glad you're here, Jackson," Maddie cooed. "But don't let Gordon see you."

Jackson stared at me as I walked past.

"Is that her?" he asked.

"*Shhh*," Maddie whispered. "She'll hear you."

"I don't care," he said. "That money-grubbing bitch sure didn't waste any time getting here, did she?"

****

I stepped off the elevator with my cheeks burning. If the town goth thought I was a gold digger, what would the rest of Bitter Ridge think? I already knew the answer to that. Courtesy of James St. Clair.

I gazed down the hall and shuddered.

The McAlister Inn had definitely seen better days. The lobby was a work of art, but the third floor looked like Norman Bates lived there: threadbare carpet, peeling wallpaper, a whiff of stale cigarettes lingering in the air. The place was shabby but oozing with character. It could be a real showstopper if someone had a boatload of money to renovate it.

Thankfully, my room was clean and cozy, although I doubted if my parents would have stayed there. I heaved my heavy suitcase onto the luggage rack and suddenly felt ravenous. I hadn't eaten since scarfing down a stale cinnamon roll at LaGuardia airport, and I was starving. It was close to eight o'clock. According to the cardboard sign on the dresser, the restaurant downstairs would be closing soon. It had looked deserted when I'd waited for the elevator, but there had been piano music drifting from the bar. Always a good sign.

I grabbed my purse and headed downstairs.

I glanced at my reflection in the elevator door and winced. The last two months had taken their toll. The gaunt, too thin face stared back at me with a haunted expression in its eyes. I rubbed my finger pads over the bluish tint beneath them that no amount of concealer could hide.

"Stop it," I said. "Just stop it."

I went in and sat at the bar, over to the side where I could watch the front entrance. Then proceeded to devour a fried chicken sandwich on homemade sourdough bread with a large order of dinner fries. The day was catching up with me, but I slowly began to relax. I sipped a glass of chardonnay and looked around appreciatively. It was the kind of dark, cheesy bar that I loved: a stuffed trout mounted on the wall, netted candle bowls flickering on the tables, a middle-aged man merrily slaughtering "Here Comes the Sun" on a baby grand. Strictly old-school like Maddie had said. Which may have explained why no one in the place except me looked like they were under sixty.

"I see you found my favorite bar," a deep baritone rumbled behind me.

I swiveled around and almost spun off into James St. Clair's arms.

"What are you doing here? Have you come to run me out of town?" I pretended to search the room behind him. "Where's the angry mob waving pitchforks and torches?"

"They're waiting outside."

"I see. Well, if I just finished my last meal, then I'm glad I ordered the fries."

He slid onto the stool next to me and signaled the bartender.

"So will the mob mind if I finish my wine? Or do I have to leave now?"

He chuckled softly. "I'm lying. I sent them home."

"You're still lying."

"Okay. Then I'm apologizing."

"You'd best be careful, miss." The bartender shook her overly processed blonde hair and winked at James. "He looks sweet enough, but believe me, he ain't nothin' but trouble."

"Actually, you're not the first person to tell me that," I said. "And I've only been in town for two hours."

"Aw, Doreen," James said. "Just when she was starting to like me."

Doreen poured him a shot of Jameson whiskey. "Is the town council meeting over already? Cause your sister just went out back with you know who."

James nodded. "No refills tonight, I'm driving. But put the lady's wine on my tab." He sipped his whiskey and looked at me. "My sister works at the inn. I'm here to pick her up, but it looks like she's out by the Dumpster spending some quality time with her boyfriend."

"How romantic."

"And now for that apology." He cleared his throat. "Would you like to sit with me at a table? My good friend Doreen will vouch for my moral character."

"He's the best," Doreen said.

"All right." I didn't have anywhere to go except upstairs. And the promise of an apology—from any man—intrigued me.

I grabbed my wine and followed him to a table near the window.

"Not too many people here tonight," he said. "More stay during the winter ski season. It didn't used to be like this. It used to be packed. At least on the weekends. The McAlister has fallen on hard times."

He lifted his whiskey glass. Candlelight sparkled across his knuckles and up the side of his hand like a fine golden spray. I studied his face. He wasn't what I would call handsome; his nose was too long for that. His face was all angles and hollows, light disappearing into shadows. A nightmare to paint. His jaw was covered with the requisite layer of five o'clock scruff that most women find sexy until it's sandpapering their faces. And he wasn't my type. I'd always fallen for the elegant, refined ones. The ones who reminded me of my father. This man was too rough around the edges and woodsy for my taste. He might have deep dark eyes and a killer grin, but five bucks said he slept in boxers and a plaid shirt.

"I'm sorry I insulted you back at Laurel Haven," he said. "You're right, I don't know you. And I had no right to judge. I hate it when people jump to conclusions about me. So, I'm sorry. I apologize."

"Apology accepted."

An elderly couple got up and began to dance beside the piano. The woman slid her arms around the man's neck and smiled when he leaned down and whispered in her ear.

"They're cute, aren't they?" James said.

"They remind me of my parents."

"Your parents look like Syd and Elsie Fogleman?"

"No, the way they're dancing, gazing into each other's eyes as if they're the only two people in the world. My parents were like that."

"Then you were lucky." His eyes met mine.

"Why does Melvin dislike you so much?"

"Melvin dislikes everybody. Even his wife." James laughed. "Especially his wife."

"Why were you at the nursing home tonight? Checking on Pris?"

"I was picking up my mother. She volunteers at Laurel Haven, and her car's in the shop. She insisted I pick up my sister tonight, who doesn't drive to work in the hopes that her boyfriend, who my mother neither likes nor trusts, will give her a ride home. So I've basically been sent here to thwart young love."

"What do you do for a living? When you're not picking fights with the locals or protecting your sister's honor?"

"I restore houses. Really old, really big houses. The

kind you have to pay an entrance fee at the front gate to look at."

A man in a mechanic's jumpsuit sauntered up to our table. He stared at James then wrinkled his nose as if he had walked into a horse stall that needed to be mucked.

"James," the man said. "How are things, buddy?" The man's auburn goatee bobbed up and down on his beefy chest. His hand gripped a metal toolbox.

James stared at his drink, then lifted the whiskey without looking up. "Hey, Delbert. Working kind of late, aren't you?"

"The freezer in the kitchen's out again."

"I'm sorry."

"I'll just bet you are." Delbert pulled a handkerchief from his back pocket and wiped the back of his neck. Then he glanced at me. "Sorry you had to hear that, ma'am. But if it weren't for your friend here, I'd be home tonight with my family studying God's word instead of working an extra job to make ends meet."

"Not now, Delbert," James said quietly.

"You wouldn't know about working two jobs, would you, Jamie-boy? You only know how to swindle your neighbors out of their hard-earned money. Proverbs says, 'Lying lips are an abomination to the Lord.' God won't forget you betrayed the people who put their faith in you. You're the devil, James St. Clair. No wonder that pretty little gal left you standing at the altar."

James let go of his glass like a discharged torpedo. It bounced once, splashing whiskey on the tabletop before rolling sideways against the webbed candle holder.

Doreen tossed James a bar towel and glared at Delbert. “The freezer, Del.”

“I best see to it, then.” Delbert tipped his cap to me. “Ma’am, I feel it’s my Christian duty to warn you about this man. If you’re gonna keep company with him, you need to ask our Lord and Savior to protect you.”

“Delbert!” Doreen stood at the kitchen door with her hands on her hips.

Delbert hoisted his toolbox. “I’ll be praying for you, miss.”

I waited until Delbert had disappeared through the swinging kitchen door then stood and extracted a twenty from my purse.

“Don’t let Delbert scare you off,” James said. “He’s the head honcho at one of the churches on the other side of Crow Mountain. He’s an extremist. And a little scary. Take anything he says with a grain of salt.”

I avoided James’ eyes. “I need to go. It’s been a long day.”

He leaned back and folded his arms across his chest. The same haunted look I saw in the mirror every day washed over his face. “Then don’t let *me* scare you off. What just happened was—”

“You don’t need to explain.” I stepped back toward the door.

“Delbert is real big on sharing his religious views, which, I’ve come to realize, includes holding a grudge. The eye for an eye thing, I guess. So please don’t—”

“Really, it’s all good. No conclusion jumping here.”

“Right.”

"Goodnight." I turned and made a beeline for the elevator.

My self-esteem had taken a colossal hit when Kent left me for someone I couldn't compete with, and the last thing I needed was a man in my life the local bartender described as trouble. Everyone I'd seen interact with James so far, except Doreen, had a huge ax to grind. Red flags everywhere. Which made me want to know just how close he was to my Aunt Pris. And why.

Back in my room, I made sure the chain on my door was secure, then unzipped my bag and flung the canvas flap back. I stared at my belongings. My shoes were lined up end to end across the flexible lid. Which was something of a miracle because I always arranged them side to side. *Always.*

I pawed through my clothes looking for the card the TSA handlers leave telling you they've searched your checked bag. It was usually lying on top, but this time there was no card. Anywhere. And where was the luggage lock? I was sure I had snapped on the little red lock with the black swivel numbers. The combination was always the same: 3-3-0. Van Gogh's birthday. Hadn't I put it on? After getting the emergency call telling me about Pris' stroke, I'd been in such a hurry to make a plane reservation and get to her, I'd packed like a criminal on the run. And the Uber had gotten there faster than I'd expected. Had I forgotten to lock the damned suitcase?

My heartbeat thudded in my ears.

Someone had been through my luggage. If not an airport baggage handler, then who?

I checked the contents again. Sweaters, jeans,

jewelry, pastel pencils, art supplies—it was all there. Even my prized NYU baseball cap. The only thing out of place was my makeup bag tucked beneath my best silk blouse. I'd packed at warp speed before and never been careless enough to risk the accidental mingling of moisturizer and silk. I wouldn't have dared. I was the daughter of two world travelers, schooled in the fine art of packing by the best. And I had done them proud. Except for failing to lock my bag.

Should I report it to the front desk? Call the police?

What would I tell them? That my shoes were turned the wrong way? That my mesh makeup bag wasn't where it was supposed to be? That I'd been just a little rattled since the day Kent's brains had been blown across the room?

The police would ask questions. Questions I wouldn't know the answers to. Then they would make a great show of dusting for fingerprints, sprinkling and powdering and touching everything I owned until I wanted to curl up and scream.

I sat on the bed and took a deep breath.

I couldn't let myself panic. This was nothing like the Asheville break-in. This was a simple case of an airport TSA employee forgetting to include the search card. Or maybe the contents of my bag had shifted in flight. I'd seen baggage handlers throw bags into the belly of an airplane like they were made of Styrofoam. Everything was fine. I was overreacting.

I thought about calling Esther, the one person I could count on to be the voice of reason in my life. But her new baby still wasn't sleeping through the night, and I had imposed on her enough. I hadn't brought my laptop computer. I didn't want to lug it through airport security and if I needed the internet, I had my phone. Now I was glad I'd left it in New York. If someone was searching through my life, that would be the first place they'd look.

I needed sleep.

Deep, uninterrupted, REM sleep.

I closed my eyes and let my mind drift to the edge of a dream until it tricked me into believing everything was all right. Until the sound of squealing tires dropped me onto the bus that killed my parents.

I tried to hold on as the bus careened around one hairpin curve after the other. I could see my parents sitting in the back with Kent. My mother was waving frantically to me to join them, but I couldn't move. I wanted to warn them they were going to die. but every time I tried to stand, the rickety bus swerved to the side and slung me back against the seat. When I jolted awake, my fingers were clutching the chenille bedspread so tightly they ached.

And then I heard it.

A loud, pulsating beep that would not go away.

I fumbled for the lamp switch. The bright light popped on and seared my eyes. A bitter stench stung the inside of my nose. I sat up. Wisps of blue smoke seeped into the room from beneath the door, twisting and spiraling like fog rising from a riverbank.

As the adrenaline kicked in, giving me the kind of clarity I could never awaken from the soft cocoon of sleep and muster on my own, I stared at the door in horror.

The McAlister Inn was on fire

Chapter Three

I scrambled out of bed.

The switch in my brain flipped to Survival Mode and my instincts pushed the fear aside and took over. I grabbed my jeans off the chair and pulled them on over my sleep shorts. I stuffed my feet into my already tied athletic shoes, threw on my cotton jacket, threaded my purse strap diagonally across my chest, and slid my phone and its charger into my jacket pocket. I was operating on automatic, ticking off boxes in my head.

I somehow remembered to feel the door for heat before I unlatched it. All those fire drills at school I had been forced to participate in were finally paying off. I threw the safety chain, pushed the handle down, and tumbled into the empty hall.

Plumes of gray smoke filled the air. My eyes watered. I dabbed them with the corner of my jacket. The hall was empty. *Where was everybody? Was I the last to get out? Were people still asleep in their rooms?*

I wiped my eyes again and turned toward the back hall. Through the thick smoke, I could just make out the green exit light glowing like kryptonite over the stairway door.

Wait a minute. *Had I heard someone crying?*

Beneath the relentless cadence of the fire alarm, I could hear a low-pitched wail coming from the room across the hall.

"Hello?" I rapped on the door. "Is someone in there?"

"Help me," a muffled voice cried.

I shoved the handle down and pushed open the door.

A cloud of smoke rushed at me. Black and thick, stinking like lighter fluid. I tried to gulp in air, but the smoke came at me again, burning the inside of my nose, singeing my throat. I bunched up my jacket and held it over my mouth.

"*Where are you?*" I screamed. *"I can't see you.*"

A gloved hand came out of the cloud and clamped around my mouth. It jerked me back hard, popping the muscle in my neck. I fought for air, gasping, and wheezing while stars pulsated behind my eyelids. A hand tried to pull my purse strap over my head.

Some fuzzy, distant memory wormed its way through my brain like a soldier fighting its way across enemy lines. I'd done this before. In self-defense class at boarding school. I stopped struggling and willed myself to relax. Then slowly, deliberately, raised my right foot and kicked back against my attacker's shin. *Hard.*

In an instant I was free.

I sprinted down the hall toward the exit. When I reached the stairway door my hands shot out to grasp the door handle. But before I could touch it, two gloved hands seized my shoulders and spun me around.

A black gas mask materialized in front of my face.

I fell back against the metal exit door. I opened my mouth to scream, but no sound came out. My legs and arms turned to liquid as I slid to the carpeted floor. My attacker—Man? Woman? I wasn't sure.—grabbed my purse strap and lifted it over my head. Then tucked my black leather purse under their arm and ran.

I knew I should get up, but I couldn't make myself move.

The back of my head throbbed with my heartbeat—*Bam-bam. Bam-bam.* I reached up and touched it, fully expecting to pull my hand back covered in blood. The lump, still growing, felt remarkably intact.

I stared down the length of the deserted hallway. The air had begun to clear. Curls of gray smoke hung suspended in the air, floating languidly toward me like miniature ghosts on the prowl. I held onto the metal door frame and pulled myself to my feet. I pushed the fire door open and stumbled down the narrow stairwell.

Seconds before the heavy door clanged shut behind me, I heard the sound of sirens echoing in the distance.

****

"I think we can take that oxygen mask off now."

I sucked in one last breath before parting with it. My lungs had stopped feeling like they'd been flung into an incinerator, but my throat was still dry and raw. The doctor bending over me looked like Andy Griffith during the *Matlock* years: a thick shock of white hair; a friendly, toothy grin. When he'd leaned over to unfasten my blood pressure cuff, he'd smelled of peppermint laced with bourbon.

I raised up on one elbow. Pain shot through the back of my head. *"Ow."*

"Easy now," the doctor said. "You've got a big old goose egg back there."

I held the plastic ice pack and tried it again, only slower this time. After the initial change in altitude, the pain subsided to a dull pulsing thud.

"Mom, she's sitting up." Maddie from the front desk stood beside an older, taller version of herself, a striking woman with kohl-lined brown eyes and short black, perfectly coiffed hair swept across her forehead. A rather severe starched white collar framed her exotic looking face.

"I'm Olivia. I'm Maddie's mother." She sat beside me on the stretcher. "Are you all right?"

"I think so," I said.

"I'm a friend of your Aunt Priscilla's." She flashed her gypsy eyes at Andy Griffith and smiled. "And this is Dr. Hugh Turner."

"Just call me Doc."

"Hugh, are you sure we shouldn't take her to the emergency room?"

"No, no, she'll be fine. Fine as frog's hair." He grinned at me. "She never lost consciousness and her lungs are clear. Are you allergic to anything, Mrs. Chandler?"

"Bubble bath," I said groggily.

He laughed. "Then we're in business. Your head's gonna feel like hell, though. I've got some pain meds in my bag that I'll give you. I wouldn't drive anywhere until tomorrow. No aspirin, at least for a few days. And call me if you feel any nausea during the night." He fished around in his doctor's bag for a two-capsule blister pack and his card. "Take one now but wait six hours to take the other one. And only if you need it. Try to get by on ibuprofen if you can."

I nodded obediently.

"Madelyn!" Olivia waited until the girl looked up from her phone. "Get Emory some water so she can take this pill. There's a bottle in my purse."

"Were you and Maddie here when the fire started?" I asked.

"No, we were starting up Gray Top Mountain when we heard the sirens. I knew something awful must have happened, so we turned around and came back."

"Mrs. Chandler?" A tall, uniformed man stepped out from behind the parked yellow fire engine. "I'm Sheriff Will Riley."

"What about the fire?" I suddenly felt panicky. "No one has said anything about the fire. Did everyone get out? Was anybody hurt?"

"There was no fire, ma'am."

"No fire?" My throat closed up like a clogged drain. The wracking coughs that followed shook the flimsy stretcher until Olivia grabbed Doc Turner's arm for support.

"No fire." The sheriff watched me closely. "Someone wanted us to think there was a fire, but they only set off a few smoke bombs. We found some oily rags burning in a coal bucket in Room 310, the room across the hall from yours."

"Was anyone hurt?" I said.

"No, ma'am. Counting you, only six guests are staying at the inn. As soon as the alarm went off, they went outside. But they were all on the first floor. You were the only one staying on the third floor, and it looks like whoever did this just wanted to evacuate it. They did a pretty good job of it, too. Did you see anyone?"

"Yes, I saw him—her—I'm not sure which. They pushed me into the fire door and stole my purse."

"This one?" The sheriff's deputy handed me my black leather bag. "Thanks, McBride. We found it outside near the service entrance, ma'am. Would you mind checking the contents?"

The fifty-dollar bill and three twenties were still there. None of my credit cards were missing. My box of pastel pencils was intact. Whoever had grabbed my purse hadn't been after my money. Nor felt the fervent need to dash off a quick sketch.

The sheriff, whose boyish face made him look too young to be sheriff of anything, sighed and checked his watch.

What was it with North Carolina cops? Were they all rude and insensitive? The detective in charge of Kent's murder had acted like an ill-mannered child. Two minutes after meeting me he'd laughed and said, "I read your statement, Mrs. Chandler, and I'd like to know what kind of woman can be married to a man for four years and not know he's gay?"

Sheriff Riley checked his phone. Again.

I cleared my throat. "Am I keeping you from something?"

"Sorry, I'm waiting on a call." He regarded me with amusement. "So besides getting your head slammed into a fire door, have you noticed anything unusual here at the inn? Anything strange or out of the ordinary?"

"Besides the fact that it's practically deserted?"

"Besides that," he said.

"I think someone searched my luggage while I was at dinner."

"And you didn't tell anyone?" Sheriff Riley said.

"No, sir." Four pairs of eyes stared at me in disbelief. Five, counting Deputy McBride's. "I was pretty sure, but I wasn't positive."

Riley checked his notes. "You told my deputy you heard someone crying for help in the room across the hall from yours."

"Yes, but when I opened the door, someone grabbed me and—"

"—tried to steal your purse," Riley finished.

"Yes."

"So this hotel fire was staged by someone wanting to steal her purse?" Olivia said. "That's ridiculous. Why go to all that trouble? Why not just take it off her arm when she's looking the other way?"

"That's what we're gonna try and find out, ma'am." Riley pocketed his little notebook. "I don't want to scare you, Mrs. Chandler, but it sounds like what happened here tonight was directed solely at you."

"Great," I said.

"I know your apartment in Asheville was broken into." If he knew that, he knew about Kent's murder. "If someone went through your luggage and stole your purse, maybe you've got something they want. Any idea what that might be?"

"No, sir."

"If somebody thinks you have something worth stealing and will pull a stunt as risky as the one they pulled tonight, you need to be careful." He glanced at the doctor. "How's she doing, Doc?"

"She'll be fine," Doc Turner said. "But for the next twelve hours or so, in case there are unforeseen complications, she really shouldn't be alone."

"I know you're a stranger in Bitter Ridge," Sheriff Riley said, "but is there anyone—"

"Nonsense, Will," Olivia said briskly. "Emory's not a stranger. She's Priscilla Austen's niece, and she's coming home with us."

"Oh, no." What little control I had over the situation began to slip away. "I couldn't impose on you like that. I can stay in a motel tonight then go to my aunt's house tomorrow."

Olivia and Doc Turner exchanged glances.

"I don't think Pris' house is inhabitable at the moment," Olivia said. "No one has lived in it for almost two years." She patted my arm. "Now, don't be silly. Maddie and I are up on Gray Top Mountain, just a couple of miles from here. And we have plenty of room, don't we Maddie?" Maddie nodded, looking at her phone. "If Pris knew what had happened, she would want you to stay with us. She would *insist* on it. Wouldn't she, Hugh?"

"That's very kind of you," I said, "but I don't think—"

"You might as well stop arguing with her," Maddie said, glancing up. "She always gets her way."

I looked at Sheriff Riley for support, hoping he would speak up if this was a bad idea. I didn't know these people and the last thing I wanted to do was camp out in some stranger's house on top of a mountain. Maddie seemed nice enough, but her goth-hipster boyfriend reminded me of the guy in a horror movie who pulls the legs off spiders when no one is looking. Olivia looked normal, but this southern belle/steel magnolia thing she had going was beginning to get on my nerves.

"It's okay, Emory," Sheriff Riley said, softening his tone. He could have been talking me down from a ledge. "I can vouch for Olivia and Maddie. I've known them for years, and they'll take good care of you." He handed me his card and smiled reassuringly. “And if you need me, here’s my number.”

“Then it’s settled,” Olivia said brightly. “You’re coming home with us.”

Ten minutes and one very large pain pill later, I was floating up Gray Top Mountain sprawled across the back seat of Olivia's dark blue Cadillac. Sheriff Riley had assured me Olivia's house was one of the safest places I could be, a fact that drove itself home when I noticed that the myriad of security cameras bolted to the trees were pointing at a ten-foot electric gate.

The lights from her house sparkled through the trees, making it look more like a ski lodge than a residence. The stone, wood, and glass façade jutted out from the side of the mountain like a page in a pop-up book. Landscaped to the max and illuminated with the kind of tasteful outdoor lighting that doesn’t come cheap, a multi-leveled wooden deck connected the two stories with a series of ramps and steps before winding down a manicured hill to a rock-enclosed pond. The effect was breathtaking.

“I know a gate like this may seem excessive,” Olivia said. “But during ski season, this place is crawling with tourists.”

“You wish,” Maddie said under her breath.

“It's beautiful,” I said.

“Oh, do you like it?” Olivia waved her hand as if it were some little studio apartment she'd fixed up herself. “My son built it for me.”

I caught her eye in the rearview mirror. “Your son’s a builder?”

“Good God, no,” Olivia said. “He's an architect specializing in historical restoration. He's been a consultant for the Biltmore House in Asheville, the Hague House in Charleston, all sorts of famous places. If you're into historic homes, you've probably heard of him. James St. Clair?"

"Your last name is St. Clair?" I pushed myself up.

"Well, yes," Olivia shot me a puzzled look. "You knew that."

"No, I didn't." I pressed my forehead against the back of the driver's seat. Then banged it a few times until it began to throb again.

"What's the matter?" Olivia said.

"I've met James. At Laurel Haven." Oh, man, I did not want to do this. "Is he home now?"

"I doubt it," Olivia said. "He and Tess were going to a movie after he dropped Maddie at the house. Then Maddie realized she had some more work to finish, so I picked her up instead."

Maddie snorted softly.

"Tess? Is that his wife?"

Maddie snorted again. "No, but she'd like to be."

"Tess is our houseguest," Olivia said. "She's the daughter of my dearest college friend. She's stayed with us every summer since she turned thirteen while her parents go on archeological digs. She and Maddie are like sisters."

"Yeah, *right.*" Maddie wrinkled her long nose, deepening the dimple on the left side of her face exactly like James St. Clair. Why hadn't I noticed the resemblance?

I was already plotting my escape. First thing tomorrow, I would call a taxi and get back to the hotel. By then, the sheriff would have released my belongings and I could go to Aunt Pris' house. No matter what shape it was in, it had to be better than staying with the St. Clairs. With a little luck, I could be down Gray Top Mountain and gone before I ran into James.

Olivia parked the car in a garage large enough to house a pet elephant and led the procession through a tastefully decorated mudroom into the kitchen. I glanced around. Someone had been watching *way* too much HGTV. A nine-burner gas stove, stainless steel appliances, caramel brown granite countertops, a kitchen island big enough to land a plane on. A small plane, but still.

Maddie immediately disappeared into another room, still on her phone. I followed Olivia through a long dining room that opened up into a living space with giant overstuffed sofas and an enormous river rock stone fireplace. What was it with these people? It was like Papa Bear's house on steroids. Why was everything so huge?

We made our way up a winding staircase to the second floor.

Olivia flung open the door at the end of the hall. "Is this all right?" She gestured around the spacious bedroom.

"I think I can stand it." Ten-foot ceilings with timber beams? A hand-painted bed and dresser set that looked like works of art? A quilt depicting a mountain river scene as beautifully wrought as any watercolor? I ran my hand over it reverently.

"Beautiful quilt, isn't it? It was done by a local woman—Alpha Hoskin. Strangely enough, she lives on Holly Berry Road right down from your aunt Pris. I think she's watching the house for her." She pointed to an alcove. "The bathroom's through there. I'll get you one of my nightgowns. Are you hungry? I can warm something up if you—"

"I'm fine. I just need to sleep." Dr. Turner's magic pill had stopped my head from feeling like it had been hit with Thor's hammer, but I was exhausted.

I glanced up. Olivia was watching me.

"Thank you for rescuing me tonight," I said.

"Don't be silly." Olivia switched on the bedside lamp. "It's the least I can do for Pris. After all, she's giving us our lives back." She smoothed her black hair back from her temples. "Fresh towels are in the closet. I'm one floor down if you need me."

"After a hot shower and some sleep, I'll be good as new."

But I wasn't.

The too soft mattress kept me awake until the pain medicine wore off, leaving me with another headache pounding the base of my skull. I rummaged in my purse for some ibuprofen then flipped on the bathroom light.

"Yikes," I said, recoiling from my reflection. My dark blonde hair hung in damp matted curls around my face. My eyes were bloodshot beyond recognition. I touched the ruffled bodice of Olivia's high-necked nightgown and laughed. If Kent could see me, he'd say I looked like Laura Ingalls on a three-day binge.

I needed air. I felt like I hadn't taken a real breath in hours.

In New York, I would sneak out the top floor door of our apartment building marked No Entry and climb the metal stairs to the roof. Tonight, I would have to make do with a backyard that looked like the mountain version of Gramercy Park.

I opened the louvered window shade and looked

out. The tall chain-link fence surrounding the St. Clair property appeared reassuringly secure. If I stayed near the house, I could slip outside for a quick hit of oxygen without anyone knowing.

I slipped on my cotton jacket, which smelled like I'd been pumping gas for the last two hours, and padded downstairs barefoot. I unlocked the beveled glass door leading out to the patio and braced myself for the soul jarring burglar alarm that was sure to follow. When nothing happened, I stepped over the threshold and eased onto the cedar deck. The night air swirled around me, soft and thick and damp. I pulled the lapels together, then tiptoed halfway down the cedar stairs and crouched in the shadows.

The low rumble of thunder echoed in the distance. Strings of puffy clouds raced across the three-quarter moon. Rectangular wooden planters filled with pink and white begonias sat balanced on the deck railings. As the wind moved through them one by one, the evergreens behind the fishpond swayed in the same uneven rhythm. It was too dark to see the mountains, but come morning, layers of them would be wrapped in a blue haze stretching across the horizon as far as the eye could see.

What was I doing there? My time on Crow Mountain had come and gone. Pris and I had spent the last twenty-two years exchanging Christmas and birthday cards and little else. When she woke up—and I had to believe that she would—she might not be so happy to see me. She might remember why she stopped asking me to visit. Or worse, she might *not* remember, and then I would never know.

But here I was, still chasing the dream. Back in the

Carolina Blue Ridge Mountains, the only place that had ever really felt like home. Aunt Pris used to say these mountains were her strength, her backbone, a sturdy place to rest her soul. While I was here, maybe they would find it in their big mountain hearts to do the same for me. Because I needed that kind of strength now more than ever. Since I'd left New York, someone had been systematically trying to turn my life upside down. And until I discovered who it was and why, I didn't have a chance of getting it back.

I leaned my head against the damp railing. The sharp woody scent of cedar pricked my nose. Flashes of me racing down the hall then getting grabbed ran through my head. I still couldn't believe it had happened. Someone in Bitter Ridge wanted something I had. And after the McAlister Inn fire that wasn't a fire, I was beginning to realize they would go to any lengths to get it. I needed to calm down and figure out who was behind this and who, if anyone, I could trust.

My luggage. My purse. My God. What would anyone want of mine? I owned a few pieces of art which were neither expensive nor promising and some unusual mementos my parents had picked up on their travels from around the world. I made decent money as a portrait artist, but my income fluctuated wildly depending on how many commissions I had lined up. There were still months when I had no commissions at all and had to dip into the savings I'd squirreled back, a fact I had kept from Kent during our marriage because my pride wouldn't admit to him that my success was hit and miss. The internet business I'd started of turning photographs into pastel portraits had become tedious and artistically unfulfilling, but it had kept me solvent and sane after Kent died without having to deal with actual human beings.

Could it be something of Kent's they were after? Something he'd kept hidden? He was good at keeping secrets. In fact, he'd been a master at it. After his death, I'd packed the few possessions he hadn't moved out of the apartment and sent them to his parents. I'd kept nothing except the gold wedding band he'd thrown at me from across the room and his cell phone.

Kent's death.

Hard to even think those words, much less say them out loud. It was all still so surreal.

Maybe everything that had happened in Bitter Ridge was karma. Maybe the Universe was finally giving me exactly what I deserved. Kent's death had been my fault. And no matter how much he had deceived me, or betrayed me, or reduced my sad little trusting heart to shrapnel, I could never forgive myself.

I laid my head on my knees and closed my eyes. I rocked my body back and forth, like a child trying to soothe itself when sleep will not come. Then at last, in the cool dark shadows of the night, I began to cry.

Oh, God, I am so sorry.

I hadn't loved Kent for a long time. At the end of our marriage, I hadn't even liked him. But I had never wished him dead.

"Emory?"

I raised my head.

James St. Clair stood on the top deck looking down at me.

The lights from the eaves spilled over his broad shoulders, catching the outline of his cheekbones, the square set of his jaw. His unbuttoned flannel shirt had been rolled up at the sleeves over a white T-shirt, the sides gently flapping in the breeze. His faded jeans were pulled snug across his thighs. And he was barefoot. Okay. Deep breath. The man standing above me might be the black sheep of Bitter Ridge, but he sure as hell knew how to make an entrance.

****

James started down the staircase. “In that old-fashioned nightgown with your hair curling every which way, you look like a character in a Jane Austen novel,” he said.

“I did not take you for a Jane Austen guy.”

He laughed. “Well, I’ve never actually read any of her books. But I’ve seen the trailers for some of the movies, and there always seems to be some woman running around in a long nightgown with hair hanging down her back.”

“You got that right.”

“And your last name is Austen.”

“Maiden name. Which I’m thinking of taking back.”

He sat on the step above me. “Are you okay? I heard about the fire.”

“I’m fine.”

“Olivia said you hit your head.”

“I did. But I guess being hardheaded has finally worked to my advantage.”

“Mind if I sit with you? You don’t have to talk if you don’t want to.”

“Sure,” I said. “It’s your house. Which I discovered after I got here.”

He pulled a folded handkerchief from the back pocket of his jeans and handed it to me. “You've been crying."

"Nothing gets by you, does it?"

"Not much."

"So what gave me away? The red snotty nose or the wet puffy face?" I dabbed at my eyes. "Sorry. I don't usually sit around blubbering like I didn't get invited to the prom. I didn't wake you, did I?"

"No, I just got home."

I began to cough. Long wheezing wracks that sounded like a freight train. "I'm okay," I croaked.

"You don't sound okay. I could make you some hot tea. Fix you a drink."

"No, I'm—"

"I'll get you a drink."

"—fine."

He went back to the house then returned a few minutes later with a bottle of water, a bottle of Jack Daniel's Tennessee Honey Whiskey, and two shot glasses. He poured us each a whiskey and handed one to me."

"Drink up," he said. "It's good for you."

I knocked it back and gasped as the amber liquid burned a path down my throat. He cracked open the water bottle, then drank his shot and refilled my glass with the strong sweet whiskey. I smoothed the folds of Olivia's nightgown over my knees.

"I know some of your history," he said, "from talking to your Aunt Pris. It can't have been easy. You must be missing your support system in New York."

"I am. But it's basically dwindled to one: my friend Esther. After my husband was killed, most of the people I knew in New York pulled away from me. They started acting weird. As if they thought my bad luck was going to rub off on them and they'd be next."

"I don't believe in luck."

"Neither do I. Not anymore." I sipped my whiskey. "So, how was the movie? Your mother said you were going on a date with…what's her name?"

"Tess. Tess Winslow. And it wasn't a date. I don't date."

"Okay."

"Tess is like family. She's stayed here every summer for years. It was getting late, so I drove around for a while. I always head to the mountains when I need to cool off."

"Cool off from what?"

James ran his hand back through his hair. "From the town council meeting. From running into Melvin Owens at Laurel Haven. From seeing Delbert Jenkins at the bar. After a while, the people in this town wear me down."

"I haven't met Tess yet."

"Her mother is my mother's best friend. She graduated from boarding school a few weeks ago. She's Maddie's age. Just a kid, really."

I laughed. "Well, I guess you know what floats your boat."

"She's like a sister to me. She's had a rough life."

"Boarding school can be tough. And I know because I was a boarding school brat for nine years. I'm sure Tess and I have a lot in common."

"God, I hope not."

"So, are you on the Bitter Ridge town council?"

He stretched his long legs out in front of him. "Nah. I just show up at meetings to thumb my nose at the locals and make a few waves. It keeps them on their toes. You heard Delbert's opinion of me tonight. He's in the not-so-silent majority."

"Is what Delbert said true? Did you cheat your neighbors?"

He poured himself another shot. "No, but there are plenty of people around here who think I did."

"If it isn't true, then why do you care what other people think?"

"Because I'm not the only one it affects." He sighed. "Two years ago, a big corporation blew through here called Mountain Sports, Unlimited. The man running the show was a weaselly little guy named Ron Weber. I was just starting to make a name for myself as an architect, and when he discovered my family owned a sizable chunk of Gray Top Mountain, he thought he'd hit pay dirt. His company had drawn up big plans to develop Gray Top as a ski resort. And not just a few slopes and a place to rent ski boots, either. I'm talking about a hotel, an alpine village, a gift shop, the whole nine yards. A little too commercial for my taste, but the people in Bitter Ridge could have used the kind of money it would generate."

"Go on."

"Not only had Mr. Weber not been able to secure enough financing, he hadn't bothered to read the surveyor's report, which stated that 86.9 percent of the mountain was solid granite. The cost of developing Gray Top Mountain quadrupled overnight. I was too proud to accept help from my father, and it blew up in my face." He downed the Jack honey. "It's taken two years, but I've reimbursed every person for their original investment. And they still hate me."

"But why?"

"Because I waved the good life in front of them then snatched it away. I don't blame them for not trusting me. I just wish they weren't still taking it out on Mother and Maddie." He gestured toward the gate bathed in a bright security light. "That's why it looks like Ft. Knox around here."

"Has your family been threatened?"

"It's been a while, but yes. A fence this intimidating is probably overkill, but I can't let my guard down."

"What would it take for you to get back into the town's good graces?"

He shrugged. "I don't know. Maybe developing one of the other mountains."

"Another ski resort? Which one could sustain something like that?"

"Only one," he said. "Crow Mountain."

"Well, that won't happen. Pris will never sell the Austen property." I yawned, in spite of myself, then smiled. "And where would the crows go?"

James stood and held out his hands. "Come on, Alice. You need to get some sleep before you fall down another rabbit hole."

I let him help me up. "At least my headache is gone."

I started up the stairs. "I thanked your mother tonight for letting me stay here, and she said, 'It's the least I can do for Pris because she's giving us our lives back.' What did she mean by that? Are you seriously thinking about developing Crow Mountain?"

He sighed. "Mother's always hopeful something around here is going to change for the better. As for Crow Mountain, I'm not sure it could be developed without securing your family's property. The estate cuts across the top of the ridge then winds around the north face covering most of the eastern side including Stoney Creek."

"Sounds like you've done your research."

"The extent of the Austen property is common knowledge around here."

"It's also a moot point because Pris will never sell."

"The backside is the best."

I raised my eyebrows. "The backside of Crow Mountain?"

"I'll have to take you hiking up there sometime. It's magical."

"All the more reason not to build a condo and a ski lodge on it."

He picked up the whiskey bottle and stopped. "Did you hear that?" His gaze shot to the dark house looming behind them.

"I didn't hear anything."

"Must have been an owl."

I gathered my nightgown and started up the steps. At the top of the landing, James stumbled.

"What's wrong? Are you okay?"

"Yeah," he said grudgingly. "I stood up to speak at the council meeting tonight, and Nancy Darnell's kid kicked the fire out of my shin."

A scratching noise echoed above us.

I glanced up. A three-foot wooden planter teetered back and forth on the cedar railing, its pink and white begonia blossoms shaking up and down.

James grabbed my shoulder and jerked me back. I heard a crack and looked up again, just in time to see the planter flip off the railing and plummet toward us.

Chapter Four

The planter smashed onto the deck a scant six from feet where I was standing, spraying splinters of wood and black dirt across the deck.

"Evening, Tess," James said without looking up.

"Sorry. My bad." A young woman with straight brown hair cascading over the left side of her face leaned over the balcony. "I heard voices. I came to see who it was."

"You knew damned well it was me out here." James nodded in my direction. "This is Emory Chandler. Emory, meet Tess. At your own risk, of course."

"Hello." I wondered just how close a call we'd had. And if this girl—Tess—had pushed the planter off the railing on purpose. Just a feeling I had, and I was probably way off base, but I wasn't getting any warm fuzzy vibes of remorse from her. Quite the contrary. Maybe she'd been trying to overhear our conversation and had leaned over too far and slipped. But if it had been an accident, then why was she smiling like she'd cracked the code on the Rosetta Stone? "You'll have to excuse me," I said, "but I need to pack it in. I'm leaving in the morning."

"Don't let me keep you," Tess said.

A light went on in the upper bedroom, illuminating the left side of the patio.

James cursed softly. “Great, Tess. Now you get to explain to my mother what just happened.”

The girl’s voice took on the singsong pleading of a little girl. “Please, James. Don’t make me do it alone. Olivia won’t get mad if you’re here.”

I hurried back to the house and opened the glass door. Olivia was running down the staircase tying a silk flowered robe around her waist.

“What’s going on?” she cried. “What was that noise?”

“It’s all right, Mother,” James shouted from the patio. “Just a little accident. Right, Tess?”

I ran up the stairs and locked my bedroom door. I kicked off my shoes and dove into the huge four-poster bed, pulling the soft quilt up around my neck. The sooner I got out of the St. Clair house, the better off I would be.

I closed my eyes, but I couldn’t relax.

Had James been trying to convince Pris to sell her Crow Mountain property to him? Was he cozying up to her to convince her to part with it? He had admitted that Crow Mountain couldn’t be developed without purchasing the Austen lots. Had he discovered in his research that my father still owned some of those lots when he died? And, as his sole beneficiary, they had been passed down to me?

I curled into a ball. Did the property I now owned—much less than Pris, but still considerable—have something to do with the attempted robberies? I couldn’t imagine that it would. Whatever the thief wanted had to be something tangible I could stash in my purse.

All of this was hitting too close to home. And too

soon since Kent's death.

After the Asheville apartment had been cleared as a crime scene, I had repacked the boxes and had them hauled to a storage unit outside of Bitter Ridge. At the time, I hadn't wanted to deal with sorting the bittersweet accumulation of our four married years together. But I think part of me still held onto the hope that one day I would recover from everything that had happened and move back to the mountains.

I sat up in bed.

The storage unit.

I flung the quilt back and ran to the dressing table. I rummaged in my purse, then checked my keyring for the two padlock keys to the storage unit. Both of them were missing.

The knot in my chest sank to the pit of my stomach.

I dropped onto the padded dresser chair, still holding my keys, and stared at the trees outside the arched window. Was the person who had stolen my purse looking for my storage unit keys? How did they even know I had rented a storage unit? Or which one?

I knew I was grasping at straws, but the fact remained that the keys that were there before were not there now.

Who had I told about the storage unit besides Esther? No one.

Who did I trust?

No one.

****

Early the next morning, I called the only taxi in town to come to get me.

I crept downstairs to the kitchen in my smoke

saturated clothes, hoping I'd be able to figure out how to open the electric gate, the only thing standing between me and freedom. It was terrible to think of it like that. Especially after Olivia had been so welcoming. And I felt bad about it. But the truth was that, even though Olivia St. Clair had opened her home to me and been the epitome of southern hospitality, there was something about the woman I didn't trust.

"You're up early." Tess sat perched on a wooden stool at the end of the kitchen island, sipping something steaming out of a mug. "You didn't sneak downstairs to steal the good silver, did you?"

"I'm leaving."

"Uh, huh. Well, it's a long walk back to Bitter Ridge." She swung her shoulder-length hair to the side, making it ripple like a sheet of silk. Even in a simple pink quilted robe, the girl exuded wealth and privilege.

"A taxi is coming for me."

"I know. My room's next to yours. I heard you call them." She crossed her legs and leaned back against the tile wall. "That's why I came downstairs. I wanted to see what you looked like in broad daylight."

"And now that you've seen me?"

Tess smiled. "I don't think I need to worry."

"Thanks," I said lightly. "Just what a girl likes to hear first thing in the morning."

"You're hardly a girl. In this light, you look older than Olivia."

I held my tongue. It was early. I hadn't had my coffee yet. And I wasn't about to take this girl's bait. I'd spent half my life dealing with boarding school brats who used their words as weapons against anyone who didn't fit in. And this was no different. I was older and less brittle now, but I still knew a mean girl when I saw one.

"Let me give you some advice," Tess said. "James and I are together, so you might want to keep that in mind the next time you go sneaking around his house in your nightgown."

"Olivia's nightgown."

"I saw you with him."

"We were sitting outside on the stairs. I'd had kind of a bad night. I'm his mother's houseguest. He was being nice to me."

"You were both laughing. He touched your arm. He poured you drinks. Then you did shots together. I could tell you were trying really hard to make him like you."

"Oh, honey." I had never called anyone *honey* in my life. "There is absolutely nothing between—I only met the guy last night. Look, I'm leaving in like…ten minutes. And I don't think I'll be back. So you don't have to worry."

"Good." Tess' amber-brown eyes stared at me like she wanted to rip out my spleen. Which was good. Because now I was sure that trusting her would be like throwing a sirloin to a Rottweiler and expecting the dog to bring it back.

"Can you open the electric gate for me?"

"My pleasure." Tess went to a small control panel beside the back door and flipped one of the switches. The electric gate came to life, grinding in the distance like the soft whir of a can opener.

"Your ride is here," Tess cried cheerfully. "Let me get the door for you. Sorry to see you go. Bye, now."

"Bye, Tess. Enjoy your day."

“Oh, I will,” she said contemptuously, letting the backdoor bang shut behind me.

I over tipped the taxi driver, who I was sure had been awakened out of a deep sleep to fetch me, and ran inside Laurel Haven. I hurried down the hallway, barely missing a portable hospital computer and an aide carrying a breakfast tray. My rubber-soled shoes slapped against the linoleum floor as I swung around the corner of the Intensive Care Unit. I stopped at the nurse’s station to catch my breath, which was still a little ragged from the smoke inhalation, but almost back to normal.

“Hi, I’m Emory Chandler. Priscilla Austen’s niece. Is she—”

“We were just about to call you. Your aunt is awake.”

Pris was conscious? She was going to be all right? Relief flooded over me, followed by a stab of selfish worry. *Would she know me? Would she be glad to see me? Would she want me to stay?*

“She’s not a hundred percent yet,” the nurse said. “Her speech has been affected and she’s having some double vision. Normal stroke stuff.”

“But she’s awake. You said she was awake.”

The nurse smiled brightly. “Yes, she’s awake. I told her we were going to contact you.”

We stepped inside the curtained enclosure. Aunt Pris lay on the bed with her eyes closed, as still and pale as the day before.

“Open your eyes, Miss Austen,” the nurse chirped. “Your niece is here.”

Aunt Pris groaned but didn’t move.

The nurse motioned for me to come closer. “Go on,

honey. Talk to her."

I stood beside the bed. Aunt Pris' thin face was turned to the wall. The soft gurgle of oxygen slid into her nose through a clear plastic tube. The monitor on the wall above her head flashed her steady heartbeat in white moving blips.

"Aunt Pris? It's Emory. Can you hear me?"

Pris' blue eyes opened. Her gaze traveled to the ceiling, to the far corner of the room, then to my face. The right side of her mouth quivered. A single tear slid from her eye and ran along the deep crease of her cheek. *"Em...Em...Emmm."*

"Why, look at that." The nurse beamed. "She's trying to say your name."

"*Mmmm...Emmm...Emmm.*" Her short nails clawed into my palm.

I took her hand. "It's okay, Aunt Pris. You don't have to try so hard."

Pris shook her head in frustration. A low, plaintive cry rose from her throat. She pushed herself up on one elbow, looked me straight in the eye, and said, "Emory," just as plain as could be. Then she fell back against her pillow, panting.

"It'll get better." The nurse picked up the Styrofoam water pitcher and gave it a spirited shake. "You should be grateful. Your aunt is truly blessed."

"What did you say?"

"I said your aunt is a lucky woman. The Lord must be watching out for her."

I gripped the metal bed railing and tried to control the burst of red hot anger rushing through me. "You think so?" I kept my voice steady. "And was He watching out for her the day a blood vessel burst in her brain? Or was He off that day?"

"Mrs. Chandler, you don't understand what you're dealing with here. Your aunt has had a major stroke. The fact that she's talking at all is a good sign." She smiled reassuringly. "Take heart, honey. Nothing is ever as bad as it seems."

No. Sometimes it was worse.

After the nurse left, Pris closed her eyes and began to breathe calmly, in and out, unaware she'd just performed a minor miracle.

I had so many questions about the Austen house on Crow Mountain and Pris' relationship with the St. Clair family, but I didn't want to distress her. My questions would have to wait until she was strong enough to answer them. No matter how long that took. It was the two of us against the world now, and I wasn't going to let her down. I patted her bruised arm above the curling strips of IV tape. "We're going to be all right, you and me." I blinked back tears. "So no worries, okay? No matter what happens, you and I are going to be fine."

Pris' faded blue eyes fluttered open, then closed. "*Emmm,*" she said.

Chapter Five

Laurel Haven's residential wing was a short ten-minute walk from the hospital. I stood in the middle of Pris' room and stared at my father's portrait. I had taken my time painting it carefully in oils, and I was proud to say, it was one of my best.

His likeness looked odd without a companion piece of my mother nearby; the two had been inseparable for four decades. I had wanted to paint Mother, but she had always refused, claiming that my father was the handsome one in the family. Nothing could have been further from the truth: They were both spectacular.

Preston and Alexandra Austen. Eccentric free spirits, flitting around the world on a whim and a fat bank account. They'd been so infatuated with each other, I often felt like an intrusion in their lives, the only reason to come back to a dreary house in Upstate New York they cared little about. And yet, I knew they doted on me. I was their little star. The product of their never-ending passion. And I loved them blindly.

When their bus went over the mountainside in Peru, it took weeks for me to realize they weren't coming home. I wasn't sure I realized it yet. I'd spent my life welcoming them back from one trip after another and I still expected to see them come whirling through the front door or find a postcard from some idyllic spot lying in my mailbox.

They had died never knowing they were almost penniless. Except for the property on Crow Mountain, my father's inheritance, which he'd shared with his two older sisters, was nearly gone. The one consolation I held onto was the fact that my parents would have been devastated if they'd been forced to give up their lifestyle and had at least made their grand and glorious exit before the party ended.

"Yoo-hoo."

I turned around.

An elderly woman sat in the doorway across the hall waving to me. A fluff of permed gray hair framed her small, pointed face. Thick granny glasses, positioned halfway down her long nose, magnified her watery gray eyes. Her slippered feet scooted her cumbersome wheelchair back from the door. "Come here, Emory. I want to talk to you."

"You know who I am?"

"Well, of course. I'm Etta Shipley, your Aunt Pris' friend. I've got a thermos of hot cocoa here just begging to comfort someone, and I think we could both use a drink. Would you pour? I'd do it, but I'm not too self-sufficient these days." She held up her gnarled, arthritic hands.

"I'm sorry."

Mrs. Shipley laughed. "Well, me, too. But what can you do? I'd offer you a cookie, but I polished off the last of the Oreos around midnight. I might as well tell you upfront, I'm a card-carrying chocoholic. My children used to tease me about it unmercifully."

"Do your children live close by?"

"Oh, no, they're both gone. Philip and Marcus died in a boating accident ten years ago, and my husband lost his battle with cancer soon after. I'm quite alone these days." She smiled warmly. "It's the pits, isn't it, dear? Being alone, I mean."

"Yes, ma'am. It's the pits."

"That's why I couldn't live without the internet." She gestured to the little laptop computer sitting on her tray table. "And your aunt's friendship. How is Pris doing? No one will tell me anything."

"She's awake." I tried to sound hopeful. "She's having a little trouble talking, but she knew who I was. The doctor says she'll need extensive physical and speech therapy, but he thinks she's going to be okay."

"Thank God. I've been praying for her. Now, before you pour the cocoa, look in my closet beneath that folded quilt and pull out the Manilla envelope. Pris gave it to me to keep for you. Her room was vandalized last week, and she thought it would be safer with me."

"Vandalized? No one has mentioned that. What was taken, do you know?"

"I don't think anything. The person who went into her room was only there for a few minutes. The housekeeper had gone down the hall to empty the trash can and, on the way back, she saw someone running out of Pris' room."

"Did the housekeeper get a description?"

"No, I talked to her," Mrs. Shipley said. "She was clueless and almost as old and blind as I am. She couldn't even tell if it was a man or woman."

"I thought there were security cameras in the hall."

"Only above the exterior doors, not near the rooms. It happened in the middle of the day—very disturbing. Pris kept this envelope hidden under her mattress. She made me promise to give it to you if anything happened to her. She said it's mostly keepsakes, things she wanted you to have. I think the key to the Austen house is in there and a legal document giving you medical power of attorney. Take it with you. She may be on the mend, but we don't know what this thing has done to her brain. I don't think there's much money in the estate, except for the land, of course. When your Aunt Portia's husband died—"

"Edward."

"When Edward died, he had no life insurance. And since Portia's death was deemed a suicide, the insurance company refused to pay."

I stared at her. "My Aunt Portia killed herself?"

Mrs. Shipley sighed. "Oh, sweetie, I am so sorry. You didn't know, did you?"

"No." I tried to wrap my head around what I was hearing. Why was this a secret? Why hadn't my father told me the truth about my aunt? "I thought she died of pneumonia. She was always so sickly and frail."

"Physically and mentally."

Maybe my father hadn't known the truth. Maybe Pris had kept the real cause of Portia's death from him to spare him more grief. His relationship with his sisters had always been an odd one. Nearly ten years younger, he'd been sent to live with their great-aunt in New York at the age of six after their parents' death during a meningitis epidemic. Portia and Pris had remained in the house on Crow. It was mostly logistics that kept him out of the loop: he was seven hundred miles away. He couldn't help but be excluded from his sisters' insular world in the North Carolina mountains.

"Portia took her own life a week after Edward died," Mrs. Shipley said. "They'd only been married three months when he had the heart attack."

"Father said Edward had a serious heart condition when they married."

"He did. He was eating nitroglycerin like candy." Mrs. Shipley shook her head. "Mr. Squires, their mailman, had handed Edward the mail that day then lingered in the yard to chat with Pris. Edward opened a letter, read it, then began to yell at Portia. This alarmed Mr. Squires because these were not young people; they were all in their eighties. Anyway, Mr. Squires ran to Edward and found him lying on the ground dead, still clutching the letter in his hand. His heart had just given out."

"What was in the letter?"

Mrs. Shipley's gray eyes twinkled. "Well, now, that would be fascinating to know, wouldn't it? Pris isn't very forthcoming about that part of the story. After Edward died, Portia just came apart. She spent all day in her room, then at night, she'd wander around the property like a lost soul. Her mind had always been a bit dodgy, but Edward's death pushed her completely over the edge."

"Why didn't my father tell me any of this?"

"Oh, sweetie, I'm sure Pris hid Portia's condition from him. She hid it from everyone. The neighbors thought Portia was eccentric, but I doubt if any of them knew the full extent of her mental illness. Except for that one woman. What was her name? She used to work for them. "

"Hoskin. She's watching the house for Aunt Pris."

"That's right. Alpha Hoskin. I'll bet she could tell you things that would make your hair stand on end."

I glanced out the window. The rain had finally

stopped. Fog clung to the sides of Old Baldy Mountain like strands of cotton candy. "James St. Clair and his family are friends with Aunt Pris. Do you know them?"

"Just in passing. After they built that big house on Gray Top Mountain, Olivia and Carl divorced. I've never met the daughter, but I've talked to James a few times. He seems nice—but guarded. Why do you ask?"

"After the fire at the inn last night—"

"Oh, yes, I heard about it."

"—Olivia insisted I stay at their house. I'm grateful she took me in, but I don't feel comfortable there."

"I don't know Olivia St. Clair, but Pris is very fond of James." Mrs. Shipley peered over her glasses. "Is that what concerns you?"

"What concerns me is how interested James seems to be in Pris' property on Crow Mountain. How long have they been friends?"

"A couple of years. They got to know each other when the plans to develop Gray Top fell through. James said he only had Bitter Ridge's best interest at heart, and Pris believed him. She stood by him when no one else would. She said he reminds her of Edward when he was young."

"Do you think James wants to buy the Austen property and develop Crow Mountain like he tried to develop Gray Top?"

"If he had the resources, he'd be a fool not to."

"But where would he get that kind of money?"

"I think the St. Clairs are still pretty well off. You've seen their house. And their fence. At the time, there were some rather frightening threats made against them. Some of the farmers around here have a herd mentality. No pun intended."

I sipped my cocoa. “That must have been tough.”

“It was hard on all the family, but I think Olivia suffered the most. She was ostracized by her friends, blackballed by some of the social clubs she belonged to. And yes, there are social clubs in Bitter Ridge. For a while, Olivia St. Clair ruled this town. Her standing in the community went from Queen Bee to drone in two days. Bitter Ridge may seem small and unsophisticated, but don’t let it fool you. Outlying farms make up the majority of the five-mountain spread, but the artists and craftsmen are still the heart and soul of Bitter Ridge. They lost a lot of anticipated income along with the farmers. Olivia thought they would forgive and forget, but they toppled her like a stack of Dominos.”

“I just don’t want Aunt Pris to get hurt. Or be coerced into doing something she doesn’t want to do. I don’t want her to lose her home even though she doesn’t live there anymore. It’s still her home, right?”

“Oh, sweetie.” Mrs. Shipley patted her chest. “Home is in here. Home is the part of your heart where you hold the people you love most, whether they’re with you or not.” She reached out her hand, and I took it gently. The shape of her rigid fingers pointing straight down from the high swollen knuckles reminded me of my mother's hand when she’d held it just so and created the head of a swan from shadows thrown against the nursery wall.

Later, in the elevator, I realized I hadn’t asked how Aunt Portia had died. What method would a frail eighty-year-old woman use to end her life? A gun? A razor blade? Sleeping pills?

I called the town taxi driver, apologizing again for having to drag him out to Laurel Haven for a second time that day. I would get him to drop me at the McAlister Inn to pick up my car, then figure out something to do about transportation. I couldn't keep shelling out for the airport rental. I'd be broke in no time.

"Emory Chandler?" The volunteer at the main reception desk, who I'd met the day before, reached into the pocket of her raspberry-colored smock. "I have a note for you." She handed me a white envelope. "When I got back from break, it was lying on top of the mail stack."

"Thanks." I glanced around the lobby. A young couple with a fretful toddler pushed the child's stroller back and forth as if it were exercise equipment. A teenage girl sat sprawled on a plastic chair, thumb tapping a text on her pink phone. An elderly man in overalls sat in the corner holding a battered straw hat in his hands. He smoothed the sides of his gray mustache, then caught my eye and glanced away.

I walked outside and stood beside the front door in the same spot James had ducked out of the rain the night before. I tore open the envelope and unfolded a single sheet of paper.

Three lines.

Double-spaced.

All caps.

I read the note then pocketed it. By the time the taxi arrived, my heart was drumming hard inside my chest. At the inn, I picked up my car, unlocked the door with hands that wouldn't stop shaking, and drove straight to the Haywood County Sheriff's Office in Bitter Ridge.

****

Sheriff Will Riley cleared a stack of newspapers from the chair beside his desk. “Have a seat, Mrs. Chandler. Let's have a look.”

I handed him the envelope.

“Guess I’d better treat this like a real piece of evidence.” He grinned, showing a couple of overlapping bottom teeth that were not unattractive. “That’s what they taught me to do in sheriff school.”

“Sheriff school?”

“Just kidding.” He pulled on a pair of latex gloves and carefully extracted the piece of paper from the envelope. He glanced at both sides then read the words out loud,

“*Give it back, you blonde bitch.*

Or you’ll be sorry.

Or you’ll be dead.”

He looked up. “Catchy poem. Doesn't rhyme, though.”

“I thought you should see it.”

“Yeah.” Riley sighed. “You okay? Nasty little notes like this tend to upset people.”

“I can see why.”

“Sit down, Mrs.—can I call you Emory?”

“Of course.” I dropped into the thick metal chair, dodging the stacks of papers piled on his desk. “Ever since I left New York, I’ve had the feeling someone was following me.”

“Have you actually seen anyone? On foot or in a car?”

“No.”

“Did you see anyone suspicious at Laurel Haven? At the inn?”

“No. But this feeling is so strong, I—”

"I can't arrest a feeling, Emory."

"I know." I unzipped the side pocket of my purse and pulled out my keys. "When I went through my purse after the fire—" I stopped. "Have you found out anything about the fire?"

"We're working on it."

"When I looked in my purse after the smoke bomb incident that you still don't know anything about, I didn't notice that two of my keys were missing from my keyring. They open the locks on a storage unit I rented after my husband died."

Riley frowned. "Where is this unit?"

"Store N' Lock. Out on Highway 421. Unit Number 67."

"I know where that is. I'll send one of my deputies out there to check it out."

"No, I can go myself." He raised his eyebrows. "I'll be okay. I promise not to touch anything if it looks like it's been broken into."

Riley returned the note to the envelope and pushed a lock of brown hair out of his eyes. He had one of those mischievous, ready-to-break-into-a-smile faces that probably still looked the same as it did when he was twelve.

"I've been a little paranoid since my husband was—"

"—murdered?"

"Yes." I clenched my fists on top of the desk. "Look, it's clear someone thinks I have something they want, but I don't have a clue what that could be."

"Let's talk about your husband's death for a minute. What have the police said?"

I sighed, dreading going over even the smallest part

of the investigation again. I looked into Sheriff Riley's kind eyes, a big change from the cold Asheville detective handling Kent's case, and said, "Drug money. They think a burglar on drugs looking for money to buy more drugs tried to rob my apartment, then panicked when Kent opened the door."

"But you don't buy that."

"It's Detective Logan's theory, and I've always found it hard to swallow. I mean, the intruder might have been high all right, and panicked, to be sure. But he or she still had the presence of mind to fire a bullet right between Kent's blue eyes." I got up and walked to the window. "And why would our apartment, situated halfway down a hall, be randomly targeted? If the robbery was about money, why was nothing of value taken? Even a teenager strung-out on crystal meth knows that a camera and jewelry and electronic equipment can be pawned for a fistful of quick cash. No, I think it's more than that."

Riley sealed the envelope in a plastic bag.

"My aunt's room at Laurel Haven was vandalized a few weeks ago. I don't think anything was taken, but I'm worried she could be a target like I am."

"I don't mean to criticize Detective Logan—"

"Oh, go ahead. I've been doing it every day since Kent died."

"But as far as theories go, that's a pretty lazy one." Riley sipped something from a half-full coffee mug and made a face. "Whatever this person wants, it's probably small enough to fit into your purse, or they wouldn't be looking for it there. I think the fake fire at the inn was just a gimmick to get hold of your purse and search it."

"Do you think Aunt Pris is in danger?"

"I'm sure she's fine," Sheriff Riley said. "But I'll call the security department at Laurel Haven and make sure someone is checking on her regularly."

"Thanks," I said. "I would appreciate that."

"No problem. When your husband was killed, what was the situation? Was he still living with you?"

"No, he'd moved out. I had already filed for divorce. There was barely anything of his left in the apartment. He hadn't unpacked much, so most of it was still in boxes. When he left, he just carried them out, loaded them into a U-Haul, and drove away."

"With his new boyfriend?"

I nodded. "How does everybody know this? Did somebody publish it in the *Bitter Ridge Gazette?"*

"It's in the police report."

"Of course, it is." I sat back down. "Did you read it? Can I get a copy?"

"I'm not authorized to give it to you. But as next of kin, you should be allowed full disclosure. Have you asked Detective Logan to give you a copy? If he balks, you should be able to request one through your attorney."

If I had an attorney.

"Did the report say I promised Kent I'd stay at the apartment and wait on him but instead left before he got there?"

"Yes. It also said you have an airtight alibi."

"The owner of the deli I was at remembered me. He'd seen me sitting at the corner table crying and given me a free piece of chocolate cheesecake. He was probably hitting on me, but I was too upset to notice."

"Why didn't you stay and meet Kent?"

"I…couldn't."

"Why not?"

"I didn't want to see his face again."

I had promised I would stay, but as the minutes dragged on, the fact that he'd been concealing a secret life for months, a life he knew would destroy us if I ever found out, stuck in my craw. I hated him for changing into someone I didn't know—would never know. And so I bolted.

The stubborn streak Kent had always detested in me reared its ugly head to him one last time. Instead of waiting, I drove to downtown Asheville and treated myself to lunch at the Unicorn Deli, plowing my way through an organic hot pastrami on rye, enjoying the smug satisfaction I felt at standing him up, leaving him to flounder like an actor who's been abandoned onstage by a temperamental leading lady. Only then, when the high of exacting some sweet revenge of my own began to wear off, and I realized that losing Kent meant losing my husband *and* my best friend, did I begin to sob. I couldn't bear to face an empty apartment, so I stayed at the deli for two more hours eating cheesecake, talking to the owner, drinking lavender-infused decaf iced tea, solving crossword puzzles on my phone. When I finally made it home, I found the apartment building swarming with police, my unpacked boxes overturned, and the husband I was divorcing dead on the floor.

Riley drummed his fingers on the desk. "You want to know what I think?"

"That's why I'm here."

"I think it's all connected. I think if you find out who wants something from you, you'll find out who murdered your husband. I agree with Detective Logan about your husband not being the target. I think someone went to your apartment looking for—whatever—and your husband—"

"Will you please stop calling him that?"

"Sorry." His expression softened. "Your dead soon-to-be-ex-husband just got in the way. He opened the door, surprised the burglar, and the burglar shot him. I don't think it was personal. Kent just happened to be in the wrong place at the wrong time."

"Thanks to me," I said under my breath.

Sheriff Riley shook his head sadly. He knew the deal. We both did. If I'd stayed at the apartment like I'd promised, the deadbolt would have been locked and the robber would not have been able to break in. And Kent Chandler would still be alive. This is what I carried with me. Every hour. Of every day.

"I'm not sure what to do." I bit my lip to keep it from trembling. "Or who to trust."

"Are you still staying at the St. Clairs' house?"

"I thought I had left for good, but when I stopped by the inn to pick up my car, they said Olivia had called and had my bags sent to her house."

"I think you should stay with them," Riley said. "At least until we find out who's stalking you, for want of a better word. The St. Clairs are decent people. James still has a few supporters in this town, including me. What happened with that land development deal on Gray Top awhile back tore this town apart. But greed will do that, won't it?"

I nodded.

"For now, I believe the St. Clair house is the safest place you could be. James put up those security cameras and that big fence for a reason. It's virtually impenetrable." Deputy McBride signaled to Sheriff

Riley through the glass door. “I’ve got to go.”

“What about the letter?”

“We're pretty bare-bones around here. I'll have to send it to the lab in Asheville. They’ve got your fingerprints on file from your husband’s—from before, so they’ll be able to eliminate them. But don't get your hopes up. Unless you're dealing with a moron, anonymous notes are usually wiped clean. Just be aware of your surroundings and don't take any chances.”

I laughed nervously. “And call if I wake up with a knife in my back?”

“You’ve got my number.”

“I do. Thanks. I’m going to visit my aunt’s house on Crow Mountain today.”

“Be careful up there, Emory. I’ve had to run vandals out of that house more than once. Of course, it could be because someone started a rumor that your aunt—the one who died—left some kind of treasure hidden on the property.”

“And they think I found it?”

“Don’t know about that.” Sheriff Riley said. “Just keep your eyes open. Like I said, you have my number.”

“On a very nifty business card.”

“Yes. I’m a sheriff with a business card.” Riley grinned and patted his holster. “Cool, isn't it? I love this job.”

Chapter Six

Instead of heading back to Laurel Haven, I called the number the nurse had given me to check on Aunt Pris' condition. I was rung through immediately. *Holding her own and fast asleep.* So everything was fine. I didn't have to rush back.

I drove a few miles outside of town to the storage unit. The manager went in with me, and I was relieved to find the lock still in place and everything inside untouched. Every box, every plastic container I'd so carefully packed was still taped and labeled just like I'd left it. Maybe the person who had stolen the keys couldn't locate the storage unit. I purchased a new heavy-duty lock from the manager and clamped it on the door.

I was halfway back to Bitter Ridge when a quick storm blew through, leaving the spotty remnants of a rainbow trailing across the slate-gray sky. I drove through the valley and made the sharp turn onto Holly Berry Road. Every tree, every wildflower, every bend in the road looked brand new and familiar at the same time. As the car began the steep climb through the dense hardwood forest, my heart filled with the dizzy rush of anticipation. I stopped for a moment at the small wooden bridge straddling Stoney Creek. I'd swum there almost every day when I was thirteen. Even in the dog days of August, it had been as cold as the pitcher of water in Aunt Pris' refrigerator.

I drove past the turnoff for the Joyner Christmas Tree Farm and glanced at my phone. No signal. I knew I was in the mountains, but I still didn't get it. Why wasn't there a signal? Cell towers weren't that hard to erect.

As I reached the top of the hill, the sun broke through the clouds, and there it was: the three-story gabled house of my dreams, shimmering in the distance like a mirage. I was so happy to see it, my heart squeezed hard in my chest. But my elation was short-lived. The closer I came, the more I realized that what I'd been seeing was a mirage. The white paint had peeled back to the bare wood. Shingles were either missing or falling off. Shards of broken glass clung to the porch roof. The front steps crumbled like decayed front teeth. Winters could be harsh in the Blue Ridge, but this grand old house had had its ass kicked to hell and back.

I climbed the porch steps and pulled the screen door open. My heart fell again. No need for a key. The lock had been jimmied ages ago. Anyone with the strength to push the warped door open could go inside anytime they wanted.

In the foyer, my spirits sank even lower. Spider webs tangled across the ceiling like cheap Halloween decorations. The few pieces of furniture left intact were covered in gray grimy dust. Through the arched doorway, in what Aunt Pris had always called the parlor, dirty sheets covered the high-backed Victorian sofa. Gaping holes mutilated the plaster walls. Half opened upper windows had let in rain, soaking the mildewed carpet runner on the stairs. Muddy footprints trailed across the filthy hardwood floor.

I wandered from room to room as if I were in a dream. The sounds and smells I tried to conjure from the past refused to come. Nothing of Aunt Pris still lingered there—no warmth, no memory I could hold on to. I felt cheated and sad, knowing I had waited too long to come back.

Aunt Pris had been in the nursing home for less than two years. How could her house have fallen into such horrible disrepair in that short of time? And where was everything? The soft velvet curtains, the porcelain knickknacks, the family photographs? All the homey touches I recalled with such affection had vanished. Even the paintings were gone, their ghostlike outlines still visible against the faded green wallpaper. I wandered through the upstairs bedrooms. If there were a treasure hidden inside the house, I didn't know what it could be.

A sequence of loud knocks on the back door brought me racing down the squishy rain-soaked stairs. I circled through the dining room and looked out the kitchen window. A woman, small and stout, stood beside the crab apple tree, squinting up at the house. Sprigs of gray hair hung over her white canvas sun visor. The skin beneath her eyes rested on her cheeks in bulging half-moons. She spotted me, grinned, and waved.

I shoved the back door open with my hip and went outside.

"You've got to be Emory," she said, pulling me down to her level, gathering me into a warm hug. "Oh, honey, let me look at you. All grown up now, and so pretty! Do you remember me? I'm Alpha Hoskin from down the road."

So this was the person who was supposed to be looking after Aunt Pris' house? Like hell she was. The poor house was on its last legs. It was literally falling down. This woman hadn't lifted a finger. I took a deep breath and shoved my fists into my pockets. Getting mad wouldn't solve anything. It might make me feel better. But it wouldn't solve anything.

"How is Pris?" she asked, her smiling face suddenly wrinkled with concern.

"It's going to take some time, but the doctors think she's going to recover."

"Priscilla Austen is a tough old bird. Henry and I both said it just wasn't her time yet." Mrs. Hoskin wiped her hands on the front of her dirt-streaked apron. They were working hands, rough and calloused like mine. "Emory Austen, just look at you."

"I'm a Chandler now. Emory Chandler." Though not for long. As soon as Kent's will was probated, I planned to change my name back to Austen.

"I was here when you came to visit that summer," Alpha said. "You were just a scrawny little teenager then. I used to come over and help with the cleaning and washing. Did some cooking, too. You always liked my blueberry pancakes with hot maple syrup."

"You helped out in the mornings, didn't you?" I did remember her, but as some dim light eclipsed by the bright and shining star that was Aunt Pris.

"Oh, I was over here more than that. Through the years, I've helped your aunties out in many ways, many times."

"About Aunt Pris' house—"

"This house is one of the few places you can see all

the mountains at once." She swept her hand toward the horizon. "And these mountains don't tell no tales. Do you know their names?"

"Some of them."

"Well, you're standing on Crow." She pointed to her left. "That one over there is Gray Top. The one next to it is Big Bear. And the fire tower is on Clemdon. They're part of the Blue Ridge Mountains. But Old Baldy, on the other side of the river where it runs into Stoney Creek, is part of the Smokies. The Great Smoky Mountains National Park starts at the bottom and runs west."

"Mrs. Hoskin, what happened to my aunt's house? It's in terrible shape."

"Now, you call me Alpha. You used to love my name, remember? You used to call me Alpha-Bits." Her round face crinkled into a grin.

"Let's sit down."

Alpha reached between her legs and pulled her housedress through the opening like a calico diaper. She swiped a few dead leaves out of the way and sat on the edge of the porch beneath the overhang where it was dry. She pulled off her sun visor and wiped her forehead with the back of her hand. "I know I'm a sight. I was trying to get my tomato plants out when that rain hit. Jackson—the boy who works for us—ain't showed up yet, and Henry's out in the field. I guess Jackson can let himself in the gate. He has keys to everything."

"Jackson Spencer?"

"That's right. His family lives over that hill on Holly Berry."

"I heard you were taking care of the house for Aunt

Pris."

She squinted up at me. "Well, I was, but I ain't no more. It's a mess, I know."

My irritation shot up a notch. "A *mess*? The pipes have burst. The upstairs windows are broken. The walls are bashed in. And I don't even want to know what that smell is in the back bedroom. Aunt Pris would be horrified."

"I tried to get her to fix it up before she went to Laurel Haven, but she didn't want to put no money in it."

"Where are her things? Her furniture? Her personal belongings?"

"Now, I don't know about that. When Pris broke her hip and moved into the nursing home, I thought she'd be back soon. But she never came home." Alpha glanced over her shoulder and lowered her voice to a whisper. "I told her I'd look after the house, and I meant to. But that was before Portia came back."

"Excuse me?"

"Her sister—your aunt—Portia. She comes back almost every night now."

"My dead Aunt Portia? How do you know that? Have you seen her?"

"I've seen lights moving through the house after dark. And I'm not the only one, either. Ask Henry if you don't believe me. This spring, I told him I wasn't gonna set foot in this house no more. And I haven't."

"So you think the house is haunted?"

Alpha's eyes widened. "I know you don't believe me, but it's true."

"It's not that I don't believe—" Actually, it was. I looked at her frightened face and softened my voice.

"Look, Alpha. Sheriff Riley said he had run vandals off from here several times. That's probably what you've been seeing. Didn't you notice that the lock on the front door has been forced open? And not by a ghost unless the ghost of my Aunt Portia needed a crowbar to get inside. There are footprints on the floor, and I'm pretty sure they weren't left by a ghost."

"I told my Henry, and I'll tell you: Portia Austen is back. That woman was too mean to stay dead for long."

A car door slammed in the distance.

"Have you mentioned any of this to Pris?"

"No." Alpha shook her head. "I didn't want to worry her."

"But if you were afraid to go in the house, why didn't you call Sheriff Riley? Or find someone else to look after it?"

"Mrs. Hoskin?" Gordon Spencer rounded the left side of the house and charged toward us through the tall grass. "Is everything all right?"

"Gordon!" Mrs. Hoskin clasped her hand over her heart. "Oh, Lord, is something wrong with my Henry?"

"Oh, no. I'm sure he's fine." His gaze darted over Alpha's head to me. "I was on my way to the inn and saw a car parked in Miss Austen's driveway. Then I saw Daisy loping down the road, so I figured you were up here. I turned around and came back to see if you were all right."

"That durned dog follows me everywhere." Alpha glanced at the road. "Henry must have taken her home. Let me introduce you to Emory."

"Emory and I have met. She's a guest at the inn."

Gordon looked even more like Kent than I remembered. They both had the same chin, the same blond hair, the same startling blue eyes. Gordon's eyes—Kent's eyes—locked with mine.

"Our house is the last one on Holly Berry Road," he said. "Over the crest of Crow on the other side."

"The old Cameron place."

"That's right." He pointed to the top of the hill. "Just around the curve. We're practically neighbors."

"You and your wife?"

Alpha snorted.

"I'm not married," he said. "I live with my mother—" He grinned. "Yeah, I'm one of those guys. I still live with my mother."

"As long as you do your own laundry," I said.

"He also lives with his father," Alpha said. "And his younger brother, Jackson."

"Jackson gets around," I said.

Alpha adjusted her sun visor. "I gotta go fix Henry's lunch. He's a fine man, but he turns into an ornery old goat if he gets hungry."

We followed her to the front of the house, and she waved a cheerful goodbye as she walked toward the road. I was sorry to see her go. I had a lot more questions about my aunt's house.

"I didn't realize you were Pris' neighbor," I said. "Why didn't you say something when I checked in?"

Gordon shrugged. "My family has lived here for about ten years. I had a place in town for a while, but my father's not in the best of health. We've hired someone to help my mother care for him when I'm working."

I laughed. "So you *don't* do your laundry?"

"I'll never tell." He glanced at the Austen house. "Some of the locals around here swear there's a treasure hidden inside. Portia's treasure, they call it. That's the rumor, anyway."

"That would explain the holes in the walls and the lights Mrs. Hoskin has seen going from room to room at night. I'll bet the whole town comes up here treasure hunting after dark."

"We should make it part of the Bitter Ridge Summer Festival."

"Along with watermelon seed spitting and horseshoes?"

"You got it." He grinned. "It's a shame about your aunt's house, though. This old place needs work, but it could be gorgeous. You, on the other hand, are already gorgeous."

I laughed. "You southern boys lay it on pretty thick, don't you?"

"We try." His blue eyes twinkled. "And sometimes it works."

We walked to the front porch. "So you manage the inn for your father?"

"The McAlister belongs to me. Dad signed it over two years ago. He used to be at the inn all day, but not anymore. I doubt if he even remembers what the lobby looks like."

"I'm sorry he's sick."

"No, it's fine. I love the inn, but running it can be a challenge. If I got a decent offer to sell, and I thought I could find a way out, I'd unload it in a heartbeat."

"Gordon, about the fire—or whatever they're calling it—have you found out anything?"

"Riley hasn't said much. Just that they've finished fingerprinting the place and questioning the staff. Other than that, I don't know."

"It's crazy."

"I know. Hard to believe someone would do something that destructive. And for what? The room across the hall from yours is toast. It's gonna cost a fortune just to make it habitable again. I hope Riley nails whoever did this, and soon."

"I hope so, too."

"Are you still staying at the St. Clairs'?"

"For the time being. Olivia has been really kind to me."

"What about James? Most women like James."

"I don't know him. He seems nice enough."

"Just be careful, Emory. Beneath that good-old-boy southern charm, James has a dark side." We looked up as James' green Jeep Wrangler rumbled up the road and turned into the driveway. "And speak of the devil—here he is. I can't catch a break, can I?"

James cut the ignition and swung out of the car. "Hello, Emory. Gordon."

Gordon frowned. "What are you doing up here? Slumming?"

"Jackson's hanging out with Maddie, and his truck died again. I gave him a ride to Alpha's. She said Emory was up here." He looked at me. "I didn't know you two knew each other."

"Of course, I know her. She stayed at the inn, remember?"

"An experience she's not likely to forget any time soon. And you're here because…."

"I didn't recognize Emory's car," Gordon said. "With all the break-ins, I was worried about Alpha."

"Don't be," James said. "She carries a gun in her bra." He turned to me. "Have you had a chance to look inside the house?"

"Yeah." I sighed. "It's a wreck. I thought it might be neglected, but I never expected it to be such a lost cause. It's breaking my heart."

James crossed his arms over his chest and leaned back against the Jeep. "I've been in love with this old house for years. And just so you know," he added softly, "I don't believe in lost causes."

"That's our James," Gordon said. "Always the optimist. I've heard he's trying to buy lots on Crow Mountain. Too bad someone is beating him to it."

"What are you talking about?" James said.

"Someone's trying to develop Crow Mountain," Gordon said. "Someone with a big bank account and a reputation people can trust."

"Who?" James said.

Gordon laughed. "Oh, you'd like to be the big hero this time around, wouldn't you? Make up for the disaster you caused two years ago. Well, good luck. Because there isn't a person in town who'd piss on you if you were on fire, much less sell you a lot on Crow Mountain."

"And you'll make sure of that, won't you?"

"Why don't you stop lying, James. Everyone knows how desperate you are to develop Crow. Just admit it."

James took a step toward Gordon. "Who is the buyer? Tell me."

"A Mr. Castril," Gordon said. "I'm not even sure what his first name is. He's a wealthy entrepreneur recluse living on the Florida coast. I don't think anyone has met him, but his emails sure talk a good game. So far, he's made offers to the Hoskins and Ned Joyner.

They're decent offers, too. They'd be fools to turn them down." Gordon checked his watch. "Christ, it's late. I have to get to work. Like now."

After Gordon left, I turned to James. "Do you own land on Crow Mountain?"

"No."

"Are you planning to buy land up here to develop it?"

"It has crossed my mind. But no."

"Who is Mr. Castril?"

"I've never heard of him; he may not even exist. Gordon might be bluffing. Nothing would please him more than to see me fail again."

"So you made a mistake. Why all the hostility?"

"His family-owned property on Gray Top. Their finances were affected as much as everyone else's when the deal fell through. Gordon is bitter." He gazed at the mountains in the distance. "Everyone is bitter. That's why we live in Bitter Ridge, I guess."

I sat on the front steps. "You said that if someone was trying to develop Crow Mountain, they couldn't do it without obtaining the Austen property. Is that true?"

"It would be difficult. Not impossible, but difficult."

I glanced behind me at the house. "It doesn't matter. Even if this old Victorian crumbles to the ground, Pris will never sell."

"Don't be so sure. She's happy at Laurel Haven, and this house holds a lot of bad memories for her. I don't think she'll ever come back to it."

"You're wrong. She was born here. It's her home."

"I think you want it to be your home."

I started to fire back a smartass reply but stopped.

Maybe James was right. After visiting Pris at the nursing home, I had fantasized about going back, guns blazing, and springing her from that awful one-room prison. It was one of the most depressing places I'd ever seen. But if holding on to a falling-down house on top of a mountain was what *I* wanted, and not her, then I was the selfish one. It wasn't Pris' fault I couldn't stop believing that the house on Crow Mountain was the only place my heart could heal and forgive myself for causing Kent's death. I had felt that for months, and I wanted it to be true.

But who was I kidding? I didn't belong in the mountains of North Carolina. I didn't belong anywhere. I was just another fish out of water, flopping around on dry land, unable to find the sea when it was two feet in front of me. The home I thought I'd left on Crow didn't exist anymore. I wasn't sure it ever had.

"I'll follow you to the car rental place," James said. "You can turn in your car then we can swing by the garage and pick up Maddie's Jeep. Jackson said it's ready. You can drive it while you're staying with us. You okay driving a stick shift?"

"Maybe." I laughed. "Before we moved to New York, my husband had an old four-in-the-floor Mustang I used to tool around in. But that was four years ago, and my driving skills are a little rusty. Are you sure I can handle it?"

"Absolutely. Jeeps pretty much drive themselves, anyway."

"Uh-huh. And I'm supposed to believe that?"

"I wouldn't lie to you."

James followed me down the narrow mountain road. It was comforting to glance in the rearview mirror and see his Jeep splashing around the same muddy curves and bumping over the same potholes as I did. It felt safe.

I liked James. Even if I was in the Bitter Ridge minority, he seemed like a good guy who'd made one huge, really stupid mistake. But trusting him was a whole different animal.

I needed to talk to Alpha Hoskin again. I was sure she knew more than she was letting on, and I wanted to find out what she'd meant when she said she'd helped out Pris and Portia in many ways. I also wanted to know if there was a more plausible reason Alpha had stopped looking after Pris' house other than avoiding Portia's ghost. And what had happened to Pris and Portia's things? Where were the high back chairs? The marble-topped tables? The hand-blown globe lamps? Where were the mementos and the photo albums and the embroidered linens? Had Pris sold them or given them away before she moved into assisted living? Or had the people breaking into her house at night carried them out?

Tomorrow I would conduct a more thorough search of the house, starting with the attic and the cellar. There were nooks and crannies hidden in the old place that might have gone undetected by someone searching with a flashlight. There was also the large envelope Mrs. Shipley had given me. I was eager to go through the documents and find out if there was a clue tucked away somewhere. Was Aunt Pris even aware that her house was practically empty? I wished I could ask her about it. If she improved in the next few days, and the doctor gave his approval, she might be able to answer some of my questions.

My head was spinning.

But at least I had a plan. I always did better with a plan.

And, even though Tess wasn't going to like it one little bit, I also had a place to stay with a ten-foot electric fence.

Chapter Seven

"Don't be silly." Olivia scraped the meat from a falling-off-the-bone pork butt onto a platter. "Of course you're staying for dinner."

I had planned on retreating to my room, but the mouthwatering aroma of Olivia's barbecue, plus the fact that I hadn't eaten anything all day besides a cup of Mrs. Shipley's cocoa and a stale granola bar, rooted my feet to the floor.

"This is an amazing kitchen," I said, looking around. "You must love to cook."

"Cooking is much cheaper than eating out," Olivia said, "and since my divorce, I've been forced to live a bit more…frugally."

"It's nice of you to let me stay here," I said, meaning every word. "I wish there was some way I could repay you."

She wiped her hands on her apron. "You can paint my portrait."

"Really?"

"I've seen the oil painting you did of your father hanging in Pris' room. I'd love one of me just like that. But you don't have to do it in oils. Pastels are fine. Charcoal. Whatever you decide. Will you do it?"

My portraits usually took anywhere from a few days to a few weeks to complete, depending on the size and the background. If I did something small for Olivia that I could knock out in a day or two, I would still have time to spend with Aunt Pris.

"I'd be happy to," I said. "I brought my pencils and crayons with me, but I'll need to pick up some paper."

"Wonderful." She took bowls of coleslaw and broccoli raisin salad out of the refrigerator. "How will this work? Should I pose for you?"

"I'll take some photos with my phone then sketch you in pencil first. Then I'll add color. You won't need to sit for me."

Tess appeared in the doorway. "James hasn't come down yet?"

"Not yet," Olivia said.

Tess smoothed her white eyelet blouse, which showed only slightly less cleavage than a Victoria's Secret Valentine's Day ad, and glared at me. She sat on her usual stool at the end of the island and crossed her long legs. "I thought you'd left."

"Change of plans," I said.

"Then I just lost my appetite," Tess said. "I don't want dinner after all."

"You don't eat enough to keep a gerbil alive," Olivia said. "All you're eating is junk. And you need to clean up after yourself, little girl. I come down in the middle of the night for a cup of tea and there's trash everywhere. Food left out. Dishes in the sink. It's a wonder we don't have mice pitching tents under the table."

"Maddie's bringing a guest for dinner," Tess said.

"Well, it better not be that boy," Olivia said.

"Oh, it's him, all right." Tess put her hands over her heart and sighed, *"Jackson."* She smiled, clearly enjoying the discord she was stirring up. "There's

James." She smoothed her denim skirt over her narrow hips and opened the patio door. She was tall and slender enough to be a model, but as she sidled up to James, her strappy four-inch heels made her teeter from side to side like an inebriated giraffe.

Olivia moved a gallon of ice cream to the front of the freezer. "We need chocolate sauce for the sundaes." She shuffled some things around on a pantry shelf. "Here it is. Half gone, of course. It amazes me the way food disappears out of this kitchen."

I helped myself to a chip. "Sounds like you're not too thrilled Jackson is coming."

Olivia leveled her gaze at me. "That's putting it mildly."

"He's young," I said. "We all go through phases."

"You think this is a phase?" She laughed. "His parents, Helen and Frank, are friends of mine, but even they can't talk any sense into him. Have you seen his tattoos? He looks like he should join a circus."

"Everyone has tattoos now," I said. "It would be strange if he *didn't* have one."

"Maddie says she's going to marry him, but I will not let that happen. Helen says if I try to keep them apart, I'll end up pushing them together. Like Romeo and Juliet." She rolled her eyes. "Helen watches Hallmark."

"Why don't you like Jackson?"

"He works in a *garage*, for God's sake. Maddie is an A student, but she can't think straight when it comes to that boy. She'll do anything he says. Did you know he ran away from home four times before he was sixteen? He cheated his way through high school and spent a year in a reformatory for stealing beer from a 7-

Eleven. I wouldn't trust him with a dog I liked, much less my own child. And now, Maddie wants to marry him." Olivia shook her head. "Not happening. And I'll do whatever it takes to make sure of that."

Watching the soft-spoken well-mannered Olivia St. Clair morph into an angry she-cat hellbent on protecting her youngest cub was a revelation. But why should I be surprised at anything she said or did? I'd known the woman for less than twenty-four hours. And if I'd learned anything in the last two months, it was that even the most boring predictable people on earth were not always who they appeared to be.

****

After dinner, I was antsy to get upstairs and go through Aunt Pris' Manilla envelope. I had unsealed it to take out the house keys but hadn't opened any of the folders. Hopefully, I would find some receipts for Pris' missing belongings and put that mystery to rest. I tried to excuse myself and leave, but Olivia refused to let me skip out on the ice cream sundae buffet. And I had to admit, the glutton in me didn't really want to. I ignored Tess' pointed stares and piled enough M & M's and rainbow sprinkles on my vanilla ice cream to nauseate a ten-year-old.

James sat across from me at the glass-topped table. Tess scooted in beside him and dipped her index finger into his ice cream. "Oh, I see how it is," he said.

"Just a taste." Tess eyed my bowlful of fat and calories with disdain. "A taste is all I can stomach after that huge meal."

"So, Jackson," I said, not holding out much hope he would let me engage him in polite conversation but figuring it was worth a chance. "It must be nice having a grand old place like the McAlister in your family. Do you help out?"

Jackson looked at me like I'd just asked him why he never wore deodorant—a good question for another time. "My father doesn't think anyone is smart enough to work at the inn except Gordon."

"At least the rain has stopped for now," James said.

"Lucky for Emory," Tess said. "Her hair is twice as curly as it was this morning."

"I like her hair," James said.

"Well, that makes one of us," I said, gazing longingly at Tess' silky hair cascading over her thin shoulder like a dark waterfall. "I bet you never have to worry about anything as pedestrian as humidity. I used to pray for hair like yours. It probably comes with a built-in force field."

"Yes, it does," Tess said.

James laughed. "Which only reinforces my belief that Tess was dropped off at her parents' house by aliens."

Tess turned her attention to me. "My parents are on an archeological dig in Abu Simbel. I would've gone with them, but I can't stand the heat. Where are *your* parents?" Her tiger eyes held mine, unwavering and malicious. I was sure she knew exactly where my parents were.

I lowered my bite of ice cream and kept my voice steady. "My parents were travelers, too. They weren't archeologists like yours, Tess, although they were passionate about ancient history, and they had friends all over the world. My father spoke five languages. My mother spoke four. They walked and ate their way through every country in Europe and Asia without gaining a pound. They were crazy about Abu Simbel. They went to Egypt every March."

Tess wrinkled her nose. "Ugh. Why?"

"They loved the pyramids and the camel races, but knowing my parents, they probably went for the lentil soup and the guava milkshakes."

"They sound like my kind of folks," James said, laughing.

"They sound ridiculous," Tess said.

"Jeez, Tess." Maddie raised up from the crook of Jackson's arm. "Do you always have to be such a vicious bitch?"

"My parents were quite eccentric," I said. "But they were wonderful. I didn't see a lot of them growing up." I didn't point out to Tess how similar we were. She was a boarding school brat like me who had most likely been dumped at the St. Clairs' just like I had been dumped somewhere I didn't want to be for more summers than I could remember.

Olivia slid open the patio door. "Are you still here, Jackson?"

"Of course he's here, Mother," Maddie said. "You see him, don't you?" She shot Olivia a disgusted look. "Come on, baby. Let's get out of here."

After Maddie and Jackson had gone, I carried the ice cream dishes to the kitchen, eager to escape to my room. Tess suddenly came in from the patio, wobbled through the living room, and stomped up the winding stairs, no easy feat in heels high enough to reach the ceiling. I loaded the bowls into the dishwasher. On my way upstairs, I realized Tess had left the patio door open and reached for the handle to pull it closed. "You got another letter today," I heard Olivia say.

“Where is it?’ James said.

“On the table in the foyer,” Olivia said. “I thought it was addressed to me and opened it. Then I realized it was for you, so I put it back in the envelope without reading it. It looks like all the others.” There was a long pause. “It’s starting up again, isn’t it?”

James didn’t answer.

“I thought things were better. I thought we were done with all that.”

“I thought so too, Mother.”

“But why now?” Olivia’s voice quavered. “What’s happened to stir things up? Have you talked to Delbert or Connie? Made them angry?”

“They’re already angry.”

My heart began to beat in slow, rolling thuds.

I eased away from the door and retraced my steps around the dining room table, keeping close to the wall, praying I could make it to my room without Olivia or James seeing me. I passed the stone fireplace and wound my way through the maze of leather chairs to the bottom of the staircase. I looked up. No sign of Tess, so I turned and strode silently across the red woven rug to the foyer. A business size white envelope with James’ name and address typewritten on it sat propped beneath a banker’s lamp on the half-moon table. Without hesitating, I picked it up and opened it. I had to know what was in it. And I knew he wouldn’t tell me.

The paper, crisp and flat, slid out easily. I unfolded it.

You think that big fence of yours can keep her safe?

Not as long as that bitch has what I want.

Chapter Eight

No one had touched the Manilla envelope sitting on my dresser. I had placed it there meticulously, exactly two finger lengths from the ceramic lamp, quite pleased with myself that I'd thought to use a variation of the trick I'd seen once in a James Bond movie where Bond dampens a strand of hair and places it across the closed door to his hotel room, knowing that when he returns, if the hair is gone, someone has been inside.

I locked the door to my room and kicked off my shoes, then climbed onto the high antique bed. I dumped out the contents of the envelope and spread it across Alpha's quilt.

There wasn't much to see. A copy of Pris' Last Will and Testament naming me as sole beneficiary, a small life insurance policy, death certificates for Portia and Edward, the original deed to the Austen house, and a padded jeweler's box containing two pearl hatpins and a silver-filigree locket.

I pried open the locket with my thumbnail. A flat brass key about an inch long fell out and landed in my lap. I picked it up and turned it over. I was intrigued. What could a key like this open? A cabinet? A diary? A box holding the treasure everyone was so sure existed? Had my attacker at the hotel been after something as ordinary as a little brass key? It didn't seem likely. One trip to Home Depot for the right tools and you could open anything.

Three sharp raps sounded on the door. “Emory? It's James.”

My stomach lurched like someone had rocked the Ferris wheel seat.

Did he know what I’d done? Had he seen me read the note? What was I going to say to him? Confess I’d opened his mail and read the threatening letter? Tell him I knew my presence at his house might be putting him and his family in danger? Admit that I was afraid to stay but more afraid to leave?

I was so tired of being afraid.

I tucked the papers beneath the pillow shams, smoothed my hair back from my face, took a deep breath, and flung the door open.

James stood in the hallway holding a plate wrapped in tinfoil. “Oatmeal raisin cookies. Mother said to tell you how much she appreciates people who enjoy her cooking.”

“I guess scarfing down that second barbecue paid off, huh?”

“Apparently. I’m also supposed to tell you breakfast is at eight.”

“Oh, I'll be there. With my feedbag on.” The stairs behind him creaked. If James had heard it, he was choosing to ignore it, but I was sure it was Tess trying to eavesdrop. And since I was still stinging from the unkind remarks she’d made about my parents at dinner, I lowered my voice to a laughable version of a femme fatale and said, “Want to come in?”

“For a minute.” James stepped inside and pulled the door closed behind him. “I want to offer my services. Free, of course. But I’d be happy to take a look at your aunt's house to see if it's worth saving." His western North Carolina accent sounded a lot like the late Reverend Billy Graham. "Restoring old houses is what I do for a living. I could at least give you an idea what kind of shape it's in and what it would take to make it livable again."

"I would love that. Thanks."

He crossed the room and pulled open the side curtain, stirring the space between us. "You have a little balcony out here; did you know that?" He slid the glass door open, and I followed him outside. I breathed in the heady scent of pine and wild honeysuckle and gazed across the ravine to the dark forest. In the moonlight, I could just make out the outline of the mountains rolling across the horizon. "It's connected to the guest room next door." He leaned against the railing. "I'm sorry Tess was such a pill at dinner."

"I've run into girls like her before. Down deep, they're just insecure."

"Tess is about as insecure as Atilla the Hun."

"Where's your father?" I asked. "No one ever mentions him. Is he still around?"

"Not really. We don't get along very well. And last year, while he was still married to my mother, he fell in love with the twenty-six-year-old yoga instructor who was teaching him how to manage stress. They live together in Charlotte. He wanted a different life. And now, he's got one." The tiny lines around his eyes deepened.

"How did your mother take that?"

"Her pride took a big hit. And her pocketbook. My dad waited until the house was finished then left. I wish he'd never built it." He looked up. "What about you?

Are you missing the big city?"

"So far, no. There's nothing like the peace and quiet of a small town. Unless you count fire, robbery, and assault."

"Oh, I think I'd count them." The light from the room shimmered across his face.

"Tell me about your work," I said.

"Why, you need something to put you to sleep?"

"Is it that boring?"

He grinned. "Not to me. It's like finding the missing pieces to a giant puzzle. Kind of a nerdy thing to end up doing, though." He flexed his arms. "I always wanted to be the jock, the guy with the amazing biceps, but I was too lazy to go to the gym. Then I got interested in the history of old houses. I enjoy crawling around in basements and attics looking for pictures and original blueprints. Occasionally, I even break a sweat. Sometimes I come across proof that a house should be included in the national historic register, which is gratifying. The work can be tedious, but it's the most fun I've ever had."

"I feel like that when I'm painting."

"I haven't known many artists. Are they all like you?"

"Only the really talented ones."

He propped his feet on the railing like a cowboy sitting in front of the saloon on a slow day. "I'm sorry about your husband. I can't imagine suffering that kind of loss."

"I lost Kent a long time before he died. Maybe I never really had him, and I just didn't know it."

"Well, at least you're not bitter."

"Oh, I'm bitter, all right. I'm bitter as hell." I

glanced at him. "But there are two sides to every story and Kent isn't here to defend himself. If he were here, he'd tell you I have more faults than he could shake a stick at." The guilt began to pull me under. "But the worst one, the biggest one, is that it's my fault he's dead."

"How is that your fault?"

"I told him I'd be at the apartment the day he got killed. And then I left before he arrived just to piss him off. If I hadn't broken my promise and stayed, the safety locks would've been set. A Navy Seal couldn't have gotten in. Kent would still be alive."

"You don't know that."

"I do know that."

"It could've been you that was killed."

"That's what I'm saying. It *should* have been me." I forced a laugh. "Meanwhile, I'm hanging out in Bitter Ridge, North Carolina, running for my life down hotel corridors, getting my purse snatched by some creep in a gas mask, finding an anonymous note telling me to give something back to somebody."

"Someone sent you an anonymous note?"

"Yes." I looked at him. "Have you ever gotten one?"

He hesitated, and I could tell he was considering his options and it could go either way. He could tell me the truth about the anonymous letter I had read, or he could lie to my face.

"I've received a few of them in the last two years," he said.

Truth, then.

"Did they freak you out?"

"No. But I wasn't happy about it."

"Is that why you built a ten-foot fence around your house and put in enough security cameras to shoot an independent feature film?"

"After my father left, it was up to me to keep my mother and sister safe. I've gotten threats directed at all of us, but Mother refuses to move, and after everything she's been through, I can't ask her to. That's why I still live here in Bitter Ridge. That's why I do everything in my power to protect them."

If I had wanted the Universe to send me a sign that I should pack up and leave his house, that was it. Every minute I stayed I was putting his family in danger. I'm sure he felt that way, too. How could he not? Even with all the fancy security measures in place, I was an easy target.

I followed him to the door.

"Do you want to go to the Austen house tomorrow?" he said. "I have some time in the morning."

"That would be great."

"After I assess things, we can look for Portia's treasure. I'm good at unearthing clues in old houses." He stepped into the hall. "What time?"

"They're starting physical therapy with Pris in the morning, so I can't see her then anyway. After breakfast?"

"I have a conference call first thing, but it shouldn't last long."

He reached into his pocket and pulled out a business card. "My phone number. Just in case."

The curtains across the hallway ruffled softly.

"Tomorrow, then." He started down the hall. "Wear old clothes. Bring an umbrella."

"And cookies," I said.

I started to pull the bedroom door closed, but another movement across the hall caught my eye. On the far side, where the curtains spilled into a pool of chintz on the floor, I spotted Tess' neon pink painted toenails still encased in the white ankle-strap sandals. Still gently wobbling back and forth.

Chapter Nine

Ribbons of gray mist shrouded the mountains outside my window. It was early, and I squelched the urge to pull the quilt over my head and go back asleep, which is one of life's greatest pleasures on a rainy day. I cracked open the bottle of spring water sitting on my nightstand and pulled out my sketch pad and pencils.

Olivia's unique face wasn't hard to capture. The photos I'd taken of her on the patio helped reference the image I had begun to carry in my head: short pixie cut black hair, dark soulful eyes flashing with personality yet wary at the same time. Her smile was fleeting, and I decided to draw her with her mouth closed. I hated drawing teeth, anyway. The look I was going for was something between inscrutable mystery woman and tough girl power. Sketching something always helped me focus on the plans I needed to make.

Staying at the St. Clairs' house had felt safe, but after reading James' anonymous letter, I couldn't impose on them any longer. The first order of business was finding some transportation of my own. I didn't want to spend money on another rental car when I didn't know how long I would be in Bitter Ridge, but maybe I could cut a deal with one of the used car lots in the area. If I asked James to recommend someone, he would probably try and talk me out of it, but Gordon might know of someone who could help.

After pulling on jeans and an old cotton button-up shirt I had a love/hate relationship with, I went downstairs to the kitchen. I expected to see James waiting for me. Instead, I found Tess sitting on her stool, dipping pieces of a toasted frozen waffle into a jar of peanut butter.

She licked her index finger. "Did you finally get some sleep?"

"I did. Thanks for asking."

"We're on our own for breakfast. Olivia was up late last night with a migraine. Can I fix you something?"

"No thanks. I've got a granola bar in my purse."

I didn't trust this sudden rush of goodwill, but maybe I was just being paranoid. Which seemed to be the new normal for me.

"James left this for you." She slid a folded piece of notepaper across the granite countertop. "He can't text you because he's still on a Zoom call."

I opened it and marveled at his square sure handwriting. Blue ink. Straight lines. No smiley faces or hearts. I was sure Tess had already read it, but I read it out loud anyway. "Still on call. Looks like it might be a while. James."

"He said for me to drive you to your aunt's house so you can look around some on your own, then he'll meet us there later. I can drive Maddie's car back here. Jackson's taking her to work today because they're going venue shopping."

"Venue shopping? For the wedding?"

Tess folded her waffle in half like a taco. "Beats me." Her amber eyes met mine. "Maybe they're going to have a turkey shoot for the reception. Or go possum hunting. Isn't that what they do out here in the sticks? I can't understand why Maddie wants to marry that loser."

"They don't live in the sticks; they live on a mountain. And Maddie wants to marry Jackson because they're in love."

"Let's just hope he can get the axle grease out from underneath his fingernails before the big day."

I unclipped the flashlight hanging from the utility cabinet, thinking it might come in handy in a house without electricity. "Ready?"

I wasn't sure why James wanted me to go with Tess. I could have driven to the Austen house by myself and he could have met me there. I had a feeling he'd set up this little outing on purpose to give us a chance to get to know each other. Tess and I had gotten off on the wrong foot. Maybe some time alone with her would soften things up, make her see that I wasn't a threat. And maybe Matt Damon would show up at my front door and beg me to paint his portrait.

Ten minutes later, I was gripping the handle in Maddie's Jeep as we barreled down Gray Top Mountain, grateful I hadn't eaten the granola bar. The bottle of water I'd downed was sloshing back and forth in my stomach like the rinse cycle in a washing machine. I peered out the window at the gray threatening sky.

"It's supposed to start raining again and continue through the night," Tess said. "Did you bring the key?"

"The key?" I touched the silver locket at the base of my throat.

"Yeah, you know that little thing shaped like alligator teeth that opens doors?"

"We won't need a key. The lock on the front door is hanging by a thread."

She bumped over a pothole. "Are you really painting Olivia's portrait?"

"It's the least I can do to repay her for her hospitality."

"It's the least you can do to suck up and ingratiate yourself to her. I saw you and James in the hall last night exchanging phone numbers."

I sighed. "He gave me his. I did not give him mine. It's a professional courtesy. He's going to evaluate my aunt's house. It's what he does for a living."

She glanced at me sideways. "But you're attracted to him, right?" She downshifted and began the steep climb up Crow Mountain. "You can't hide that."

"He's a good-looking guy. But I'm not interested."

"That isn't how it looks to me," Tess said. "It looks like you're embarrassing yourself falling all over him." My stomach lurched as she careened around a switchback. "I mean, I understand that it must be nice to get attention from someone as masculine as James since your dead husband was…you know…gay."

"Watch out!"

The Jeep Wrangler swerved to the right. It left the road and plowed upward through a thicket of mountain laurel and chicory, bumping over rocks and clumps of black dirt. A low hanging branch whipped past my window. I swallowed another scream and gripped the sidebar as the Jeep slid to a stop between a line of boulders and a thin strip of grass that served as a shoulder on the narrow road.

"*What the—?*" Tess jumped out. "*Hey! Get out of the way.*"

A brown bloodhound sat in the middle of the road, staring at us. Her whiskered jowls dropped into caramel-colored folds that sunk into her thick neck. Long black and brown ears swung down on either side of her face like two pork chops. A tiny globule of drool glistened on the side of her soft mouth.

I got out and stood beside the car.

"Go home, you big mongrel," Tess yelled. "Get out of the freakin' road."

The dog backed up a few yards, turned around, and sat down.

"She's hardly a mongrel," I said.

The dog thumped her long tail on the ground.

I slapped my thighs. "Come here, girl!"

The dog bounded over to me at once. I let her sniff the back of my hand, then rubbed her throat and gave her a playful scratch behind her floppy ears. "What a good girl you are. Why, you're not so fierce."

"She probably belongs to the Hoskins," Tess said. "I think their house is down that dirt driveway."

"You've been on Crow Mountain before?"

"Well, sure." She looked a little taken aback. "Maddie and I were driving around one day, and she brought me up here to see where Jackson lived."

I led the bloodhound to the side of the road and knelt beside her. "Now, listen, puppy dog, I don't want you to get hurt. So you have to stay here until we drive away, understand?" I lifted a soft, droopy ear. "I need you to do this. Don't make me look bad."

Tess and I got back in the Jeep. As she drove around the wide curve leading up the hill to Stoney Creek Bridge, she glanced in the rearview mirror. "What are you? A dog whisperer?"

I turned around and looked behind us.

The bloodhound hadn't moved.

****

“Can I borrow your phone?” Tess ripped through my aunt’s front yard, barely missing the crumbling birdbath at the edge of the overgrown flower bed. “I forgot to charge mine last night, and I need to make a quick call.”

I hesitated.

“Oh, come on, Emory. I’m not going to call Abu Simbel or anything. I just need to check on my cousin Poppy. She lives in Baltimore. We’re like sisters.”

“Sure,” I said, still trying to win points with her. I fished my phone out of my purse and handed it to her.

“I’ll only be a minute,” she said. “Poppy’s having some personal problems. Her dad died last year. Go on inside. I’ll be right in.”

I nodded and closed the car door. I started up the steps and braced myself for another depressing trip through the Austen house. Hopefully, James could see the possibilities. Figure out a way to save it. I needed to look at the house objectively, and not as something I’d lost that held my best memories.

The interior was still a shock. Not only because of the water damage and sticky cobwebs hanging from the ceiling, but the disheartening fact that except for a few stained mattresses, a bashed-in sideboard, a high backed Victorian sofa, a mahogany piecrust table, and an oak hall tree standing in the foyer with a pale blue crocheted sweater hanging on its hook, everything was gone. The kitchen had been stripped bare except for a few oil lamps, some canned food I wouldn’t have the guts to open, much less eat, and a rusted waffle iron.

The air in the front room felt thick and oppressive, like something solid I had to push my way through. I walked to the brick fireplace. I'd forgotten about the two andirons on either side of the hearth—a medieval man and woman—standing across from each other with their arms outstretched. Pris used to call them Guinevere and Lancelot. They seemed sad to me, and I'd always felt sorry for them, forced to spend eternity apart holding up a blackened grate.

The sound of crunching gravel brought me lurching back to the present.

I ran to the front door.

"Tess!" I shouted, stumbling onto the front porch. *"Tess!"*

Tess beeped the horn twice and laughed, then stuck her arm out the window and waved to me without looking back. I stood helplessly, watching the Jeep speed down the road then over the hill and out of sight.

"Oh, Tess," I sighed. "Why didn't I see this coming?"

I ran to the kitchen where I'd left my purse on the counter. What was I doing? I couldn't call for help. Tess had my phone. She had trapped me at a house without running water or electricity without a car or a phone. Had she planned this? Of course, she had.

I wondered if James even knew she'd driven me out there? Or did he think I was still at his house waiting for him to give me a ride? Or had she lied to him too, and told him I wasn't going? I was beginning to realize Tess was more devious than I had given her credit for. A mistake I would not make again.

I went outside and stood on the front porch. Gray clouds swirled above Old Baldy. It was like a scene from a sci-fi movie when the camera pans upward just before the mothership appears in the sky.

Thunder cracked above my head.

Rain spit at me as the wind picked up. I went back inside.

I was angry. More at myself than at Tess. But I wasn't going to let it get to me. As long as I was stuck there, I might as well use my time wisely. After I'd explored the house, more thoroughly this time, I would walk down to the Hoskins' farm. I was sure they'd let me use their phone to call Bitter Ridge's one and only taxi to fetch me. I'd been wanting to talk to Alpha anyway.

An ardent list maker from way back—another trait that drove Kent up the wall—I pulled out a small notepad and pen. *Secure the house. Board up broken windows. Deadbolt the doors.* If I didn't do these things, and soon, whoever was breaking into the house would keep ripping it apart until there was nothing left to restore.

The rain began in earnest.

Sheets of mist sprayed across the rippled windowpanes, rattling them with each new gust of wind. I took the flashlight and started up the stairs. I glanced around, half expecting to see Aunt Portia scowling at me from the corner. But all I saw were cobwebs and dust.

Upstairs, the solitude was deafening as the rain pinged against the gabled roof. I wandered through the barren rooms, but I refused to lose heart. I still loved that old house as much as ever. And now it needed me. If James' inspection checked out, and most of the repairs were cosmetic, before I went back to my old life in New York, I would find a way to rescue it. No matter how many portraits I had to paint.

In Portia's old bedroom, the smallest of the four, I looked out the high half-moon window, hypnotized by the torrent of rain splashing on the gray slate shingles. Had Portia stood there year after year watching the seasons change? Feeling her life slip away until the day Edward Gilmore came back to Bitter Ridge? I hadn't really known Aunt Portia. But I knew what a broken heart felt like.

I ran my hand along the carved oak mantel. I'd never been allowed in Portia's room; Pris had always kept it locked. How many ghosts had taken up residence there? I sensed them all around me, both living and dead. Pris and Portia and Edward, the grandparents I had never met, me as a sarcastic thirteen-year-old on the brink of womanhood, following Pris around the house like a shelter dog who's been left by the side of the road.

As I turned to go, something behind the closet door caught my eye.

"I don't believe it." The swollen door scraped against the hardwood floor as I shoved it closed. Hidden in the corner behind the thick door stood three 16 x 20 framed watercolors. I pulled them out and propped them against the wall.

The paintings were delicate and beautifully done, all of them a swirling study in color and light. I wiped the dusty glass with the sleeve of my shirt. Each picture depicted a different view of the Austen house in summer. I looked for a signature and finally found it in the lower right-hand corner, concealed as part of the scenery. *PMA. Portia Martine Austen.* These paintings had to belong to Portia. I'd never heard of her doing any artwork, although, I supposed it was foolish, and even a little arrogant, to believe I was the only artist in the family.

Two of the paintings showed the side yard with Old Baldy looming behind it in the distance. Two girls stood beside a grape arbor in the third painting while a small boy sat perched on a wrought iron bench, dangling his chubby legs over the side. Was this a portrait of the three Austen children? Was the little boy my father, Preston? I was astonished that Portia's pictures had survived in a house that had been vandalized from top to bottom.

I stacked the watercolors beside the bedroom door, then pulled out the little flashlight I'd found in Olivia's garage. Time was slipping by. I needed to finish my search and head to Alpha's house. I checked out the other three bedrooms and the attic. The only thing I discovered of any consequence was a baby quilt stuffed in the back of a closet that must have belonged to my father. The handsewn blue and white squares were musty and ragged and water stained. But I knew I would cherish it forever.

I shoved the swollen basement door open and held on to the banister as I made my way down the narrow steps. The rain beat against the two pie-shaped windows near the ceiling, letting in a few wispy shafts of diffused light. The cellar air felt cold against my skin. As I descended the well-worn steps, I ran my hand along the cinder block walls. The last thing I expected to see when I reached the bottom were papers strewn everywhere. Heaps of them. In every shape and size. They tumbled out of two steamer trunks pushed against the wall, sat stacked in the corners, covered the concrete floor like Bourbon Street the day after Mardi Gras.

I picked up a few scraps and turned them over: a receipt from the Blue Ridge Greengrocer dated 1959, a 1978 insurance claim for Pris' old Pontiac, a handwritten invitation to Katharine McAlister's wedding. Portia and Priscilla's entire lives had been scribbled on these snippets of paper. It would take days to go through them all.

Along the side walls, open shelves held empty canning jars and a few rusted gardening tools. The rest of the basement had been emptied. No furniture, no boxes of mementos, no moldy photograph albums, or old clothes. Nothing that could be unlocked with a little brass key.

I checked my watch. It was almost noon. If James was meeting me here, then where was he? Oh, right. He wasn't coming. Tess had seen to that.

I mentally wrote *Transportation ASAP* on my notepad. I had to find a car of my own to drive. I was resourceful, but with my trips to the nursing home and Crow Mountain, I couldn't manage without one. Another mental note for my list: check the Classifieds in the *Bitter Ridge Gazette*. If I had to get a temporary job waitressing to pay for a used car, then so be it.

I started for the stairs. Again, something caught my eye. A few feet away from the old coal furnace, a small, slanted door about four feet high was nestled in the corner almost buried behind a stack of wooden planks. It was a miracle I had even noticed it.

I knelt and flipped the metal latch. The tiny door swung open. I crawled inside and turned on the flashlight. At the top, carved letters, rudimentary and childlike, encircled the perimeter. I pointed the light toward the space above the door.

P-A-P-A.

I scooted back and pulled my feet toward me until the door sprang closed and clicked. I moved the light horizontally along the top of the room as each new letter came into view.

PAPA WILL BURN IN HELL

"Dear God," I whispered. "What is this place?"

Whatever it was, it was giving me the creeps. Some of the letters formed deep grooves as if someone had taken a sharp object and dug it into the wall over and over again. Had someone locked a child in this room? Who would do that? My grandfather? He'd had a reputation for being stern and strict. But which child? It couldn't have been Preston, my father. He had been sent to Great-Aunt Claudia's house in Upstate New York before he was old enough to write.

How terrifying to be locked in a room like this, so far away from the heart of the house. So far away from anyone who could help you escape. What could a child have done to deserve a punishment so cruel? I was beginning to realize just how much I never knew about my aunts' lives. So many secrets. So much heartbreak. I shone the beam of light around the walls and floor one last time to make sure I hadn't missed anything. The sooner I got out of there, the sooner I could talk to Alpha or Mrs. Shipley to try to make sense of it all.

And then I tried to open the door.

Which had, of course, locked the moment it closed.

I cursed loudly, which only made me feel slightly better, then tried to bull my way out. I pushed on the door with my shoulder. Beat it with my fists. Slammed it with the soles of my athletic shoes, leaving a trail of muddy prints around the frame.

How could I have been so careless? So *stupid?* I knew what a hinge lock was. In theory, anyway. I knew it made a clicking sound and automatically locked when the door closed.

Stupid. Stupid. Stupid.

I forced myself to take slow, deep breaths. Falling apart was not an option.

James would turn up sooner or later. When I didn't come down for dinner, he would ask where I was, and Tess would have to confess that she'd dropped me off with the deliberate intention of stranding me. I wasn't in any danger. I was just stuck. Olivia would notice I was missing and call Laurel Haven. One of them would send someone to rescue me. I just had to be patient and wait.

The rain rode the force of the wind in waves, crashing against the basement windows like a wild horse kicking out of its stall. I turned off the flashlight to save the battery and huddled next to the dank wall. I'd collected blonde jokes for years—it was my right, being born a blonde—and I suddenly thought of one that seemed fitting. *What do you call a blonde skeleton in the closet? The winner of the 1996 hide-and-seek contest.*

I began to giggle. Which was another old habit of mine.

Whenever my nerves were ready to shatter, and I was trying like hell to hold it together, I got the giggles. It had always been that way. I couldn't help it. I'd gotten them the night Kent decided to walk out of my life, tripped on the alpaca rug, and skated across the hardwood floor like Johnny Weir. I'd gotten them again at the preliminary divorce hearing when the fly on Kent's tight new jeans was unzipped.

It had been a fluke I found out Kent was gay.

Four days after the movers stacked all our worldly goods in our new apartment, carefully crammed into sixty-four taped and labeled cardboard boxes, I made the mistake of borrowing Kent's phone while he was in the shower. I didn't have ulterior motives. I only wanted to check his Yelp app for a restaurant he'd been wanting to try. I thought it would be fun to surprise him with dinner reservations, so I scrolled through the alphabetical list, my heart picking up speed, life as I knew it circling the drain.

Staring at me were some of the other apps he'd been using. Gay hookup apps like Grindr and Scruff and Men4Men, which, considering our practically nonexistent sex life, explained a lot. When he finally owned up to cheating on me with other men, strangers he'd never met before, including a twenty-four-year-old guy named Conner who lived in his parents' basement half a mile from our new Asheville apartment, the sting of betrayal and the realization that for four years everything between us had been a lie was hard to take.

But take it, I did. What else could I do when the part of my heart that could love and trust without holding back had disappeared the moment I looked at Kent's phone and found out who floated his boat, and who didn't?

I stretched my legs out in front of me. Outside, the heavy rain began to let up as the storm moved away. The receding thunder had almost lulled me into a meditative state when I heard the distant banging of a screen door.

Someone had entered the house.

Someone was walking through the kitchen. Down the hall. Across the parlor floor. The footsteps became louder, nearer, slower. Then they started down the basement stairs.

Had James come back for me?

I opened my mouth to shout to him, but something stopped me cold. This wasn't James. If James were trying to find me, he'd be calling my name. He'd be shouting it, over and over again, desperate to find me.

The footsteps reached the bottom of the stairs then moved across the basement floor, uneven and soft. I strained to hear them.

Rustling sounds drifted beneath the slats, and I covered my mouth with my hands to keep from crying out. My best guess, because I couldn't see squat, was that someone was gathering up my aunts' papers and stuffing them into plastic bags.

I held my breath. Did they know I was in the house? I had left my purse lying on the kitchen counter in plain sight. Had they seen it? Were they looking for me? Baiting me? Screwing with me while I cowered behind a locked door?

Panic washed over me.

What if James came back before the thief left? If this were the same person who had trashed our apartment and shot Kent, they wouldn't have any qualms about putting a bullet into James St. Clair, a man who, by his own admission, was despised by most of the residents of Bitter Ridge.

I scooted toward the door a few inches at a time,

careful not to make a sound. Streaks of light shone through the narrow slats, disappearing as they hit the floor. If there was a wide enough opening, and I could glimpse the person's face, or even part of it, I would have some kind of description to give to Sheriff Riley. I pressed my face against the door and squinted my eyes, turning my face toward every angle, but it was no use. I couldn't see anything. And I didn't dare turn on the flashlight.

The deep silent breath I took burned my lungs. I let it out slowly. Perspiration covered the back of my neck, slid between my breasts. The courageous part of me wanted to beat on the door and let my presence be known. Find out once and for all who the killer was. A man? A woman? A surly twenty-one-year-old wearing a *Love Sucks* T-shirt? But the other part of me, the part that sat on the floor shaking like a trapped rabbit, prayed the intruder would find what they were looking for and leave.

Footsteps crossed to my door, stopped, then retreated to the steamer trunks. I pushed my feet against the wall to steady myself. I bit the inside of my hand to keep from making a sound. The basement door banged hard.

How long could I sit there with my heart pounding out of my chest and not scream for help? *Where was James? Where was Tess?*

Where was anybody?

Something scratched against one of the windows high above my head, back and forth, like metal etching glass. I felt at my side for the flashlight then curled my fingers around it. If I had to use it as a weapon, I wanted it in my hand, ready to swing.

I squeezed my eyes shut and shot up a little prayer. The only thing that kept me from completely losing it was the knowledge that as long as I stayed calm, I might remain undetected. And as long as I remained undetected, I might stay alive.

Thoughts flew through my head like ashes in a windstorm. Why would the thief want my aunts' papers? Besides my purse, was there any other evidence proving I was in the house? Why hadn’t I waited for James? Why couldn't I picture my mother's face? Or remember the things my father and I said to each other the last time we spoke?

There had to be some kind of vehicle—a van or a truck—waiting outside the house. The thief couldn't just amble across the front yard carrying a couple of bags as if they were taking out the garbage and loading them into their vehicle.

Of course, they could. We were on a mountain in the middle of nowhere. In the rain. Who would see? Who would even care?

Maybe James had already left and was driving up Holly Berry Road on his way to find me. If he saw a strange car parked in front of the Austen house, he’d know I wasn't alone. He would realize I was in trouble and call Sheriff Riley, right? Or maybe James carried his own gun. Didn't most southern boys keep a loaded firearm hidden under the front seat of their car? They did on TV.

Was the person still in the house? Had they taken all the papers they wanted? Were they coming back for more?

I clutched the flashlight in my hand and tried not to move. I didn’t have long to wait. In just a few minutes, the same heavy footsteps lumbered down the cellar stairs.

Chapter Ten

I heard a few more bags being dragged up the stairs, thumping against each step and rustling until they reached the top. The door scraped open and closed, ricocheting sound above me like a two-by-four hitting the wall.

The burglar had left.

I counted to fifty. Then to a hundred. Then to a hundred and fifty, just to make sure they were not coming back. Then I blew out a long, ragged breath and stretched my cramped legs. I dropped my head into my hands. My forehead was damp.

I turned the flashlight on, took another quick look at the letters on the wall, although I wasn't likely to forget them anytime soon, and turned it off again. The last of the adrenaline seeped through my veins. It had leeched all my energy, leaving a mantle of fatigue in its wake. I could barely hold my eyes open. I curled up on the cement floor and nestled my head in the crook of my arm. I pulled the silver flashlight to my chest and held it tight.

My mind kept drifting in and out of sleep. One minute I was in my old bedroom upstairs, listening to Aunt Pris' gentle snores echo down the hall. The next I was sitting on the steep rocky bank of Stoney Creek with my feet dangling in the cold rushing water. Then I was back in my parents' house in Upstate New York lying on the little daybed in the room off the kitchen listening to my old dog Scrapper snuffle his nose against the bottom of the back door, whining to be let in.

"Have you found something, girl?"

I opened my eyes.

"Back up, Daisy. Let me open the durn thing."

The tiny door swung open. I came face to face with a pair of muddy work boots. I glanced up, expecting to see James, but a cluster of soft whiskers nosed my cheek then brushed across my mouth, sticky and ticklish. A long wet tongue swiped my face followed by a hot blast of sweet, musty dog breath.

"I'm Henry Hoskin, ma'am, Alpha's husband. And this here's Daisy Mae. James called to see if we'd come up and check on you. I saw your purse on the kitchen counter, but I don't think I'd ever have found you down here unless Daisy picked up your scent."

Relief flooded through me. I threw my arms around the big bloodhound's shoulders and nuzzled her neck. "Good girl, Daisy," I said, hugging her tight, hysterically happy to see her again. "Daisy and I are old friends. We met earlier on the road."

"She likes to patrol the neighborhood. You all right, miss?" Henry smiled, showing off a shiny set of dentures beneath his thick gray mustache. His weathered face was the color of wet sand. His hands, when he helped me to my feet, were rough and calloused and huge. He smoothed the bib of his worn overalls and waited for me to brush myself off.

"I've seen you before," I said. "Yesterday, in the lobby at Laurel Haven Senior Care Center. You were sitting in the corner. Do you remember me?"

“I didn't notice.” He glanced away, and I knew he was lying. There was no way hadn’t seen me. We’d made eye contact.

“I was waiting for Alpha,” he said. “She’s a textile artist, but she works part-time in the Laurel Haven cafeteria. She’s waiting for us outside right now, so we’d best go.”

I pulled myself up the basement stairs. Which wasn’t easy since both my legs had turned to linguine. Alpha stood on the front porch, peering through the torn screen, clutching a hunting rifle. “Lord, child, are you okay? James called and asked us to check on you. Then Henry couldn't find you. That's when I let the dog out of the truck. I knew if you were somewhere in that house, our Daisy would track you down.”

“Is James coming to pick me up?”

“No, we’re gonna ride you home,” Henry said.

“Hurry up. We need to go. I don’t like it here.” Alpha glanced behind her at the Austen house. “Henry, get that durn dog in the back of the truck, and let's go.”

Once we were settled in the cab, and Henry had ground the gears a few times, I glanced at Alpha's hands cradling the rifle in her lap. They were trembling worse than my own.

“*Look out!*” Alpha screamed.

Henry slammed on the brake and swerved, barely missing Jackson Spencer standing beside the birdbath.

“Where'd he come from?” Henry shouted. “Did you see that? He came out of nowhere.”

Alpha rolled the window down. “What are you doing out here, Jackson? You're soaked to the skin.”

Jackson licked raindrops off his sullen mouth. “I was out hunting when the storm blew in.”

"It's been raining for two hours, son," Henry said. "Where's your gun?"

"In my truck, sir. Parked down by the creek. The front wheel got stuck, so I started walking."

"Well, get in the back with Daisy," Henry said, "and I'll drive you home."

Jackson looked at me. Was that resentment simmering in his pale blue eyes? Was he angry? His upper lip curled back from his front teeth like Elvis. "No thanks," he said. "I'll walk."

"Well, suit yourself," Henry said.

"That boy's gonna drive us all crazy." Alpha raised her voice over the driving rain. "Now, do you believe that mud story? Where's he been with that gun, Henry? Not down by the river. There wasn't any mud on his boots."

"He probably cut through the woods," Henry said. "Drier in there."

"I want to stop by the house before we take Emory home," Alpha said. "You need to put on some dry clothes, or you'll catch your death."

"Stop fussing, woman," Henry drawled. "You know I can't stand a woman who fusses."

"You'll be thanking me when you don't catch pneumonia," Alpha said. "Remember, Sadie Burnett caught it last year. Couldn't get her breath and almost died trying to get to the phone to call for help. While you're changing, I'll call James and let him know Emory's safe."

The truck bumped across the loose gravel and out onto the road.

As we rounded the curve, I glanced out the back window at Jackson Spencer. He was still standing in the rain with his hands shoved deep into the pockets of his black jeans. His long, wet hair was plastered to his narrow face. He suddenly smiled at me and nodded. As if he, and he alone, knew the secrets to the Universe.

****

We stomped our shoes on the mat outside the Hoskins' house to shake off the rain. As soon as we were inside, Henry excused himself and went upstairs to change his overalls. It didn't seem likely that he would catch his death—or anything else—in a pair of slightly damp pants, but Alpha was adamant. I had a feeling Henry Hoskin spent his days doing whatever Alpha wanted him to, and I wondered if he hated it as much as the dogged expression on his face indicated he did.

Since Alpha hadn't had any qualms about letting the Austen house fall apart, I expected the small clapboard house she shared with Henry to be a filthy rundown shack. Nothing could have been further from the truth: the inside was cozy and spotless. High oak shelving ran around the perimeter of the living room filled with whimsical carved wooden animals. On the interior walls, antique tools and old family photographs were displayed alongside some of the most exquisite homemade quilts I had ever seen, giving the place a warmth that was friendly and openhearted.

Alpha, clearly in no hurry to take me home, sat me down at the round pedestal table in the kitchen and put on a large copper kettle to boil. She set out two turquoise mugs decorated with butterflies flitting in and out of the word *Dollywood*. When the tea was ready, she pulled out a bottle of Wild Turkey bourbon from under the sink and poured a healthy dollop into each cup. "Now, if any of them nosy women in town ask about this, I'll say it ain't so. But I think we could both use a good strong snort right about now, don't you?"

I nodded yes and eagerly sipped the burning liquid, feeling my legs stop trembling for the first time since Henry found me.

I was still shaken. Still unable to process what had happened or who to trust, so I kept silent about someone breaking into the Austen house while I was trapped in the basement. Alpha and Henry seemed like honorable people, but I wasn't taking any chances. I would call Sheriff Riley and tell him about it when I got my phone back from Tess.

Above us, on the eating alcove wall, Alpha had hung rows of framed photographs of a smiling, sweet-faced girl with Henry's eyes, showcasing her life from kindergarten to college graduation.

"Is that your daughter?"

"Oh, yes." Alpha's eyes sparkled like shiny black beads. "Her name's Angel. I named her that because she looked just like a little angel when she was born. Still does."

"Does she live around here?"

"Oh, no, she lives in Denver. She teaches at the university there. Forty-three and not married, so I don't reckon I'll be getting any grandchildren."

"Forty-three's not too old these days."

"Maybe. Don't seem likely, though." Alpha's eyes misted over. "She was gonna take a job in Asheville, which would have been closer to home, but she got her heart broken by a man here in Bitter Ridge and moved out to Denver. I never did find out who he was. She wouldn't tell us. I think she was afraid Henry would kill him." Alpha sighed. "Angel's a daddy's girl."

"Most girls are. If they're lucky."

"She couldn't get over being cheated on. That's when she decided to leave and get as far away from here as possible. And she's never been back. Not once." Alpha sipped her toddy. "Denver's expensive, but she's got a good job. We've been saving for years to move out there with her. We'd do *anything* to be near our Angel again. When she moved, it broke our hearts. Especially Henry's. He don't say much, but Angel's leaving Bitter Ridge cut him to the core."

"I'm sorry."

"That's why Henry and I are selling this place."

"Really? Who are you selling to? Did James make you an offer?" I waited, expecting her to say yes. Afraid she would say yes. I needed to know if he was lying or not.

"Oh, honey, no. And even if he did, we wouldn't sell to him. We're fond of James, but after that Gray Top mess, we're afraid to trust him with everything we have in the world. We've been trying to unload this farm for three years, and no one's made an offer we could live with until now. A man named Mr. Castril has offered us a good bit over the listing price, so we're gonna sell to him."

"I'm sleeping under one of your beautiful quilts at the St. Clairs' house. Are the rest of these on the wall yours, too?"

"They are," she said softly. "I sell mostly at festivals and a textile arts shop in downtown Bitter Ridge called Stitched. I keep a quilting frame there to work on bigger projects and they let me sell out of their store."

"I sell portraits on the internet. Have you thought of trying to sell your quilts online? I'm sure there's a market for it."

"Pris always said she thought I could make a good living at quilt making. But then she or Portia would need me to do something, so there wasn't ever time. I've gotten a lot more done since she moved to Laurel Haven." Alpha leaned back in her chair. "I gave Pris a quilt once a long time ago. A little baby quilt with yellow and blue flowers appliquéd on it. It wasn't one of my best, but I told her to pick one, and that's the one she wanted."

"Was it a quilt for my father, Preston?"

"Oh, no. For Pris' baby. The one who died."

I closed my mouth and tried not to look as shocked as I felt. I'd never heard of Pris having a baby, much less a man in her life.

"She had it out of wedlock, but no one except my family and Portia knew. We helped her hide it from the town. Back then, you could do that. Especially way up here on the mountain." Alpha's calloused fingers wrapped around her mug. "I was there the night it was born. I was only fifteen, but I brung that baby into the world." Her gaze drifted toward the window. "Tiniest baby I'd ever seen—a little boy. He only lived two days."

"Was he sick?"

"Most likely. He wouldn't stop crying, and he wouldn't nurse. My mama tried to feed him with a rag soaked in warm sugar milk, but he just lay there, mewing like a little kitten. I don't think he would've lived long anyway."

"Did you call a doctor? Or take the baby to the

hospital?"

"That was during the war, Emory. There weren't any doctors in Bitter Ridge; they'd all gone overseas. I fell asleep one night sitting beside Pris' bed and when I woke, the baby was gone. Pris started screaming for me to find it. Then Portia came in and said the baby had died. I ran downstairs and looked all around—inside, outside—but I couldn't find it. The baby was just…gone."

"What are you saying?"

"I'm saying that Portia done killed that baby. It was so small and weak; it wouldn't have taken much to snuff out its little life. Later, I saw her sitting on the porch humming to herself and smiling. I asked her what she thought the baby's father would say when he found out she'd killed his son. She turned her head and looked at me just as strange. Then she flew at me. Like a crazy person. Tried to tear my hair out. I thought she was gonna kill me."

"Who was the father, Alpha?"

"Only one man it could have been—Edward Gilmore." Alpha fanned her face with the bottom of her apron. "Talking about it brings it all back. When Portia was having those spells, she was a devil straight from hell. Once I saw her scratch herself with a broken jar until she bled. I heard her talk to people who weren't there. When your grandfather was alive, he'd take forsythia branches and switch her, then lock her in the basement till she quieted down. But that night—the night she came at me—I'd never seen anything like it. If my papa hadn't pulled her off me, I'd be dead now. When your daddy was two, Portia tried to drown him in the cistern. By the time Pris got to him, Portia was dangling him over the hole. That's when Pris decided she couldn't keep her little brother safe no more."

"So she took my father to New York to live with his Great-Aunt Claudia."

"It was Portia's fault she had to send little Preston away," Alpha said. "Everything was always Portia's fault. But Pris still took care of her."

A knot formed in my throat. The only sound in the room was the soft burble of the kettle sputtering on the stove. "No one told me what Pris' life was like here with Portia. I didn't know."

"You and your father didn't want to know."

"My family let Pris down. I let her down."

"Your parents knew Portia was mentally ill, but they didn't care. Not as long as their lives weren't disrupted."

What Alpha said was true. Preston and Alexandra Austen had lived in the insulated world of cruise ships and five-star hotels, despising any unpleasant news that might spoil their travel plans. Even I had kept things from them. It wasn't the first time their eccentric lives had seemed selfish and cruel. But it was no excuse.

"Did you know my grandfather?" I asked.

She nodded. "He was a godly man. He put up the money to start that little church on the other side of Crow Mountain—the Living Waters Pentecostal something-or-other. The one where Delbert Jenkins preaches."

"Delbert Jenkins is a preacher?" I recalled the scene in the McAlister Inn bar when he came to repair the refrigerator and stopped to berate James.

"Delbert is more of a hellfire and damnation Bible-thumper than this area is used to, but he has a following. He's the moral compass at that church and thinks the rest of us are going straight to hell." She laughed. "Not sure if I trust someone who's that sure of himself, though."

Henry ambled down the hall and stood in the doorway. "Alpha been talking your ear off?"

"She's been telling me about my family." I had a thought. "Mr. Hoskin, would you help me put some locks on Pris' house? I need to secure it as soon as possible."

"I'll take care of it this afternoon," Henry said. "I have some extra locks in the tool shed."

"But not for free. I'd insist on paying you."

"No, ma'am," Henry said.

"And all those papers in the basement? I'd like to clear them out. If you could help me load them into Maddie's Jeep tomorrow I'd be happy to pay you for that, too."

"I'll do it," Henry said. "But I won't accept no payment."

"And I'm going to need a car of my own to drive. I can't keep borrowing the St. Clairs. Do either of you know of a—"

"Will Riley has an old Volkswagen beetle he's been trying to get rid of. Belonged to his niece. It's parked behind the sheriff's station. I'm sure he'd let you drive it free of charge."

"Oh, no. I'd want to pay him. I couldn't just let him loan it to me."

"You want to pay him, too?" Henry smoothed the sides of his mustache. "You're not used to having neighbors, are you, Miss Emory?"

"No, sir."
Henry nodded. "Didn't think so."

Chapter Eleven

Some people knocked back a couple of stiff drinks when the world around them became too difficult to fathom. I took baths. Although, technically, after drinking two cups of Wild Turkey tea in Alpha Hoskin's kitchen, I was doing both.

I made sure my bedroom door was locked—not that it would do much good with a snoop like Tess in the house—and peeled off my clothes. I leaned over the edge of the deep claw foot tub, tossed in a bath gel from the glass jar on the counter, and turned on the tap. Minutes later, a cloud of scented steam enveloped me like an embrace. I pulled the elastic band from my ponytail and lowered myself into the warm water. My frizzy hair floated and swirled on the surface like tangled ropes of seaweed. But I didn't care. All I wanted was comfort. And lots of it.

The vanilla mint-scented bath oil, living up to its promise of bliss on the expensive label, wiped the dank smell of the basement room from my memory. It cradled my bones, eased the feeling of dread I hadn't been able to shake. I leaned back and closed my eyes and let the water pool around my neck. Then finally allowed myself to think about Aunt Pris' baby.

Pris would have been eighteen and Portia, sixteen. Poor Pris. Both parents dead, a three-year-old brother and an emotionally unstable sister to care for, the father of her child living far away in England, which is where Edward Gilmore was from. Stuck in a backward mountain town full of people who would probably have shunned her if they knew she was knocked up without the benefit of marriage.

Pris had hidden her pregnancy. And when the baby died, she'd hidden the fact that it ever happened at all. But being pregnant and single wasn't the stigma it used to be. If something like that happened now, who would care?

I thought of James. His Jeep hadn't been in the garage when I'd come back, and I'd jumped out of the Hoskins' truck and hurried upstairs before I could run into Tess or Olivia. I wasn't sure how I was going to handle what Tess had done to me, whether she considered it a joke or just wanted me to leave. Either way, I was not cool with it, and I wanted her to know that. I'd been terrified James would return to the Austen house while the robbery was still in progress. If he had shown up and surprised the burglar, he might be lying dead on the basement floor with his head in a pool of blood and a bullet hole between his eyes like Kent.

"Don't go there," I whispered, struggling to push the image out of my head.

It had been two months since Kent's death. Plenty of time for the memory to soften around the edges and begin to fade. But it hadn't. It hadn't faded at all. I'd played the *what-if* game more times than I could count, and I always came up lacking. But one thing had become painfully clear—nothing would ever change. I could spin scenarios out of the air for the rest of eternity, and it would still be my fault Kent was dead.

I dunked my head under the water and came up

sputtering as the image of Jackson Spencer sparked behind my eyes. What had he been doing wandering around outside the Austen house in the rain? His family lived over the crest of Crow Mountain down from the Austen property, so he could have been going home through the woods as he said. But Alpha hadn't believed his hunting story. And neither had I. There'd been something in his face and the condescending tone of his voice, that had set off warning bells that he was lying.

If Jackson had stolen my aunts' papers from the basement—and he'd had every opportunity to do so—what had he done with them? Had he toted them into the woods where he had parked his truck? Stashed them down by the river? Hidden them beneath a tree? It was possible. He was young. He had the strength to lift a couple at a time. If he had come back for a second load and seen Henry's truck parked in front of the house, he could have lied to cover his tracks. The look on his face as we'd driven away had given me chills. As if he knew something the rest of us didn't.

I wasn't going to tell anyone about the robbery until I talked to Sheriff Riley. If the thief found out I'd been in the basement, and thought I was on to them, things could get uglier than they already were. I'd had a close call at the Austen house. And until I discovered exactly what the thief had been searching for in my aunts' papers and why, I needed to be more cautious. And smarter. Because today, intellectually speaking, falling for Tess' story, getting myself stranded, then locking myself in a basement room had not been my finest moment.

The second Tess had dumped me and driven away,

I should have walked down to the Hoskins' farm or made my way up and over the mountain to the Spencers' house. I never should have risked going inside by myself. I knew the house wasn't secure. I knew it had been ransacked on a regular basis. It was the equivalent of a too-stupid-to-live heroine climbing the creaky attic stairs in a haunted house to check out a noise. In the dark. With a candle. During a thunderstorm.

I fished out the natural sponge and dribbled warm water onto my shoulders. If the Hoskins hadn't told James about seeing Jackson lurking around the yard, should I mention it to him? The boy was dating his sister. If Maddie were my sister, I'd want to know if her boyfriend had done something shady or suspicious. The kid had a rap sheet longer than my resume. It wasn't hard to see why Jackson was attracted to Maddie, but what Maddie saw in him had me baffled. Maybe the boy was acting like a punk with a gigantic chip on his shoulder because he had more anger churning inside than he could deal with. Or maybe he just didn't give a damn. But somewhere beneath his ill-fitting jeans and the motor oil under his fingernails, I had to admit that he had a certain appeal. Most girls had a guy in their past they dated to piss off their overbearing mothers. Maybe Jackson was that guy.

And what about the Hoskins? They came across as a sedate version of Ma and Pa Kettle, but I suspected both of them knew more than they were letting on. I doubted if anything escaped Alpha. Hadn't the woman practically broken her neck getting to the Austen house that first day I'd stopped by? Henry seemed trustworthy, but he had hedged about not recognizing me at Laurel Haven, and I was certain he'd seen me there.

I dried my hands and reached for my phone, which had been mysteriously lying on my bedside table when I returned. I needed to Google all these people and see what I could find out. But doing that kind of research would take forever on my phone, so I texted Esther and asked her to overnight my laptop. She texted back immediately saying she was going to take the baby for a walk and would get it to the post office within the hour. God, I loved Esther.

I leaned back again and tried to relax.

"Emory?" James knocked on the bedroom door. "Hey, are you okay?"

"I'm fine."

"Could you prove it, please?"

"I'm in the—just a minute."

I climbed out of the tub and wrapped myself in one of the oversized towels hanging on the rack. I blotted my dripping hair and wound a smaller towel around my head then padded to the door, leaving wet footprints on the hardwood floor. Before I opened it, I pulled the heavy towel tighter around my chest.

The startled look on James' face made me laugh as his gaze traveled from my face to my toes and back again in record time. "I didn't realize you were—"

"—naked?"

"No, I…sorry."

"It's okay. I was two minutes away from turning into a raisin, anyway."

"I talked to Henry, and I just had to see for myself that you were all right."

"I'm good, thanks."

"I had no idea you and Tess had left without me. When she got back, she said you wanted to spend some time at the house by yourself and sent her away." His eyes held mine. "She left you there, didn't she?"

"That she did."

"I'm sorry."

"I think Tess should be the one to apologize, not you."

"Just wanted you to know that Henry has already put the locks on the house, and I'm going over later to help him board up the broken windows."

"You don't have to do that."

"I know I don't. But I'm going to anyway." He looked at me anxiously. "Henry said he found you trapped in the basement."

"I accidentally locked myself in one of the rooms. Daisy found me." I tugged the towel up a little higher.

"Well, I can see you're all right." He laughed softly. "Do you have any idea how hard it is to keep my eyes above your shoulders right now? Very nice shoulders, by the way. Very nice everything."

"If I don't dry off, you're going to have to refinish the floor."

"I'll let you get dressed. I just wanted to—are you going back to Laurel Haven tonight?"

"Yes. I haven't seen Pris all day. I'm going to help feed her dinner."

"I thought I might visit her later. Do you think that would be all right?"

"I'm sure she would like that. She hasn't had any visitors except me."

I mashed my lips together to keep from telling him about the intruder in the basement. It would have been so easy to blurt out what had happened. To confide in him, ask for his advice. But something held me back. I wanted to trust James. I did. But I couldn't. Not yet.

I needed to step back and take a breath. And I needed to be smart.

Being smart would help me figure out the secrets buried in my aunt's house before it was too late. Being smart would keep me alive.

****

I crawled onto the bed and shook out the contents of the Manila envelope for the second time. Before I went to Laurel Haven, I wanted to go through it and make sure I hadn't missed anything. If the thief had been looking for a specific document, it might still be hidden in the ones Aunt Pris had entrusted to Mrs. Shipley. If there was a clue I'd overlooked, I needed to uncover it.

Some of the papers were stapled together in packets, some loose. I looked at them carefully, folding them back one by one, until a long brown envelope I hadn't seen before fell from between the pages of her life insurance policy. I unwound the closure string and dumped the contents. Fourteen receipts from Avery Hospital in Winston-Salem, North Carolina, tumbled across the bed. Each one listed the date of release for Portia Martine Austen and was stamped *Paid in Full*.

Avery Hospital?

I had never heard that name mentioned in our family. But according to my father, Portia had fought to regain her strength from one illness after another her whole life. Why would she go to the same hospital year after year? Was she receiving some kind of special treatment she couldn't get at the hospital in Bitter

Ridge? The most recent receipt showed a five-year-old phone number. To save time, I grabbed my phone and called it. If the number wasn't valid anymore, I'd resort to Google.

After a polite recorded message informing me about the free initial consultation for new patients and two minutes of bossa nova elevator music, a woman's clipped voice switched on and said, "Avery Hospital. How may I direct your call?"

"Would you mind telling me what kind of hospital Avery is?"

"Psychiatric."

"Thank you." I ended the call and stared at the receipts. *A psychiatric hospital?*

Alpha had been right. Portia wasn't just quirky and in delicate health, she was genuinely mentally ill. I glanced through the paperwork again, looking for a diagnosis, but there was nothing else.

The last thing I wanted to do was upset Pris, but I needed to talk to her. I would imagine that having a mentally ill sister and a baby out of wedlock were family secrets she would have guarded with her life, but I needed answers. And if Pris wasn't able to give them to me, maybe her best friend Mrs. Shipley could.

I finished getting dressed and made my way down the curved hallway to knock gently on Maddie's door.

"Come in! As long as you're not my mother."

Maddie lay on her bed propped up against a mound of pink ruffled pillows, on her phone.

"Can I borrow your car for a little while? I want to visit Aunt Pris."

Maddie took her keys out of her back pocket and tossed them to me. Then she looked up and grinned.

"So if James asks about you, what should I say?"

"Tell him she's moving to a motel," Tess said, appearing in the doorway. "I'll be glad to drop her off."

I gave Tess my best smile. "Nice to see you again." I pocketed the keys and tried to walk past her, but Tess stepped to the right, blocking my way into the hall. "What were you and James talking about a few minutes ago? I thought I told you to stay away from him."

"You told me not to run around the house in my nightgown."

"So now I have to add: *Don't open your door wearing nothing but a bath towel?*"

"Leave her alone," Maddie said. "It's not Emory's fault James likes her. You're just jealous."

"Shut up, Maddie," Tess said. "At least I'm not the one drooling over a guy who smells like dirty socks and axle grease."

"At least I have somebody to drool over," Maddie shot back. "Who do you have? A thirty-six-year-old man who doesn't know you're alive?"

Tess grabbed my arm. "I'm serious, Emory. Stay away from him."

"Are you threatening me?"

"Take it any way you want," Tess said.

I held her gaze without flinching. "You can try to intimidate me all you want, little girl, but you're in the major leagues now. And if I ever hear you say another hateful thing to Maddie about Jackson, you're going to wish you'd gone to Abu Simbel with your parents."

"*Oooh,* I'm scared," Tess said. "What are you going to do, hit me with one of your paintbrushes? Choke me with that kinky-assed hair of yours?"

"No," I said. "I'll tell James."

For a minute I thought Tess was going to slap me, but instead, and to my immense relief, she pushed past me and walked out.

"I haven't seen her that angry since she broke a fingernail opening a jar of Nutella," Maddie said.

"For some reason, that girl brings out the worst in me."

Maddie laughed. "Uh…could it be because she's a total bitch? I just wish she'd stop making fun of Jackson."

"I saw him earlier. In the yard at my aunt's house."

"Yeah, he texted me. He said he was walking home because his truck stalled out in the woods. He said Mr. Hoskin gave him the fisheye." She picked at a loose thread on top of the comforter. "I know people don't like Jackson. He can be kind of rough on the outside, but that's just a defense mechanism. With me, he's soft and sweet. He's working three jobs, so we'll have enough money to get married. What he really wants to do is work at the McAlister, but Gordon won't let him near it. Jackson has some great ideas on how to improve the old place, but Gordon won't listen to him." She rolled onto her side. "Anyway, James likes you, and it's absolutely killing Tess."

I wrapped my arms around the bedpost. "Maybe we're being a little hard on her. I know what it's like to feel deserted by your parents, and it's no picnic. Loneliness can bring out the worst in people."

"Tess is mean. She deserves to be lonely."

"No one deserves to be lonely."

"Well, Tess does. And if she's as jealous of you as I think she is, you'd better watch your back." She picked up her phone. "Are you really gonna paint my mom?"

"I owe her a big favor for letting me stay here."

Maddie shrugged. "Sooner or later everyone owes my mom a favor."

I left and went downstairs. When I reached the landing, I heard voices arguing in the living room. I knew I should have left then, but something kept me rooted to the bottom step.

"James promised he would get it for me," Olivia wailed.

"You'd better hope he does," Doc Turner said. "He's your last chance."

"This has to work," Olivia said. "Why does Carl think he has a right to be vindictive? *I'm* the one he dumped for a twenty-seven-year-old who'll leave him as soon as he pays for her Triple-D implants."

"This isn't the way to turn things around with your ex, Olivia. You'll regret it."

"Do you know what I regret? I regret spending the last two years in this town being treated like I've got leprosy. Bitter Ridge used to be a wonderful place. I used to love living here."

"You loved being a big fish in a little pond."

"It doesn't matter. All the other fish hate me now. I've lost the respect of everyone in this community. And all because of that damned land deal that didn't go through."

"It's been two years, Olivia," Doc Turner said wearily. "Let it go."

"I will *not* let it go. That bastard I was married to owes me. I don't care what's in the divorce settlement."

"You made out like a bandit in the divorce settlement."

"Because I didn't contest it. Well, I'm contesting it now. Carl owes me for not suing that woman for alienation of affections. I still might. And what am I going to do about Gordon Spencer?"

"Pipe down. There's someone on the stairs. It's probably Tess. That girl sneaks around like a fox in a hen house."

"Who's there?" Olivia called. "Tess?"

"It's me." There was nothing I could do but hold my head high and walk into the room.

"Why, look, Olivia," Dr. Turner said. "It's my old patient. How's that head of yours, young lady? You're looking fine. Fine as frog's hair. Isn't she looking fine, Olivia?"

"Yes, Hugh." Olivia pasted on a bright smile. "You remember Dr. Turner, don't you, dear?"

"Of course."

"Call me Doc."

"I'm sorry you heard us arguing," Olivia said smoothly. "Just some unpleasant business concerning my ex-husband. Come and have a coffee with us. Get her a cup, Hugh."

"No, thanks." I could feel my cheeks burning. "I didn't mean to eavesdrop. I just wanted you to know that I'm moving into a motel later today. The Thompson Motor Lodge right next to Laurel Haven. I appreciate everything you've done for me, and—"

"No!" Olivia cried. "You can't. Thompson's is a rattrap. You don't want to stay there. Please, Emory, don't leave. Stay here a few more days."

"I would love to." I hoped a lightning bolt wouldn't take me out for lying. "You've been so kind, but I really—"

“Please, Emory.” Olivia brushed her navy skirt. Her slide-on sandals clacked softly as she walked toward me across the hardwood floor. She put her hands on my upper arms. Her dark eyes bore into mine. “If you leave now, James will blame me. He’ll think you left because of something I’ve done.” Her voice dropped to a whisper. “I haven’t done anything wrong, have I?”

“Of course not.”

“Then stay. Please. Your safety means so much to us. I heard what occurred at the Austen house today, and I would never forgive myself if you moved out and something happened to you.” Tess snorted softly in the stairwell. “Please, Emory. Say you’ll stay. At least until you finish my portrait.”

“Okay. All right.” She was making me uncomfortable. All I wanted was for her to let go of my arms and get out of my face.

After I agreed to stay, Olivia’s tone did a complete one-eighty. In a heartbeat, she went from pleading and desperate to sweet and charming. Was she some kind of passive-aggressive genius who knew which buttons to push to get her way? There were many conflicting sides to the lady, and I wasn’t sure I trusted any of them.

As soon as I left the room, Tess grabbed my arm and jerked me into the foyer. “And they think *I’m* a sneak. I saw you listening at the door. If James knew what you were really like, you’d be out on the street in two minutes.”

“Does he know what you’re really like?”

Tess’ amber eyes narrowed. “Don’t push me, Emory. I don’t like to be pushed.”

“No,” I said, turning to go. “And neither do I.”

Chapter Twelve

I woke up early and dragged the little makeshift easel I'd crafted out of a cardboard box to the window. In New York, I was a night owl, hanging out with friends at my favorite piano bar, sipping chardonnay, staying up late watching old movies. Kent was hardly ever home at night and my hours were my own, so it hadn't mattered. But here in Bitter Ridge, my body clock seemed to have reset itself. Granted, I hadn't had much sleep while I'd been there, but I had discovered the unexpected pleasures of watching the sun come up over the Blue Ridge Mountains while working on Olivia's portrait.

It was coming along pretty well, as far as a slightly rushed pastel went, and it was a relief to bury myself in the work again. Painting and drawing had always had the power to transport me. And having a purpose, something to complete as quickly as I could, had turned out to be a blessing.

I dressed and headed out to Laurel Haven in Maddie's Jeep in time to grab a pastry at the hospital coffee bar and have breakfast with Aunt Pris before her therapy session. Afterward, I found Etta Shipley in her room sitting by the window stirring sugar into a mug of blackberry tea.

Mrs. Shipley was fast becoming one of my favorite people. I marveled at this woman who had traveled the world as a military wife, lost her entire family, and managed to keep her wry sense of humor completely intact. In her eighty-three years, she'd not only seen it all, she still remembered most of it. It didn't seem fair that she had ended up in an assisted living facility being cared for by nurses half her age who patted her head like she was their cherished lapdog and called her Honey and Sweetie and Darlin'."

"Bipolar Psychosis," Mrs. Shipley said.

"That was Portia's diagnosis?"

"Yes. I've been thinking about her this morning. She went to that psychiatric hospital in Winston-Salem for treatments on and off for years, until she decided she didn't want to go and stopped."

"Maybe they couldn't afford it anymore."

"Maybe. I know that by the time Edward came back into their lives, their savings were running low. Then, of course, he had a heart condition. His medical bills must have been astronomical. Of course, all medical bills are astronomical. You ought to see mine."

"Didn't Edward have any money of his own when he returned?"

"I don't think so." Mrs. Shipley peered over her thick lenses. "Seems he had a bit of a gambling problem that he enjoyed flaunting with the locals. I heard he made quite a killing."

"Gambling? Here in Bitter Ridge?"

"Don't look so shocked, Emory. Frank Spencer used to host a weekly poker game in one of the rooms at the McAlister. Apparently, Edward never missed one. You know, he married Portia after only being back here for two weeks. Which was quite a surprise since Edward Gilmore was your Aunt Pris' beau when they were young."

"I had no idea she even had a beau until yesterday."

"Oh, yes. The two of them were deeply in love, but your grandfather forbade it, which, of course, made them all the more desperate to be together. I don't know how he managed it—paid Edward off or threatened him—but he forced Edward to leave Bitter Ridge and go back to England. Soon after, your grandparents contracted meningitis and died. But by then, Edward Gilmore was long gone. I know Pris wrote to him, but he never answered. It was strange when he came back. I mean they were all old then, but I don't think his feelings had changed. I think he wanted to be with Priscilla, not Portia."

I didn't ask about the baby. I didn't feel it was my place to divulge something Pris may have kept secret from Mrs. Shipley. If Edward and Pris were in love just before he left for England, then the baby had surely belonged to him.

"How did Pris feel about him coming back after all that time? Did she still love him?"

Mrs. Shipley shrugged. "I don't know. It had been so many years since she'd heard from him. So much had happened. He hadn't been strong enough to stand up to her father and had abandoned her. Pris must have resented him for that. When he showed up here, he was all alone in the world. He had no family left in England. His heart was failing. I'm sure he knew he didn't have long to live. I think he wanted to spend the time he had left with Pris. If Pris didn't want him, then marrying Portia was a way to do that."

"Did he know about Portia's mental state?"

"Hard to tell. Pris said Portia had always had periods in her life when she was normal. but then her behavior would become more erratic and violent, and Pris would have to send her back to Avery. Pris said the meningitis Portia had survived as a girl had damaged her brain and left her physically frail. At least that was one theory. She was always a difficult woman."

"And when she killed herself?"

"Oh, that was a sad business."

"How did she—no one's told me how she died."

"It's pretty gruesome, dear. Are you sure you want to hear this?"

I nodded.

"She buried herself alive."

"But how could she—how could anybody do that?"

"After Edward died, Portia started wandering around at night. Pris decided to fill up the fishpond in the side yard for fear that Portia would lose her footing and fall into it. Pris had the pond drained, leaving a hole about four feet deep."

"But how—"

"Bags of sand. The lumberyard had delivered them late in the afternoon and stacked them around the empty pond. The workmen were slated to come back the next morning and fill it in. That night, Portia slit the bags with a knife one by one. Then she lay down in the hole and waited for the sand to pour in on top of her. She was old and fragile. It didn't take long for the weight of the sand to crush her."

"How could anyone do such a horrible thing?" My voice quavered.

Mrs. Shipley took my hand. "She wasn't in her right mind, dear. When Edward died, it broke her heart.

I'm sure she didn't think she could live another day without him."

"Is that what true love is supposed to feel like?"

She laughed. "That's what the movies would like us to believe."

I rose to go and put my teacup in the sink. "One more thing. You said you didn't know the St. Clairs well, but they're friends with Pris. The Austen property is key in developing anything on Crow Mountain, and although James says he's not interested in buying property up there, Gordon Spencer believes otherwise. If James is lying, and Pris has promised him first right of refusal on our property, of which she owns the majority, I want to make sure he's not using their friendship to take advantage of her. His mother Olivia volunteers here, so I thought—"

"I'll ask around. See what I can find out."

"Would you? Are you sure it wouldn't be too much of an imposition?"

Mrs. Shipley laughed. "Don't be silly. I'd love to help. And all I'll have to do is sit here and listen. From Miss Marple to Jessica Fletcher, people have been confiding in sweet little old ladies since the dawn of time."

****

The long twisty corridor snaking between the medical wing and Aunt Pris' room had always seemed a little nightmarish to me, like the bright light you hope to see at the end of the tunnel when an eighteen-wheeler plows into your mini-bus. I walked past the nurse's station and headed left toward the tiny lounge. As I neared Pris' room, two male voices raised in anger ricocheted off the walls. Was that James who'd just let the S-word fly? And then the B-word? Who was he arguing with?

"God Almighty will strike you down, James St. Clair," the other voice boomed. "Our Lord in heaven doesn't abide liars, and neither will I. If Miss Austen promised to sell you her property on Crow Mountain, then tell me now. I have a right to know."

I came around the last curve and stopped. James and Delbert Jenkins stood face to face outside Pris' room, glaring at each other.

"Just answer the question." Delbert jabbed James' chest with a well-worn copy of the New Testament.

"You poke that Bible at me one more time," James said, "and you'll be eating it for lunch."

"Is Miss Austen selling you her lots on Crow Mountain or not?"

"Answer him," I said quietly.

James spun around. "I didn't know you were there."

"Surprise."

Delbert looked at me, his auburn hair sticking up in the crown of his head, his bloodshot eyes a little wild. With his Bible held under the crook of his arm and his hand poised in the air he looked like a preacher waiting to put the fear of God into a roomful of sinners. I could see him taking the same stance behind a pulpit.

Delbert turned to me. "Several months ago, my church approached Miss Austen about leasing her house and some of her property on Crow Mountain then buying it from her when we can raise the funds. A fire destroyed our sanctuary two years ago. We've been holding services in the chapel, but we've outgrown it, and we're desperate to find a new location. We want to build a church on Crow Mountain like the one we planned to build on Gray Top until James here got greedy and decided a ski resort would be more profitable." He raised his Bible. "Luke 12:15. 'Be on your guard against all kinds of greed.'"

"Your church didn't lose any money," James said. "I gave the deposit back to you."

"That's not the point," Delbert said. "You promised to help us, then went back on your word. Our congregation needs a bigger place. We're running out of options. You're trying to stand in the way of good people who believe in the Lord. Don't you have any shame?"

"It's a church," James said. "You can build a church anywhere. Crow Mountain is *not* your only option. Why are you taking this so personally?"

"Personally?" Delbert's thin face turned the color of pickled beets. I half expected steam to come shooting out of his ears. He brought his voice down a couple of octaves, an effective maneuver I'd seen evangelists use on TV, and said, "This church is my life. It means everything to me. The congregation is trusting me to see this through, and I'm not going to stand by and let you ruin it for us again." He nodded toward Pris' door. "Everybody knows you've spent the last six months ingratiating yourself to that poor woman, so she'll sell her land to you."

"That's not true," James said.

"Miss Austen's father—your grandfather, Mrs. Chandler—donated the money to start our church. It's part of your family's heritage. Miss Austen promised me she would consider the matter, but then we never heard anything. I think James talked her out of leasing to us. You ask your aunt if you don't believe me." He scowled at James. "And then you might want to say a prayer for James St. Clair's black soul." He started down the hall. *"Greed,"* he said under his breath. "Nothing but greed."

"Well, that was fun," James said. "Pastor Delbert is the gift that just keeps on giving."

"I felt sorry for him. He's trying to do the best he can for his church family. He seems desperate."

"Delbert always seems desperate. Besides preaching about all the ways we're going to hell, his life's purpose is exacting revenge from me. He takes every opportunity to discredit me in any way he can, and he revels in it. *Unreliable James. Lying James. Piece-of-crap James.* I've heard them all. And I've heard them all from him. Delbert may be doing the best he can for his family, but I'm doing the best I can for mine."

A low moan escaped Pris' room.

"Emory and I are out here, Miss Austen," James said.

"We must have woken her up."

"She was asleep when I got here," James said. "I was waiting in the hall for you when Delbert showed up. He doesn't understand how fragile she is since her stroke. I'm sure he thought he'd be able to talk to her directly and plead his case."

James followed me into Pris' room. He stopped just inside the doorway, and I couldn't help but notice that his broad shoulders practically filled it up.

Pris' long gray braid spilled across her left shoulder. Her creased hands, dotted with age spots and angry dark bruises, clasped the top of the white thermal bedspread. Her blue eyes, brighter than I'd ever seen them, gazed at James with complete adoration. She tried her best to smile with a mouth that still wouldn't quite work, but she was delighted to see him.

The sudden pang of jealousy that pricked my heart threw me off guard. It wasn't a significant amount. Just enough to raise my hackles. Just enough to make me feel ridiculous. The unabashed affection on Pris' face as she looked at James fascinated me. Was she thinking of Edward, her long-lost love? Or of the baby boy she had cradled for two days then spent the rest of her life wondering what he would have grown up to look like?

"How are you doing, Miss Austen?" James smiled at her. "You're looking good."

"She was a little down in the dumps earlier," I said. "I couldn't get her to talk to me."

"What's the problem?" James said.

"I don't know. When I first got here, she'd just come back from physical therapy, and I found her sobbing into a towel. I think the extent of the physical damage and the kind of therapy it's going to take to recover has finally hit home."

"She's depressed," James said. "That's to be expected." He smiled at Pris. "I'm sorry. We're being rude talking about you like you're not here."

I smoothed the fluff of gray hair back from her forehead. "Her doctor won't be in until tomorrow. I'm not sure what to do. She seems happy to see you, though."

James leaned over the bed railing, and Pris blinked up at him. Her hand fluttered toward his face then dropped.

"Now, what's this I hear about you not talking?"

He took her hand in his and held it gently, like a baby bird he'd scooped off the ground. “Do you remember two years ago when the people in this town were ready to hang me?”

“*Oonngh,*” Pris groaned.

“That's right,” he said. “You weren't having any of it. You got in that old green Pontiac of yours and drove down Crow Mountain to the council meeting. Then you marched up the aisle like Moses parting the Red Sea. You told them I was a man of my word and they were fools for not believing me. I'll never forget the power in your voice. Why, you shut Melvin Owens right up, and no one's ever been able to do that.”

Pris smiled.

“You were a pistol that night.” He chuckled softly. “And you’re still a pistol. Can you say my name? Miss Priscilla, you've gotta try. Because if you don't, you'll never get your speech back. And then who will I get to kick Melvin’s butt for me?”

“*Sjzhe,*” Pris whispered. “*Szsmas.*” She squeezed her eyes shut and worked her mouth up and down. “*Gzamaz. Jamz!*”

“Close enough.” He kissed her withered cheek. “Now, are you gonna finish that green Jell-O, or can I have it?” He grinned at me. “Unless you want it.”

“It’s all yours.”

“Sell,” Pris said.

James looked up. Our eyes met.

“What did you say, Aunt Pris?” I said slowly. “Did you say *sell?”*

“Sell…James.” Pris was still gazing at him as if he were the moon and the stars all wrapped up into one big pot of Carolina grits and gravy.

I moved the hospital tray table to the side and smoothed the folds of her thermal blanket. "What are you trying to say, Aunt Pris?"

Pris pushed herself up onto one elbow. "House. Crow."

"Are you saying you want to sell your house to James?" I said gently.

"House," Pris cried. *"Crow."*

The muscle in James' jaw clenched and unclenched. "I think I need to tell you something. Let's step outside for a minute."

I followed him down the hall, walking briskly, dodging one of the mobile computer carts that were always in the way. He ducked into the corner waiting room overlooking the grounds.

"What do you need to say to me?" I stood beside the window with my arms crossed tightly over my chest, waiting.

"I wanted to put off telling you this until Pris was out of the woods."

"She's out of the woods. Spill it."

James swallowed, and I braced myself for the worst.

"The day before she had the stroke, she asked me to come see her. I thought she wanted to talk about fixing up the house. I'd known for some time it was in bad shape and had tried to warn her that houses don't bounce back on their own. I knew she was thinking about selling and I knew if she didn't begin repairs on the house—and soon—it would be too late."

I stared at him.

"But when we met, she had thought up this Grand Plan to restore my reputation. Make everyone in Bitter

Ridge sorry they'd ever doubted me. She had it all figured out. Which is something that means more to her than it does to me."

"Oh, I think it means a lot to you."

"Pris said she wanted me to buy the Austen house. She doesn't think she'll ever be able to live there again."

"Just the house?"

"Well, no," he said. "The surrounding property, too. Your family owns a considerable amount of land on Crow Mountain. It goes all the way from Stoney Creek to—"

"I know how far it goes."

"Right."

"And what did you say when she begged you to buy her out?'

"I said I would consider it. She's my friend. I didn't want to hurt her feelings."

I leaned against the windowsill. "See, that's a little shady to me. Pris is an eighty-three-year-old woman, alone and vulnerable, sitting on a piece of property that you need to buy to redeem yourself in this town. You have to understand why I would question your motives."

"I know it looks suspicious," he said. "But Pris and I *are* friends. She's always been on my side. Hell, my own mother wasn't as supportive as Pris has been."

"And she just came up with this plan on her own?"

"Everyone knew that someone—Mr. Castril, as it turns out—was making generous offers to property owners on Crow. I think that's what gave her the idea."

"What about Delbert and his church? He seemed pretty sure Pris was going to help him until you changed her mind. *Did* you change her mind?"

"Pris never mentioned Delbert or his church to me. But he isn't hurting financially. I hear the Living Waters Pentecostal Church is doing quite well since they've started televising their services locally on Sunday morning. Delbert is getting noticed by some very prominent evangelicals. He has the ambition. All he needs are a few well-connected parishioners willing to foot the bill and that little Pentecostal church could be his ticket to the major leagues."

"Then why does he work two jobs?"

James laughed. "My personal opinion? I think he wants to get away from Connie, his wife. Not that I blame him. Not that anyone would blame him."

"The town council meeting you talked about to Pris. How long ago was that? And why didn't anyone in Bitter Ridge except Pris believe your story?"

"You'll have to ask them." His deep baritone lowered to a growl. "It's been almost two years, but people around here have long memories. Whether or not those memories are accurate doesn't seem to matter."

"You're holding on to those memories just as tightly as they are."

"Bitterness is a hard thing to shake." He smiled and shrugged.

"Especially in a place called Bitter Ridge."

He crossed to where I was standing. "I have to go to Charlotte this afternoon on business. I should be back in a couple of days, but I'm worried you might…"

"What? Fall apart?"

"I'm worried you might still be a little freaked out about getting trapped in the basement at the Austen house. I just want to make sure you're gonna be okay while I'm gone."

"I'll be fine," I said, mocking his slow, deliberate drawl. "Fine as frog's hair."

He laughed softly. "You're not making fun of the way I talk, are you?"

"Of course, not."

"When I get back on Saturday, will you have dinner with me?"

"I thought you didn't date."

"It's not a date. It's a chance to put our heads together and see if we can figure out what this person who's harassing you might be after."

I sucked in a short, ragged breath and let it out. I wasn't sure I wanted to go to dinner with him. But I wasn't sure I didn't want to, either.

"It's just dinner," he said. "You don't have to shave your legs or anything."

"You do remember we live in the same house?"

He grinned. "How could I forget that?"

"So, will you pick me up at my bedroom door? Or should I meet you in the garage?"

"I'll pick you up."

"Then I'll shave my legs."

Chapter Thirteen

Daisy kept pace with the Jeep while I jolted down the Hoskins' driveway. She loped beside me, long ears swinging, yowling her signature bawl a few times to warn the house that company was coming. As soon as I got out of the car, she bounded over to me and, in one swift motion, jumped up, placed her huge soft paws on my shoulders, and looked me in the eye.

Henry wandered out from behind the barn. "Get down, Daisy," he scolded. "Let Miss Emory be." Tiny sticks of straw clung to his plaid shirt. A wet stain had spread across the bottom of his overalls. "Alpha's working at Stitched today." He wiped his creased neck with a folded bandana. "I been hosing down my mule, Seraphina."

"You have a mule named Seraphina?" I scratched Daisy under the loose folds of her neck. "Of course, you do."

I glanced at the neatly mown fields behind him. A vegetable garden with long straight rows of newly planted tomatoes and beans stretched across the lower meadow near the house. A cockeyed scarecrow, fashioned out of a red plaid shirt and a string of aluminum pie plates, stood guarding it in the sun.

"You have a beautiful farm, Mr. Hoskin."

"Farming's a hard life, miss. We've thought about chucking it more than once. But I guess it's just in our blood."

"Looks like you do pretty well."

"This old place has almost gone under a couple of times, but we've managed to survive. But now, Alpha and I are getting too old to break our backs every day. And we miss our daughter."

"Alpha says you're going to sell."

"Yes, ma'am." He nodded. "Someone's offered us a good bit over the appraised value. We'd be crazy not to accept it."

"Would you sell to James if he wanted to buy your farm?"

"I don't think so." Mr. Hoskin glanced down. "Look, Miss Emory, I've known James for a long time, but I can't let friendship get in the way of what's best for me and Alpha. Doesn't matter, though, because James never made me an offer."

"I was just curious."

"He was over here this morning helping me board up the broken windows at Pris' house. He's a good man. If he'd asked his father for help back when the Gray Top deal was falling through, things would've turned out all right. He just let his pride get in the way." Henry smiled sadly. "Let me wash my hands, and I'll be ready to help you to load up them papers."

"I still wish you'd let me pay you."

Henry smoothed the sides of his mustache with his thumb and forefinger, a signal that he was about to say something surprising. "I won't accept no money. But I'd sure like to drive that Jeep Wrangler."

I handed him the keys and laughed. "Be my guest. This car hates me."

"It ain't a mule, Miss Emory. You're the boss. You

have to tell it where to go, then hang on and enjoy the ride."

"I'll remember that the next time I back over one of Olivia's rose bushes."

I was relieved not to be behind the wheel as we bumped our way over Stoney Creek Bridge. Henry was enjoying himself, and I felt relaxed enough to ask him if he knew what Pris had done with the things in her house.

"I don't know where it all went," he said. "I guess people just carried it out piece by piece. Except for that trunk."

"What trunk?"

"After Portia married Edward, Pris asked me to keep one of Portia's old trunks at our house. It was just a small thing—a little lady's trunk. I don't think she wanted Portia to know she'd taken it, so I stored it in our root cellar."

"Could you show it to me?" I clutched the silver locket around my neck. "If it's locked, I might have the key."

"It ain't there no more. Someone stole it a few weeks back."

"What was in it? Do you know?"

"Letters, mostly. Some photographs." He glanced at me. "Alpha looked in it. Portia was always talking about her treasure, so Alpha wanted to know if it was in the trunk. She didn't want to be hiding something in our root cellar somebody would come in and kill us for."

"Yeah." A chill settled in my chest. "I get that."

"Look, I know you think Alpha just stood by and let your aunt's house fall apart, but it was in bad shape when Pris moved to Laurel Haven. I was always after

Pris to get things fixed, but she never got around to it. She was too dependent on Alpha fixing everything that needed fixing. Even your grandparents relied on Alpha to do things for them."

"I'm sorry. I shouldn't have jumped to conclusions."

Henry chuckled. "My daughter would say that was bad karma. Whatever that means."

"Alpha told me about Angel. She's a teacher out west?"

"Angel." He whispered her name like a prayer. "She's a teacher. In Denver." Pain washed over his craggy face. "After she got her heart broken a few years ago, she couldn't stay here in Bitter Ridge."

"It's hard to recover sometimes."

"What that man did to my little girl don't even allow thinking about." He downshifted hard and jolted the Jeep around a sharp curve. "Alpha doesn't know this, and I want to keep it that way, but when Angel was in college, her boyfriend slapped her around one night and broke her wrist. She didn't trust no man after that. But then this fellow in town decided he liked her. At first, she wasn't having any of it, but he kept on and on, swearing she could trust him, begging her to give him a chance. He wore her down until she finally said yes. Then he cheated on her."

"That's terrible."

"She's never been the same." Henry's giant hands flexed then stiffened as he gripped the steering wheel. He caught me looking at them. "Don't worry, miss, if I were gonna wring his sorry neck, I'd have already done it. One day, that man will get what's coming to him. There's a river of justice that flows through this world and sooner or later, it's gonna reach his front door."

"Well, I hope he knows how to swim."

Henry nodded. "I hope he drowns."

The new lock Henry had installed on the front door gleamed in the late morning sun. We worked for an hour without making small talk, stuffing the papers into the plastic trash bags I'd filched from Olivia's kitchen and hauling them to the Jeep. It took a lot less time than I had anticipated, but it was still hard work. Drops of perspiration slid between my breasts, a gentle reminder of how out of shape I'd become since Kent's death. I'd never been a gym rat like Kent, but anyone in New York City will tell you that just living there is a workout all on its own. After he was gone, I spent far too much time hiding inside Esther's apartment when I should have been outside pounding the pavement trying to get my life back.

Henry pushed the last bag into the back of the Jeep. "That's the last of it, Miss Emory."

A red Mustang tore down the road and squealed to a stop beside the house. Gordon Spencer got out, adjusted his gray sport coat, and flashed me a blinding smile. He looked sharp in his dark striped tie and crisp white shirt. But then I'd always had a weakness for the wrinkle-free starched shirt types.

"Hey, Mr. Hoskin," Gordon said. "How's it goin'? I bet all this rain has been a welcome sight to your garden."

"Yep," Henry said, never looking up.

"How's Daisy doing? I'd sure like to take her out with me again when hunting season starts up." He turned to me. "The Hoskins have this great bloodhound named Daisy Mae."

"I've met Daisy," I said. "She's a beauty."

"Henry used to let me take her deer hunting, but that was a long time ago, wasn't it, Henry? Man, I've never seen a dog with a nose like that. She can find anything. Once, I bagged two turkeys and a wild boar. With her help, of course."

"Jackson takes her hunting now," Henry said.

Gordon glanced at the Jeep. "Are you getting rid of stuff? What's in the bags?"

"Bat guano," Henry said. "Cleaning out the attic."

Gordon laughed softly. "I see."

"Are you on your way to work?" I asked.

"Yeah, I came home to check on my father. I saw you out here and wondered if you'd like to join me for dinner tonight at the McAlister? Sounds a little lame to ask you to eat at my hotel, but I'm expecting a shipment, and I have to wait for it." I hesitated. "Aw, come on." He grinned, crinkling his pale blue eyes. "There's molten chocolate lava cake on the menu."

"Well, all right, then." I laughed. "How can I possibly resist that?"

I'd planned to work on Olivia's portrait, but there were so many unanswered questions about my aunts, I couldn't pass up the chance to talk to someone who lived so close. Gordon drove up and down the mountain several times a day. He might know what was going on at Pris' house just as easily as Alpha or Henry.

After Gordon left, Henry carried Portia's watercolors to the car and stacked the frames behind the front seat. He didn't say much on the way back to the farm, but it was a comfortable silence. He'd worked without a break and was surprisingly strong for a man his age, although I guessed working on a farm every day kept him in shape. In the driveway, he turned the Jeep around and pointed it toward the road.

"Thanks again, Mr. Hoskin."

"You take care, Miss Emory." He tipped his straw hat and leveled his gaze at me. "I know this tiny little town ain't what you're used to, but most cities are alike no matter what size they are. There's good people, and there's bad people. The trick is figuring out which is which."

****

By the time I'd driven back to Laurel Haven to visit Aunt Pris then backtracked to the St. Clairs' to change for dinner with Gordon, I hadn't had time to unload, or even think about, the bags of papers stashed in Maddie's Jeep. I checked the foyer on my way out, but there was no sign of a package for me. If Esther had gotten my laptop to the post office before it closed yesterday, it should arrive soon.

I corralled my hair at the nape of my neck and fastened it with the ebony clasp my mother had sent me from Sri Lanka. I threaded the delicate silver and pearl loops through my ears she'd sent me from Bali then slipped on the silver ring she'd bought me in Jaipur. These were little talismans of strength for me. Things she had touched. Things she had chosen for me that she loved, hoping I would love them too. They were also memories she had tried to give me without actually being there. I spritzed a little perfume on my wrists and smoothed the skirt of my blue summer dress. I should have borrowed an iron from Olivia, but ironing was not in my wheelhouse, and, as my jet-setting mom always rationalized, "How will anyone know if it's real linen unless there are wrinkles?"

I walked into the garage just as James was getting out of his Jeep. He held a post office issued mail package that could only be my laptop.

"Wow," he said, smiling appreciatively. "You clean up nice."

"Thanks. I tried really hard. Is that for me?" I pointed to the box. "I'm expecting a package from my friend Esther."

"I ran into the mailman at the gate. Well, not literally; he's still breathing. But he gave me this to give to you. Are you on your way out? Do you want me to put it in your room?"

The thought of leaving my laptop in my unlocked room with Tess on the prowl didn't feel like a smart move. "No, thanks. I'll store it in the backseat of the Jeep. It'll be okay until I get back." I shifted the box under my arm. "Henry said you helped him board up the windows at the Austen house this morning. Thank you for that."

"You're welcome."

"So, what are you doing here? I thought you'd be in Charlotte by now."

"I was almost there, but then I turned around and drove back."

"You what? Why?"

"I know you just lost your husband a few months ago."

"I lost him a lot longer than two months ago."

He gently clasped his hands around my upper arms. "I thought we might—you're attracted to me, right?"

"Well, I don't know." I tried to laugh it off. "You live in a fabulous mountain retreat. You know how to rock a plaid shirt. And you're the most hated man in three counties. Who wouldn't be attracted to that?"

He lowered his head and grazed his lips across mine. So fast that I wasn't able to stop the sharp intake of breath from echoing across the four-car garage.

Okay. I wasn't sure this is what I wanted to happen. Or where I wanted it to go if it did.

I could barely remember what a kiss was supposed to feel like, much less which bases I wanted to cover. How long had it been since a man had held me? Since someone else's heartbeat had thudded beneath my cheek? It had been three years since Kent had made me believe he wanted me. Two since he'd stopped pretending I was anything to him at all.

James whispered my name. Then he kissed me. Hard. Dead on the mouth. I swayed, then steadied myself, then took a step back.

"Sorry," he said. "But I've wanted to do that all day. And all day yesterday. In fact, pretty much from the first moment I saw you getting out of that ugly rental car in the pouring rain."

"Until you realized who I was."

"It didn't make any difference."

I pressed my fingers to my lips.

"You're not gonna lose your lunch, are you?"

"No. I just wasn't expecting that."

I wasn't sure I wanted to open that door again. Because once that door is open, there's no going back. And yet, during our six-second kiss, James had managed to make me forget everything: the danger I might be in, the fact that I didn't trust him, the raw ache I'd carried inside me since the day Kent had confessed he was batting for the other team.

What would my life have been if I'd met someone

like James first? Before I'd blithely handed over four years of my life to Kent Chandler and been saddled with the kind of baggage most men would kick their way through a brick wall to get away from?

"I have an idea," he said. "Let's get out of here and go for a drive. We can park on the scenic overlook. Watch the sunset from the top of Old Baldy."

"I don't—oh, God, what time is it?" I grabbed his wrist and turned it toward me to read his watch. "I have to go. I am so late."

"Where are you going?"

I opened the Jeep door, threw my purse onto the passenger seat, and slid under the steering wheel. "To the inn. I'm having dinner with Gordon Spencer."

"You've got a date with Gordon?"

"It's not a date. It's—dinner."

He ran his hand back through his hair. "I don't believe this. I drive all the way back to see you, and you're going out with that—"

"I didn't know you were coming back tonight. You invited me out for Saturday. Today is Thursday."

"I know, but you have a date with—"

"It's not a date."

"You keep saying that."

"I keep saying it because it's true."

"Then cancel it."

"I…can't."

"You mean, you won't."

"I don't want to cancel. I need to find out what's been going on at my aunt's house, and Gordon lives on Holly Berry Road right over the mountain from it. He might have some information."

"You're going on a fishing expedition?"

“Okay…yes. And while I'm there, maybe I'll throw another line in the water and ask about the bad blood between the two of you.”

“And I’m sure he’ll give you a straight answer.” He dug his hands in his pockets. “Just take everything Gordon says with a big jigger of salt.”

“That’s what he said about you.”

“Okay, fine. Go meet Gordon. Ask what you need to ask.” He flashed me a quick smile. “See, I’m smiling. Just to let you know I’m okay with whatever asshole you decide to have dinner with.” He opened the mudroom door. “I won’t leave for Charlotte for a couple more hours. If you’re not doing anything after your date that’s not a date, give me a call. I’d like to know what you find out.”

“I’ll be sure and take notes.”

“And do yourself a favor: Don’t order the flounder. Gordon catches it in Stoney Creek on his day off.”

Chapter Fourteen

The narrow dining room in the McAlister Inn was more than half full, which surprised me after hearing Gordon talk about how bad business was. The inn seemed to get most of its restaurant customer traffic during the day. Except for an ice cream stand, a barbecue joint, and the Lone Wolf Tavern, there weren't many places to eat downtown. By six, most of the shops on Main Street had already closed.

I waited at a window table, methodically shredding my paper straw wrapper and wadding it into little balls, wondering exactly how I was going to bring up the goings-on at my aunt's house on Crow Mountain to Gordon. It could be tricky. I didn't want to piss him off. Because even though I didn't consider having dinner with Gordon a real date, I was pretty sure that's what he thought it was. Unless he had an ulterior motive and wanted to ply me with wine and molten chocolate cake to make sure I wasn't going to sue the inn for gross negligence, mental anguish, and a knot on the back of my head the size of an Everlasting Gobstopper.

I brushed the straw wrapper balls aside and moved on to the paper napkin beneath my wine glass. I'd sat there for twenty minutes, and all I could think about was James.

Maybe I should call him and apologize.

But for what? I hadn't done anything wrong unless

it was going out with a man he despised. I was still trying to wrap my head around the fact he'd kissed me.

"Sorry, I'm late." Gordon slid into the empty chair across from me. His blue eyes crinkled. "But I've got a great excuse: The bakery truck hit a white-tailed deer on the Blue Ridge Parkway. All twelve pies for our Sunday buffet were rolling down the highway like hubcaps. If we'd gotten it on video, it would have gone viral."

I laughed. "Just another boring day at the McAlister."

"Not for long." He signaled the bartender for a drink. "Don't say anything, because it's not official, but it looks like I might be selling the inn. I've finally gotten an offer from Mr. Castril, and it's a good one. That man has been jerking me around for weeks, but if everything goes according to plan, I could be free of this place by the end of the month."

"You're kidding."

"No, ma'am." He laughed. "But keep your fingers crossed. I'm still negotiating." He glanced around the ornate dining room and sighed. "I never thought anyone would be interested in buying this old mausoleum. I've been wanting out for years."

"So being an innkeeper isn't your thing, huh?"

"It's the money, honey. The inn is old, and it needs a lot of work. It eats up everything we make just to keep it open."

"You said business was down, but I had no idea."

"After James botched developing Gray Top, a lot of families around Bitter Ridge, including mine, never quite got back on their feet." He lowered his voice. "My father is a recovering alcoholic. He made some poor financial decisions for this place while he was drinking. Which is why he put everything in my name last year."

"What about Jackson? Doesn't that cut into his share of the inheritance?"

"Jackson doesn't care about the inn. And even if he did, he doesn't have the brains to run it."

"I thought Jackson did care about the inn."

"He has some cockamamie ideas, but he doesn't know the first thing about running a business. If I hadn't stepped up to the plate and taken over, Jackson and my parents would have lost everything. They could still lose everything."

"Well, I hope it works out for you."

"Me, too." He paused while the waiter handed him a Belgian beer. "I just need to locate some paperwork and iron out a few things. Then I'll be free of this place and my life can start."

"You said Mr. Castril is a billionaire living somewhere on the Florida coast?"

"That's right. I only communicate with him through emails and text messages. Isn't that wild? I mean, a recluse in this day and age? I've Googled him every which way but Sunday, and I still can't find out anything. Why he's zeroed in on Bitter Ridge and Crow Mountain, I'll never know." He sipped his beer. "And I don't care. Not as long as he comes through with the cash."

"Has he made an offer to buy your parents' house on Crow?"

"Not yet. But if he buys enough land to put up the luxury cabins he wants to build, then he'll have to. If your aunt doesn't sell the Austen house to him, the ski resort will be smaller than the one planned for Gray

Top, but it's still gonna be a sweet deal: a string of specialty shops, an infinity pool on the edge of the mountain, kayaking in Stoney Creek, zip lines through the forest. Real estate around here will go through the roof. This will save Bitter Ridge." He leaned back and grinned. "And James will be left out in the cold."

"You sound exceptionally happy about that."

Gordon shrugged.

"Aren't you worried that turning Crow Mountain into a mini-Disneyland will kill the beauty of it? You live on Crow. You know how magical it is up there."

"It's a big mountain, and I love hanging out on it just as much as the next guy. Can't say I'm too crazy about all those damned crows living there, but I'm a realist. Unlike James Tree-Hugging St. Clair. And I'm not buying all that environmental crap he's trying to feed the town council."

"What are you talking about?"

"At the last council meeting, James had the balls to ask them to hire somebody to make sure part of Crow Mountain is set aside for a nature preserve. He damn near got booed out of the building. I thought Melvin Owens was gonna go for his throat. The Bitter Ridge council doesn't want him near that mountain, and he knows it. If he wants a nature preserve, let him build one on Gray Top. We all know Crow is going to be developed one day, and it's no secret that the St. Clairs stand to make a huge killing on the property they own up there when that happens."

"The St. Clairs own property on Crow Mountain?"

"The St. Clairs own property everywhere." Gordon's gaze shot to the door. "The driver's here. I need to speak with him."

"Emory." Olivia and Doc Turner were suddenly standing by my table.

"You look lovely tonight, dear," Olivia said. "Doesn't she look lovely, Hugh?"

"Lovely," Doc Turner said.

I glanced behind her. "Did James come with you?"

"Honey, he's in Charlotte." Olivia raised her eyebrows. "Isn't he?"

"No, he's here in Bitter Ridge. I think he's driving back to Charlotte later."

"He's…*here?*" Even in the soft glow of the table lamp, I could see the color drain from her face. "How do you know that?"

"I saw him. He arrived just before I left the house."

Olivia turned to Doc Turner. "James promised he would see his father tonight. He knows how important this is to me. Why would he drive back?" She stopped and looked at me. Her dark eyes narrowed. I could see the wheels turning in her head as the light bulbs flashed on one by one. "Oh," she said flatly. "He came back to see you. I guess Tess was right about something going on between the two of you."

I started to protest, then remembered the kiss. I hadn't done anything to facilitate James driving to Charlotte then turning around and driving two hours back to make a pass at me. Sure, I found him appealing, in an unlikely opposites-attract kind of way, but I never would have made the first move. It had been too soon after Kent's death. I wasn't ready to trust anybody again. Much less the town pariah.

Olivia glared at me. "You're a guest in my home, Emory, and I've enjoyed having you. But I think you've crossed the line. James is doing everything he can to get his life back, and the last thing he needs is another distraction. Do I make myself clear?"

"Yes, ma'am." I glanced at Doc Turner, who gave a little shrug.

"Good." Olivia gathered up her chiffon wrap and tossed it over her shoulder like a mountain scout going out into the snow. "Take me home, Hugh." She glowered at me once more for good measure. "I need to talk some sense into my son."

****

The dinner with Gordon hadn't gone as planned.

He'd either not known anything about my aunts' lives, didn't care, or wasn't talking. The only good thing that had come of slogging through a two-hour meal of greasy chicken piccata, acidic Chardonnay, and soggy chocolate cake, was finding out that James wanted to save the integrity of Crow Mountain. It couldn't have been easy to beg a roomful of people who openly loathed him to put aside their hatred and consider building a nature reserve on Crow. I wished I'd been there to hear him. I wish I'd seen the look on Melvin Owen's face.

I knocked on Mrs. Shipley's door and went inside.

She sat propped up in bed reading the newspaper. "One thing I despise about having arthritis is that I can't do the crossword puzzle anymore. Ironic, isn't it? I'm probably the only person on this floor who knows a six-letter word for *marsupial* and I can't hold a pencil long enough to fill in the squares. I love puzzles—crosswords, anagrams, crypto-quotes."

"Let me help you." I took the newspaper from her. "I'll give you the clue. Then you tell me the answer and I'll write it in for you."

Mrs. Shipley's gaze traveled past me to the doorway. "Maybe later, dear."

"Hello," James said. "I hope it's not too late to stop by."

I glanced up. The newspaper I was holding slid to the floor.

"Come in, young man," Mrs. Shipley said.

"You remember James, don't you?" I said. "He has a habit of scaring the crap out of me when I least expect it."

"Well, I do like a man of mystery." Mrs. Shipley laughed. "Hello, James. Good to see you again."

"You're a hard woman to track down, Emory Chandler."

"Not really," I said. "You just have to know where to look."

"I'm finally on my way back to Charlotte. You weren't in the hospital wing, so I tried your aunt's room. I thought you'd already left until I heard that Yankee accent coming from across the hall."

"Are you making fun of the way I talk?" I looked at Mrs. Shipley in mock disgust. "This is a man who sounds like Johnny Cash and he's making fun of *me*?"

"I do not sound like Johnny Cash. Nor do I sing like him."

Mrs. Shipley chuckled. "I think you both sound delightful. Now, go somewhere and talk. Get out of this old woman's room. *Shoo!"*

I followed him outside to a bench near the side entrance. The breeze ruffling through the trees smelled like rain. A low roll of thunder echoed and rumbled across the deep meadow. The rain was moving back in, probably sooner than later.

"I was going to call you," I said. "I need to apologize."

"I'm the one who's sorry. I've always been jealous of Gordon Spencer, and I overreacted. He just rubs me the wrong way."

"Why would you be jealous of Gordon?"

"I was always the nerdy kid hanging out at home reading books and playing video games. But I wanted to be one of the golden boys. You know, the athletic type who wins the race and gets the girl. Like Gordon."

"Gordon's worried about the inn."

"He should be worried. It's been going downhill for years." He motioned for me to sit beside him on the bench. "After you left to meet Gordon, someone called you on our house landline—a Detective Logan from Asheville. Said he'd tried to call you yesterday."

"Tess had my phone. When I got it back, I never checked the calls." My stomach hardened into a knot. "What did he say? Is there any news about Kent's murder investigation?"

"He was updating his files and wanted to know if you were still being followed. And if you had received another anonymous letter."

"He must have talked to Sheriff Riley."

James looked at me. "Are you being followed?"

I blew out a long sigh. "Okay, first, just let me say that Detective Logan is a real piece of work."

"I already figured that out." His eyes met mine. "Emory, is someone following you?"

"I'm not sure. Sometimes it feels like it when I'm driving to and from Laurel Haven. But then I look behind me, and no one's there. You know how curvy that road is. Someone could be after me, and I'd never see them."

"Have you gotten another anonymous letter?"

"No."

"Well, that's a relief. Have you told Sheriff Riley about someone carrying out your aunts' papers while you were locked in the basement room?"

"Not yet."

"And why not?" He shook his head in frustration. "A lot of people are trying to keep you safe, Emory, but you're not making it easy."

"I don't want to put anyone else in danger. Not until I discover what this person is after."

"You should have told Sheriff Riley."

"I know. I'm sorry."

He raked his hand back through his hair. "Is there anything else?"

"Before you left, I overheard part of an argument between your mother and Doc Turner. Olivia said you had promised to get something for her. She sounded pretty desperate to have it."

"And you think this has something to do with your aunts' papers getting stolen? Do you think it was me?"

"Of course, not." I hadn't considered that, but it wasn't out of the realm of possibility. He would have to have known I was locked in the basement, though. And for the life of me, I don't see how he could have.

"I'm not accusing you of anything," I said. "Or your mother. I'm just throwing things out there. Grasping at straws."

I didn't tell him how little I trusted his mother. And I still wasn't sure why.

"I told you my father lives in Charlotte," James said. "Mother wants him to deed some of the property back to her that she feels she lost unfairly in the divorce settlement. Now that he's living with his girlfriend, Mother thought he might be more receptive. She asked me to talk to him about it while I was there. I'm not sure why she thinks he'll listen to my opinion."

James's explanation sounded convincing enough, but I wasn't sure I was buying it.

We walked to the parking lot. "There's something I'm curious about," he said. "Where did you go the day Kent was killed? You said you left your apartment before he got there. Where did you go?"

"I went to downtown Asheville for lunch." I glanced at him. "I have an ironclad alibi if that's what you're worried about."

"I just wondered."

"So did a lot of other people."

We stopped beside Maddie's Jeep.

"I wish I didn't have to go to Charlotte," he said. "What are you gonna do while I'm gone?"

"Spend time with Aunt Pris. Work on Olivia's portrait. Try to figure things out."

"At least Detective Logan is keeping in touch with you."

"He never says much. I keep thinking that if I could just get a look at his files and read the interviews with my neighbors in the apartment complex, I might be able to uncover something he's missed. You know, step back and see the big picture. If I could do that, maybe I could determine—at least in my head—if Kent's murder were a freak incident or if it's connected to what's happening to me here in Bitter Ridge."

"You really think they're connected?"

"My apartment in Asheville was robbed. My

luggage was searched. I got a note telling me to 'give it back.' Yes, I think it's connected."

James leaned against the car door. I was afraid he was going to reach for me, and I wasn't sure if I wanted him to.

"Look, Emory, I know you can take care of yourself. But I've lived in this town half my life. There are people I can talk to. People who might know something about your aunts that we don't. We could join forces."

I nodded.

"While I'm gone, I want you to promise you'll stay at my house with my mother and Maddie. I'll know you'll be safe there. And I don't want you going back to the Austen house alone again, understand? When I get back the day after tomorrow, we'll search it together. We'll take the place apart board by board if we have to."

It had been a long time since anyone had worried so much about my wellbeing. I smiled, but I didn't promise anything. "Thanks. You are making me feel better."

"You're gonna be okay." He hugged me to him and kissed the top of my head. "I just don't want you to take any chances while I'm gone."

"I won't."

He laughed. "I should probably get that in writing." He pulled back and looked at me. "Keep your phone with you. Keep it turned on. And keep the damned thing charged."

"Yes, sir."

"I'm gonna make sure you stay out of harm's way if it's the last thing I do." He stepped back and cocked his head to the left. "Because in case you haven't noticed, Emory Austen Chandler, I think I'm falling in love with you."

"Don't be silly. You've only known me four days."

"What has that got to do with it?"

"Everything. We don't know each other."

"How long did you know Kent before you married him?"

"Eight months."

"And you still didn't know him."

"No, but we sure looked great together—blonde, blue-eyed, and tall, like matching Swedish bookends." I fumbled for my keys. "But you're right. I didn't know him. Thanks for reminding me." I slid the key into the ignition. "It's always good to remember I don't have a built-in bullshit sensor where men are concerned. That is something I do not want to forget."

I threw the Jeep into reverse and backed out of the parking space, barely missing a dented red pickup truck with a confederate flag decal on the cab.

James stood watching me leave, but I didn't care. All I wanted to do was get away. He was getting too close. I didn't trust him.

I steered the Jeep across the parking lot and onto the dark highway without slowing down. I didn't want to slow down. I wanted to escape. Maybe from myself most of all. As I passed the abandoned Texaco station half a mile from Laurel Haven, two headlights cut on from behind a stack of oil drums. It never occurred to me that it might be unusual for a vehicle to hang out in such a deserted spot. My head was still back at the nursing home, standing by the car. I hardly noticed when the car pulled onto the road and settled in behind me.

Driving through the meadow at night, with those huge, slightly oppressive mountains surrounding me, brought home the fact that at heart, I was still a city girl trying to feel at home in the middle of nowhere. The mountains had felt like home when I was thirteen. But not now. Not while I was alone. I loved the feel of the forest, the dark shadowy magic that only wildflowers and fir trees in moonlight could generate. But deep inside, I longed for an all-night deli and bright-as-day billboards flashing above me. Maybe I was one of those grass-is-always-greener people who constantly yearn for what they can't have and will never find true happiness. True happiness. What did that even mean?

I sighed and turned on the radio. Why was this road always so dark? I needed some sunshine in my life. Once Aunt Pris had recovered, maybe the two of us could move to Florida. Or Scotland where in spring and summer, it's still light outside until 10 p.m.

The car behind me switched its headlights to bright.

I moved to the right side of the road to give it a wide berth, then slowed down so it could pass me. The car cut its brights off and dropped back.

A few minutes later, it cut them on again, edged closer to me, then dropped back. I turned the radio off and squinted into the rearview mirror. My heart picked up speed as I realized that the car behind me was screwing with me, and there was a very good chance I was in trouble.

On a two-lane road.

In the middle of nowhere.

Chapter Fifteen

The road leading away from Laurel Haven bypassed the town of Bitter Ridge and wound sideways through the valley. Low rolling clouds, gray tufts of cotton against the ink dark sky, drifted overhead before disappearing behind the mountains. The sky began to spit just enough rain to smear a fine spray across the windshield. *Nit-shit rain*, Kent used to call it.

I headed around the first bend. A slash of white light seared the left side of my face. I glanced in the rearview mirror.

When had the car behind me gotten so close?

Its headlights had switched to bright again and, in the last few seconds, the car had crept up until it was almost touching my rear bumper. Just close enough to blind me. I glanced at the speedometer. The needle quivered as it passed fifty.

Was the car trying to scare me? Or were its intentions more sinister? If I slowed down, it would plow into me. Or run me off into some poor farmer's freshly planted tobacco field. I couldn't think about that now. I had to stay focused. I snapped the mirror to its non-glare setting and fixed my eyes on the road.

Rural Route 620. I knew it well. Makeshift fresh produce stands, a bait shop painted like a trout, Beryl's Hometown Barbeque and Beans. Each one closed and deserted after dark. Neatly kept farmhouses, so welcoming in the daylight, were scattered throughout the lush valley. But banging on a strange door didn't seem like a very sane option. I didn't know many people in town, and trespassers weren't always welcome. Especially after dark. It was common knowledge in the county that whoever opened their door to a stranger was well within their rights to shoot first and ask questions later.

I fumbled in my purse for my phone.

I could call Sheriff Riley. Or 911. If there was 911. I could call James; except he was on his way back to Charlotte. No, Sheriff Riley was my man. I gripped the steering wheel with one hand and finally located my phone in the side pocket of my purse under a stick of medicated lip balm and a mini bottle of hand sanitizer. I unlocked it with my thumb and glanced down to find my contact list.

The car bumped my back fender.

I lunged forward. My phone flew out of my hand. It skittered across the passenger seat and shot into the narrow, impossible-to-reach space between the seat and the door like it was skydiving into a slot canyon. Then it disappeared altogether.

I grabbed the wheel with both hands.

No phone. *No freaking phone.*

Unless I pulled over and tried to dig it out with my fingers, which might be a little tricky with a car clinging to my back bumper, I was royally screwed. I had no choice but to keep going. I was alone, trying to navigate the Mother of all Jeeps down a dark curvy road with a crazy person on my tail. I couldn't stop now if I wanted to.

If I could make it to Bitter Ridge, I would be fine.

The access road was poorly marked, but I thought I could find it. The center of town had streetlights, and people buying ice cream cones at Barney's, and the blessed sanctuary of the Haywood County Sheriff's Station. But I had to find the turnoff. And to find it, I would have to backtrack. There were plenty of places to pull off and turn around. All I had to do was pick one and go for it.

I glanced in the rearview mirror again.

No way could I turn around and backtrack. With a little luck, I could manage the gearshift. But as long as the car behind me was hugging my rear bumper, I didn't dare slow down. Turning the big Jeep around would be risky. Too risky. I had to keep going until I made it to Gray Top. Once I turned left and started up the mountain, the car behind me would be forced to reduce its speed to maneuver the hairpin turns. If something didn't give, both of us would crash through the metal guardrails and hurtle down Gray Top like toy cars flying off a kitchen table.

I rounded a deep curve and met an oncoming car. But before I could flash my headlights to signal for help, it disappeared into the night. Maybe the driver had seen the car behind me and realized I was in trouble. I had passed them just as quickly as they had passed me. But it was something—a glimmer of hope I didn't have two seconds ago. If one of the passengers in the oncoming car called the sheriff, help could be on its way in a matter of minutes.

I glanced down. The speedometer was nearing sixty.

Then I remembered where I was, and my little glimmer of hope rose and fell in the span of a heartbeat.

The sight of two cars gliding bumper to bumper down a mountain road wouldn't alarm anyone. In the boonies, no one would raise an eyebrow. We would look like a bunch of rowdy teenagers coming back from the local pool hall with a couple of shots of moonshine under our belts, playing chicken, and daring each other to stop on a lonely stretch of road. In that part of the country, it happened all the time.

I plunged into another deep curve and managed to snag a quick glance over my shoulder. The car behind me was a dark color—either black or navy blue or green. And it was large. As large as Olivia's big blue Cadillac.

My mind was racing.

Was it Olivia's Cadillac? Were Olivia and Doc Turner chasing me back to the house? How ridiculous would that be? Had providing me sanctuary at a house fortified like Ft. Knox only been an elaborate trap? And what about Doc Turner? He might be a senior citizen, but he looked agile enough to have chased me down the hall the night of the fire and strong enough to have pulled me into a room. Who would suspect that the kindly country doctor giving me oxygen was the same man who, only minutes before, had slammed my head into a metal door?

Could it be Jackson behind me? He worked in a garage with access to all kinds of cars. And he had enough anger boiling beneath his carefully crafted Goth/Hipster façade to propel him across the meadow like a maniac. Which is exactly what the big dark car behind me was doing.

Could James be back there? I didn't want to think of him as a suspect, but how could I not? Borrowing his mother's car and coming after me instead of driving back to Charlotte was…crazy. I had just left him in the Laurel Haven parking lot. But I hadn't seen his Jeep parked anywhere. Which car had he been driving? And why would he be driving the car behind me? To frighten me into staying at his house until he returned? To run me into a ditch for the fun of it? Was I so far off in my judgment of him and the attention he'd paid me that I'd been completely fooled? I'd been fooled before. Which made me suspicious of everyone.

I tried to concentrate on the road, but I couldn't stop glancing in the rearview mirror. The headlights were as close as ever.

The Jeep bumped over a pothole. The stuffed plastic bags behind the seat rustled. And just like that, it all became terrifyingly clear. *My aunts' papers. The person behind me was after my aunts' papers.*

I had almost made it through the valley to Gray Top Mountain, but time was running out. If the person chasing me wanted to physically stop my car and take the trash bags from me, they'd have to do it here, on this deserted road, while I was a sitting duck. Once I made it up Gray Top and inside the blessed safety of the St. Clairs' electric gate, all bets were off.

My anger flared as a fresh spurt of adrenaline shot through my veins, clearing my head, giving me courage. I stepped on the accelerator and moved ahead in a steady burst of speed. No matter what happened, I wasn't about to hand over my family's property without a fight.

The mountain turnoff loomed in front of me.

I pushed in the clutch then eased my right foot onto the brake. As I slowed down, I prayed that the car behind me would have enough survival instincts to do the same.

The big Jeep Wrangler skidded left across the wet pavement, squealing all four tires at once. My foot slid off the clutch. The Jeep sputtered and shook until I jammed my foot back on the pedal and shoved it to the floor. I pulled the gear shift knob down and straightened the wheels. Then I glanced to the right. Two headlights appeared out of nowhere, then two more behind them. I couldn't tell how many cars were barreling down Rural Route 620 toward me, but they were coming fast.

I checked to see if the back of the Jeep had cleared the road then stuck my head out. The car following me screeched to a halt halfway across the highway, forced to let the string of cars go by before turning left.

That was the break I needed.

I threw the Jeep into first gear and stepped on the gas. The car sailed around the foot of Gray Top, skidding across the wet pavement like a greased hockey puck before righting itself. Miraculously, it let me downshift without trying to buck me out of the car and began the long, steady climb to the top. Portia's watercolors banged against the front seat.

As I took the first hairpin curve like a seasoned old pro, my ears popped with the sudden shift in altitude. Halfway through the next switchback, I heard the convoy of cars honk as they raced past the turnoff. *Nothing to be alarmed about*, I thought with a sly smile. Just a bunch of rowdy teenagers driving back from the local pool hall on a dark rainy night.

I arrived at the St. Clairs' gate just as the gentle rain turned into a gully washer. I pushed the remote button clipped to the sun visor and quickly keyed in the four-number code, then waited for the chain-link panel to slide open.

Relief flooded through me.

It was over. I'd done it. I was safe.

I glanced in the rearview mirror. No one would dare chase me onto the St. Clairs' property. Not with a six-foot chain-link fence and enough surveillance cameras hanging from the trees to rival a corner on Times Square.

Two headlights appeared out of nowhere. My heart slammed into my throat. A car roared up behind me and squealed to a stop inches from the back of Maddie's Jeep.

The electric gate ground to a stop halfway open.

I keyed in the four numbers again with shaking hands. The lights on the gate blinked twice and flashed on. The chain-link panel began to move. "Come…*on,*" I cried. "Only three more feet and I can get through."

The gate stopped. Then started. Then stopped again.

The bulb in my brain flashed on. The gears on the gate weren't going crazy. The car behind me had the same automatic gate controls that I had. Every time I tried to open the gate, the driver behind me closed it.

Only one person could be that despicable. And find it funny.

Rage and adrenaline rushed through me, a reckless combination I had no control over. Without thinking, without even considering the fate I might be sealing for myself, I jolted the Jeep into park and set the brake. I got out, slammed the door, and stomped back to the dark blue car.

"Open this window." I slapped the wet glass with both hands. *"Open it."*

The tinted window on the big luxury car lowered like liquid smoke draining from a tank. Tess smiled and batted her amber eyes. "Hey, Emory. You look upset. Are you having a bad day?"

"It was you?"

"Sorry about the gate. I guess my finger must have slipped on the release button." She held up her middle finger, pretending to inspect it, then swiveled it toward me.

"That's it," I said. "I've had enough. Get out."

"What?"

"Get out of the car."

"Seriously?"

"Now."

Tess got out of Olivia's car and stood beside the open door, using it as a barrier between us. I couldn't blame her for looking terrified. I'd seen my reflection in the car window: wet curls plastered to my face, hands gesticulating wildly in the air, words spewing out of my mouth like some subterranean demon had possessed my soul. I looked like an escapee from Avery Hospital.

"Just chill, okay?" Tess pulled her jacket closer around her. "Stopping and starting the gate was a joke. I said I was sorry."

"How long have you been following me?"

"I wasn't following you."

"The hell you weren't. What were you trying to do back there, give me a heart attack? I almost wrecked Maddie's Jeep trying to make that turn. We both could have been killed. Why were you following me?" I took a step toward her. *"Answer me."*

Tess' eyes widened. She raised her hand, and for an instant, I thought she was going to slap me, but instead, she cupped it over her eyes to shield them from the pounding rain.

"I wasn't following you."

"I drove all the way here from Laurel Haven with only one car behind me. And it looked a lot like this one."

"I came from the other direction. I was coming back from the Walgreens on Taylor's Point when I got behind a bunch of cars. I drove over there to pick up Olivia's migraine medicine. I swear, Emory, it wasn't me behind you."

Silhouetted against the glow of the big car's interior light, with her arms wrapped tightly around her waist and her bottom lip trembling, Tess looked as vulnerable as I'd ever seen her. I almost felt sorry for her. Then I remembered how hateful she'd been to everyone except James.

If Tess had followed me, she'd gone to a lot of trouble just to scare me.

I wiped the rain off my face and shivered. My flimsy cotton dress had soaked through to the skin. As I watched Tess shaking in the driving rain, the fight went out of me. Until I had irrefutable proof that she had been driving the car that had been following me, I had to give her the benefit of the doubt. At least for the time being.

"I'm done with you," I said. "Get in the car."

Tess got in and slammed the door. She wiped the rain off her face and curled her dark wet hair behind her ears. The old Tess was back, safe now inside her tooled leather cocoon. She glared at me with the kind of contempt any sane person would not want to provoke. I glanced past her to the empty front seat. No purse. No prescription. No little white bag from Walgreens. "I thought you said you went to the pharmacy."

"I did, but they were out of arsenic." She started the engine.

"You wouldn't lie, would you, Tess? About going to the pharmacy? Or following me up the mountain? Or hooking up with James?"

"You're crazy." She laughed, but I knew I'd hit a nerve. "One of your aunts buried herself alive, didn't she? Olivia said she'd never met an Austen who wasn't certifiable." She laughed again. "And you married a man you didn't have a clue was gay. Or maybe he was straight until he met you."

"I don't think it works that way."

"Your life sucks, Emory. You really should think about getting some professional help."

I stepped back and stared at her.

I had to give the girl props for one thing: She might be a vindictive brat, but she did have a point.

****

If there was such a thing as adrenaline withdrawal, I was in the throes of it.

My arms and legs buzzed with zappy kinetic energy. Like I'd run six miles uphill or knocked back one too many Red Bulls.

I waited until Tess went inside then parked the Jeep close to the mudroom door. I hauled the heavy plastic bags—one at a time, eight trips in all—up to my bedroom and pushed them against the wall beneath the window. I dug my phone out from under the front seat and retrieved Portia's framed watercolors from the back. I made a cup of ginger apricot tea I found in the pantry and grabbed a half-eaten bag of Oreos off the counter.

I took a quick, scalding shower, washed my tangled mass of hair in record time, corralled it into a ponytail, and threw on my sweats. I was a woman on a mission. And my mission was to go through my aunts' papers and find out, once and for all, what someone would chase me up the side of a mountain in the pouring rain to retrieve. If the answer wasn't in those bags, I didn't know where else to look.

The driver of the car behind me had been careful. They had positioned their front bumper close enough to ram the Jeep but had only made contact once without leaving a traceable mark. Running me off the road and rendering me unconscious—or worse—while they stole the papers had been their main directive. I was sure of it. If there was an incriminating piece of evidence stuffed into my aunts' trunks that the thief hadn't carried out of the basement, it now belonged to me.

I sat cross-legged on the floor and sipped my tea. Then I stuffed an Oreo into my mouth and went to work.

Once I got organized, it went quickly: glancing over each paper, smoothing out the wrinkles, stacking it in an orderly pile. I sifted through unused coupons, old grocery receipts, birthday cards, and magazine articles. There were a few sentimental pieces I could understand saving, but most of it was useless crap. Four hours and four papercuts later, I opened a bag and spotted an envelope lying on top addressed to Mr. Edward Gilmore. I opened it and pulled out two folded pieces of paper. Typewritten on a real vintage typewriter was one line: *Edward Gilmore—Portia intercepted this letter from Pris and kept it from you.*

I leaned back against the bed and unfolded the second one. I held the fragile yellowed paper in both hands and read the flowery handwritten script:

My darling, Edward,

I hope this letter reaches you, my love. We have a child now. A beautiful baby boy. He was born here in the mountains and I named him after you. My parents are both with God now, and Papa can never hurt us again. We can be married like we planned and spend the rest of our lives together. Please come back to me. I love you, Edward. Please come home.

Your Pris.

I pressed the letter to my heart, imagining Pris writing to the man she loved with news of their baby, then waiting and waiting for the reply that never came.

I studied the envelope. It was postmarked from Bitter Ridge, North Carolina, two years ago last April, just after Portia and Edward had been married. Mrs. Shipley said Edward was reading a letter when he had the fatal heart attack. Was I holding the weapon that had killed my uncle just as surely as a knife or a gun? But who could have sent it? And why?

Had they known Edward had a weak heart? Mrs. Shipley said it was common knowledge that he was taking nitroglycerin. But why send this letter to Edward? After more than sixty years, what did the person who found it hope to gain? Did they think Edward was wealthy because he had married one of the Austen sisters and planned to blackmail him? But who would care? In this day and age, no one would give a damn he had fathered a child out of wedlock.

But the concealed death of a child? His child? Something like that could shake the close-knit town of Bitter Ridge to its core.

Edward had been Portia's obsession for more than fifty years, and she wasn't playing with a full deck. Would she even understand what it meant if someone threatened to tell Edward what she'd done and blackmailed her? Would she respond to the letter or hide it in her trunk to make it go away? And when Portia didn't respond, did the blackmailer go ahead and make good on their threat by sending the incriminating letter to a man with a bad heart? The shock of reading about the son he never knew existed could have killed Edward Gilmore. Which may have been exactly what the blackmailer hoped would happen.

But who was blackmailing them? And why would they think Portia and Pris were rich? They owned a great deal of property, but they weren't exactly rolling in—I stopped. *Portia's treasure.* Everyone in Bitter Ridge had heard there was a treasure hidden in the Austen house. Not everyone believed it was true, but it was a cinch the whole town knew about it.

I refolded the letters and placed them back in the envelope. In the morning, I would take them to Sheriff Riley. He would know what to do.

I slid the envelope beneath my pillow and crawled into bed. Then I switched off the lamp and pulled the soft quilt up over my shoulders. Exhaustion wrapped around me like a warm cloud, trying to pull me under. I thought of the unopened package on my dresser. Tomorrow, when I'd had some rest and was thinking clearly again, I'd set up my computer at Laurel Haven and see if I could research the people I had major misgivings about: Jackson Spencer, Olivia, Tess, Alpha, Doc Turner, James. I'd tried to Google a few of them on my phone, but the reception on the mountain had been so spotty, I'd given up.

I hoped the letter I'd found wasn't another dead-end. Blackmail was a personal, stake-through-the-heart crime executed by the same kind of cowardly person who hurts people from a distance by sending anonymous notes. I didn't think we were dealing with some notorious thief whose fingerprints were on file in an FBI computer. Whoever sent this letter knew Pris and Portia. May have even been friends with them. And had somehow uncovered their darkest secrets.

I gazed out the window.

The pounding rain, reduced now to drizzle, ran down the windowpane like a game of Plinko, leaving geometric patterns crisscrossing the glass. The sky had already begun to change from black to indigo as the sun made its way up and over the mountains.

I slid my hand underneath the pillow and touched the envelope.

"It's okay," I whispered, thinking of Aunt Pris, then of myself. "Everything will be okay."

Chapter Sixteen

"Emory? It's almost noon. Are you all right?

I blinked at Maddie, trying to bring her face into focus. Was I dreaming? Or did the blistering sunlight streaming across my face mean I was awake?

"Mother sent me to check on you." She glanced around, surveying the stacks of papers and plastic bags. "Where did all this trash come from? It looks like Tess' room, except hers is filled with candy wrappers."

I sat up and groaned. "I'm too old to pull an all-nighter. I feel like a truck ran over me." I pushed a handful of curls back from my face. "A big, ugly truck."

"Please, can I stay up here with you? Tess is in a horrible mood and Mom's going nuts because James isn't answering his phone." Tears welled up in her dark blue eyes. "I *hate* it here."

"What's happened?"

"My scholarship to Duke University came through. They sent my acceptance in the mail this morning. It's a full ride. They're paying for everything."

"Maddie, that's wonderful."

"I'm turning it down. And I'm not even telling Jackson about it."

"Why?"

"Because if I go away for four years, he'll find somebody else."

“You don't know that.”

“Yes, I do,” she wailed. “Mom says he’s holding me back. She thinks I’m throwing my life away on him. But I love him. You understand, don't you, Emory? You were married once. You understand why I can't leave Bitter Ridge.”

“I understand, but I still think you're making a huge mistake.”

“I thought you’d be on my side.”

“I am on your side. But full scholarships don’t come along every day. If you throw away an opportunity like this, you’ll regret it. If Jackson loves you—and I mean, really loves you—he'll want this for you. He'll wait for you.”

“No, he won’t.” Betrayal flashed across her face. “And I won't ask him to. I love him. Don't any of you get that? I thought you were different, Emory, I thought you'd understand. But maybe Tess is right: You don't care about any of us.”

“Talk to Jackson,” I said. “Let him know how important this scholarship is. Give him the chance to come through for you.”

“And what if he doesn’t?”

“Then he doesn’t, and you’ll know what kind of man he is. Believe me, it’s always better to know.”

Maddie looked at me as if I had just told her to skip naked through the town square. “That’s a load of crap. And I’m not falling for it.” She walked to the door. Before she slammed it, she looked back over her shoulder. “I’ll show you. I’ll show everyone.”

I was glad I wasn’t eighteen anymore. Eighteen was brutal. An eighteen-year-old girl’s heart, in the span of two minutes, could ache with tenderness then shrivel up, turn black, and die.

I rolled out of bed and ripped open the sealed postal box holding my computer. Esther had cushioned it carefully between layers of packing sheets, snug in its zippered carrying case. I plugged the charger into an outlet beside the dresser and made sure the screen was still password protected. Kent and I had had an open-door policy with our computers—shared passwords, shared usernames, no secrets. Funny that for all those years I trusted him so implicitly, I had never thought to look at his phone.

Or not so funny.

I pushed the computer to the side of the dresser and stored the soft zippered case beside it on the floor. A bulge in the inside pocket brushed against my hand as I set it down. I unzipped it, expecting to find an old computer mouse I'd misplaced. When my fingers touched the hard-plastic case, the air in my lungs evaporated.

Kent's phone. Coming back to haunt me. I vaguely remembered putting it there after he died, thinking I would go through it before giving it to his parents and erase any messages or photos that might upset them. They probably assumed the police still had it. They knew Kent had decided to embrace the gay lifestyle, and were fine with it, but I didn't think they needed hardcore evidence slapping them in the face. So to speak.

How had I forgotten I'd stashed his phone with my laptop? I'd been pretty shaken up after his murder, but I'd thought I had the basics under control. I had dreaded going through that phone. I still dreaded it. Only now I didn't have a choice. If I wanted to find his killer, I needed to look at it with fresh eyes. See if there was something Detective Logan might have missed. He swore he hadn't discovered any evidence that would make him believe Kent's death was anything more than being in the wrong place at the wrong time. But I wasn't so sure.

I held down the side button and waited for the phone to light up. It sprang to life in my hand, displaying rows and rows of gay hookup apps designed to fool the average straight person. I tried to ignore them and searched for the battery gauge, suddenly feeling as if there weren't enough oxygen in the room.

My hands trembled, and I fought the overwhelming urge to smash the phone against the wall and watch it splinter into a thousand pieces. It hadn't been charged in over a month, but it still had some battery life left. I plugged it into my portable charger while I got dressed, then slid them both into my purse. I would look through it later while Pris napped after physical therapy. I had no choice but to do it. I owed it to Kent. But more importantly, because I was the one still walking on the earth and crossing the days off one by one, I owed it to myself.

****

Main Street was just as I remembered. Rain-washed sidewalks glistened in the morning sun, wrought iron benches sat in the parkway, tiny round bistro tables gathered around the fried-chicken-café-turned-barbecue-joint, which, on closer inspection, was more charming than I had given it credit for. The shopkeepers on Main loved their flowers. They hung them in baskets from streetlamps, planted them spilling out of window boxes attached to their storefronts, and grew them in neat beds around the fountain in the town square.

As I drove past *Stitched,* the textile arts store where Alpha sold her quilts, I noticed a For Rent sign in the window of the small shop next door. I wondered how much something like that would cost and, without even realizing what I was doing, I pulled over to the side and parked. I stared at the white clapboard storefront with the bright blue door and the small bay window. An old wish that I had considered long dead began to spark. A dream I had kept buried in the tiniest, most remote part of my heart began to bloom again with hope. The memory, so sweet and all-consuming; it took my breath away. I couldn't believe that after all this time, the ache was still there. As clear and perfect as ever.

I had dreamed of being part of a working artists' community in a small town long before anyone besides Aunt Pris told me I had talent. Long before my professor at art school said that capturing the human face in all its torment and beauty was where my gifts lie. Long before I was charmed by a slow-talking southern boy from Asheville, North Carolina, who'd laughed at me when I told him the Tripplehorn Gallery thought I could make a living drawing pastel portraits. He'd stopped laughing after he lost his job at the real estate office and I'd secured enough commissions to come through with the rent and grocery money. And, as it turned out, the bar and escort money, too.

I looked wistfully at the empty storefront one more time, then made myself turn away. The location, the size, even the color—was as I'd always imagined. I drove the rest of the way down Main Street feeling astonishingly happy.

Even if I never realized that old dream, it had been a good one. The best dreams stay with us and comfort us, like a well-worn blanket or a pair of strong arms holding us close. This dream had kept me warm on a snowy New York night when my husband stayed out till 4:00 a.m. It had kept me sane when the cardboard box holding my parents' ashes cleared customs. It had soothed me when nothing—not even half a bottle of Irish whiskey—could lull me to sleep. And yet, I had never dared to try to make it happen. I'm not sure why. Unless I'd thought I had too much to lose.

But the minute Kent started making noises about looking for a job in his hometown of Asheville and moving back there, it was all the prodding I needed. I was ready to leave New York without hesitation, to jump feet first into a new life and never look back. Didn't that count for something?

I parked the Jeep in front of the County Sheriff's Office, only bumping it onto the curb and back off again one time. Sheriff Riley threw down his newspaper and grinned when he saw me push open the double glass doors. I was glad to see him; I felt like he was one of the good guys. His frank, laidback attitude was refreshing and, even though I hadn't always followed his advice, I trusted him. Maybe only him.

I told him about my harrowing trip through the meadow the night before and handed him the envelope containing the two letters.

He snapped on a pair of latex gloves, leaned back in his chair, and read them. "Now, it's getting serious," he said.

"I think my Aunt Portia was being blackmailed."

"So it would seem."

"Then this letter must be what the person who tried to run me off the road last night was after, right?"

"I'm not sure." His clear hazel eyes had stopped smiling. "You're still at the St. Clairs, aren't you?"

"Yes. You told me to stay there. You said I'd be safe there."

"Well, I've reconsidered. I think you need to get out. I know the St. Clairs have a pretty impressive security system in place, but it can work both ways."

"I'm not sure I follow you."

"A big chain link fence can keep someone out, but it can also trap you inside. I can protect you more efficiently if you're staying closer to town. I can get to you faster. I can post an armed guard at the door of your motel. I can—" He leveled his gaze at me. "Look, I don't want to scare you, but this isn't the first blackmail note I've seen in this town."

"Really? Who got the other ones?"

"I'm not at liberty to say. But if the same person who sent this letter to Edward Gilmore sent the anonymous note to you, and they're desperate enough, things may come to a head pretty fast."

"I thought you didn't want to scare me."

"I lied. I do want to scare you because I want to keep you and your aunt safe. I've already got one of my deputies checking on Miss Austen, but I'll tell him to step it up." He slid the letter into a plastic bag. "Henry Hoskin said you're interested in borrowing my niece Chelsea's Volkswagen that her mother is making me sell, and no one wants to buy."

"I'd be glad to rent it from you. Let me pay you something."

He waved me off. "It's just sitting around back.

Chelsea wrecked it a few weeks ago, and she's been grounded from driving. Indefinitely. It's a little dented up, but it runs okay. She got it for a song. Jackson Spencer customized it for her."

"Customized?" I asked uneasily.

"She's only sixteen. Very big into saving the planet. And unicorns."

"Who doesn't like unicorns?"

He took the keys out of his desk and handed them to me. "Take it for a spin. If you like it, I'll get McBride to follow you to the St. Clairs' to drop off their Jeep. Then he can bring you back here to pick up the VW. *Then* you can pack your stuff and move to a motel."

"Tonight," I said, thinking of Olivia's portrait that I needed to finish. "Or tomorrow morning."

He shook his head like I was another sixteen-year-old hellbent on getting grounded. "Just keep me informed of your whereabouts."

I followed Deputy McBride to a little parking area behind the station. Sheriff Riley had been true to his word: the gray Volkswagen bug was a sixteen-year-old girl's dream. Jackson had customized the front with a little unicorn horn jutting out from the top of the trunk cover. The chassis wasn't as dented as I'd feared, but there was a large decal of a unicorn vomiting rainbows and a rash of bumper stickers plastered across the rear—*Earth Day is Every Day, I Speak for the Trees, There is No Planet B,* and a tiny one stuck to the back window that said, *Bruno Mars Thinks I'm Amazing.*

McBride laughed. "Chelsea named this car Narwhal. You know, like the horned whale?"

"The unicorn of the sea. I get it."

Narwhal wasn't exactly an unmarked vehicle, but

the price was right, and it was way easier to maneuver around the tight curves than the big Jeep. The first thing I did was pull off the pink fake fur steering wheel cover and unhook the cluster of crystals hanging on a cord from the rearview mirror. I'm pretty sure I heard Narwhal breathe a sigh of relief.

Narwhal's clutch was a little tricky, and I made a few noisy practice runs up and down the narrow streets of Bitter Ridge to bolster my confidence. Once I got a feel for it, I guided the little VW bug toward Crow Mountain and turned onto Holly Berry Road.

I had promised James I wouldn't go inside the Austen house alone, and I wasn't going to break my word. But there was no reason I couldn't drive by and make sure the new locks were still intact or see if someone had damaged them trying to break in. Afterward, I wanted to stop by the Hoskins' and talk to Alpha. If she were aware Portia had been blackmailed by someone, I was going to try to encourage her to tell me what she knew.

The Austen house looked deserted. From the driveway, I could see the shiny silver padlocks hanging from the new hasps. Relieved they were still intact, I drove back to the Hoskins' farm and bumped the car up their potholed driveway. The rain had left the meadow green and ripe and lush. Rows of plants—I think they were soybeans—stretched across the Hoskins' back field in tidy straight lines. A brown horse grazed in a fenced area near the road. Early pink roses bloomed over their trellised doorway like a fairytale cottage.

No one home except Daisy, who seemed deliriously happy to see me. Watching her romp around and hearing her joyful high-pitched howl made me want a dog of my own. Although, I suspected that Daisy was deliriously happy to see just about anybody who gave her a hug and a scratch behind her long velvety ears.

On my way back down the driveway, my mind drifted to the conversation I'd had with Will Riley. He had mentioned seeing other blackmail notes in Bitter Ridge, but whose? Had James shown him the anonymous note he had received about me? *You think that big fence of yours can keep her safe? Not as long as that Austen bitch has what I want.* Words that still chilled me to the bone.

James had admitted to receiving similar notes since he'd disappointed the town over Gray Top Mountain. Was there more than one coward in Bitter Ridge doing their bullying anonymously? Or was there only one? And what was their motivation? Money? Power? Revenge? I'd watched enough TV crime shows to know that money was usually at the top of the motivation list. *Pay up, or I'll tell.* Pay up, or I'll let the man you've spent the last fifty years in love with know the horrible things you did to ruin his happiness.

Everywhere I turned there were secrets—a stolen trunk, a murdered baby, a possible treasure hidden on my family's property. Dark secrets I couldn't begin to uncover on my own. I touched the locket at the base of my neck holding the little brass key—another secret. But what did it open? Portia's diary? Pris' trunk? A safety deposit box at the Bitter Ridge Community Bank? I knew one thing—as long as I stayed cocooned at the St. Clair's like a scared little mouse, I could never hope to uncover anything.

A bright blue pickup truck with a chassis that reminded me of a large woman's hips, came barreling around the corner of the driveway, missing the Hoskin's mailbox by inches. It screeched to a halt in front of Narwhal. Daisy, who had been following close behind me down the drive, lumbered up and sat in the weeds across the road. Her wet droopy eyes shifted from me to the truck and back again.

Jackson jumped out and tramped toward me. My pulse throbbed in my throat.

"Hey, Jackson." I forced a cool smile. "If you're looking for Alpha and Henry, they aren't home."

"Maddie said you made her cry."

I blew out a breath. "Well, technically, I guess I did, but—"

"What do I have to do to get you people to leave us alone?"

Daisy's ears pricked to attention.

"Did Maddie tell you about the scholarship she got from Duke?"

"Yeah. Not that it's any of your damn business."

"She asked my advice, Jackson, and I gave it to her."

"What did you tell her to do? Dump me?"

"No. I told her to give you a chance to show how much you really love her by encouraging her to go. I told her she shouldn't give up a full-ride scholarship for anybody. And I think anyone who wants the best for her would tell her the same thing."

Putting a loose cannon like Jackson Spencer on the defensive might not have been the smartest choice, but he would know if I wasn't being honest with him. His deep-set eyes glowered at me suspiciously. His right hand, which kept clenching and unclenching, smeared axle grease on his *Love Sucks* shirt as if it were a hand towel.

“Well, maybe she’d rather choose me than school,” he said. “Did you think about that?”

“Why does she have to choose at all? You and Maddie have a lot of life ahead of you. If you let her throw this opportunity away, she’ll regret it. And then someday she’ll hate you for it.”

“That's crap. Maddie would never hate me. She loves me. And I love her. If she's gone for four years, her family will turn her against me. Her mother’s trying to do that now.”

“Then go with her. You could apply to Duke. Or I'm sure there’s a local college nearby that would accept you. You could both go to school at the same time. Get an apartment together. Write each other’s term papers. Play beer pong on the weekends.”

Jackson stared at me as if I’d lost my mind. And I wasn't so sure I hadn't.

“I don’t need to go to school,” he said.

“Then marry Maddie and get a job in Durham. You don’t have to live on this mountain for the rest of your life. Help each other get an education.” I sounded like Miss Duncan, my crabby ex-guidance counselor. “Stop being afraid she’s going to find someone smarter with ambition.”

Jackson stepped away from the Jeep, and I knew I’d gone too far.

“Maddie and I will do just fine,” he shouted. “We'd be fine now if everyone would stay the hell out of our business.”

Daisy growled low and slow, baring her teeth. She jumped on all fours and wedged herself between me and Jackson.

"You think you know what's best for Maddie and me. But you don't. Not by a long shot." He swung himself into the truck. "We'll show you." He leaned out the window. "We'll show you all." He gunned the engine and backed out of the driveway onto the road.

I reached down and patted the top of Daisy's head. "Good girl," I whispered.

Jackson's big blue truck started down the mountain. Through the back window, I could see the butt of his hunting rifle hanging on a rack, glinting gold in the bright morning sun.

Chapter Seventeen

I settled into the vinyl sleeper chair beside Pris' hospital bed and closed my eyes. The stiff muscles in my neck relaxed into the padded head cushion. Exhaustion from the night before wrapped around me, leaving me limp. My mind drifted to a sparkling sundrenched sea then back again. I knew I should be going through Kent's phone, but all I wanted to do—all I could do—was shut down for a little while in this safe warm place and sleep.

The sound of my phone ringing jolted me out of some blessedly benign dream I would never remember. I had kicked off my shoes and drawn my feet up into the chair with my hands beneath my cheek like a sleeping child. I had no recollection of doing it. While I slept, someone had thrown a thin cotton hospital blanket over me.

I dug my phone out of my purse and cut the ringer off. Three o'clock. I'd been asleep for almost two hours. Pris was sleeping too, and I rolled out of the chair and went into the bathroom to keep from disturbing her. I looked at the caller's name on my phone and lurched the rest of the way awake.

James.

"Hello?" I said.

"Hey. Have you heard from Maddie?" His low baritone rumbled in my ear.

"No, why?"

"Because she's run off with Jackson. Tess said you and Maddie argued and you said some things to upset her."

I sighed. "Tess should be working for the CIA."

"What did you say?" he asked gruffly.

"Maddie asked my advice about accepting the scholarship to Duke, and I told her I thought she would regret turning it down."

"That was all you said? Because Tess and my mother seem to think this is your fault."

"I just saw Jackson a couple of hours ago at the Hoskins' farm, and he didn't say anything about running away." Could I really be responsible for this? Had I made Jackson feel threatened because he wasn't enrolled in college and full scholarship material?

"They left a note saying not to follow them. But what else would it say? Mother is already lying down in a dark room with the migraine she's thinking about having."

"What can I do?" I didn't wait for an answer. "I'm leaving now. I'll come back to your house and help look for them."

"I'm on the road about thirty minutes out," he said. There was a pause. "Thanks, Emory."

When I arrived at the St. Clair's, the sight of the electric gate standing open dashed any illusions I still had about feeling protected there. Although, if Tess' threats were real, and Olivia blamed me for Maddie running off with the last man Olivia would ever choose for her, I could be in more danger from someone inside the house than from any monster who could force its way through chain-link and electricity.

Gordon's red Mustang sat in the circular driveway.

I parked Narwhal outside the garage in case I had to make a quick exit and went in through the kitchen. I found Olivia sitting at the dining room table with her head in her hands. Tess sat beside her, holding a crumpled piece of paper, which must have been Maddie's goodbye note. Gordon stood behind them checking his phone.

"Maddie and Jackson have run away together," Tess said. "And it's your fault. Way to go, Emory."

"How long have they been gone?"

Olivia lifted her head and stared at me. Tears had smudged the black mascara beneath her eyes. "What did you say to Maddie this morning?"

"Not much. We talked about her scholarship to Duke. I said I thought she should accept it."

"What else did you say?" Olivia stood up and gripped the edge of the linen tablecloth. I half expected her to whisk it out from under the floral centerpiece like a crazed magician. "My daughter is missing. Do you not understand that? *Tell me what you said.*"

"They've only been gone an hour, Olivia," Gordon said. "They're fine."

"Why don't I read the note to you?" Tess said cheerfully. She unfolded the paper and spread it on the table. "'Dear Mom. I'm taking Emory's advice and leaving with Jackson. We need to get away and decide what we want to do. Don't try to follow us. I'll call soon.'"

"Emory's advice?" Olivia shook her head.

"All I said was that she should give him a chance to stand by her and not get in the way of her education. And that if they really loved each other, they could work things out."

"Work things out?" Olivia said. "By getting married? You know I do not want Maddie marrying Jackson Spencer. He's not good enough for her. He's not good enough for anyone."

"I'm standing right here, Olivia," Gordon said. "You're talking about my brother, remember?"

"Jackson loves Maddie," I said. "They love each other."

"Maddie's not old enough to buy a margarita. What does she know about love?" Olivia squeezed the back of her neck and groaned. "My migraine is coming back. Thank God James finally called. I've been waiting for hours for him to return my calls. I was so worried something had happened to him."

"I'll get you some water," Tess said.

"And *you*." Olivia glowered at me. "I took you in. And this is how you repay me? By telling my daughter to run away with a felon?"

"The charges were dropped," Gordon said.

"Oh, please," Tess said. "Five bucks says he's out robbing a liquor store to pay for their Big Macs."

"Shut up, Tess," Gordon said.

"*Your* mother isn't happy about this, either," Olivia said to him. "Why are you still here? You promised you would go look for them."

"I'm going. I'm going." Gordon pocketed his phone. "Come with me, Emory."

"Yes, go with him, Emory," Olivia said. "Looking for Maddie is the least you can do. I'll be in my room. I need to lie down before my head explodes."

As soon as she was gone, Tess turned on me. "Why don't you leave?" she hissed. "No one wants you here."

"Let's try Taylor's Point," Gordon said. "If they're hanging out with Jackson's friends, his truck will be easy to spot."

"I thought you said I was going with you." Tess stood with her hands on her hips.

Gordon flicked the collar of her robe and laughed. "You're not even dressed. It'll take you forever to get ready, and you know it."

"But, Gordon, you said—"

"I say a lot of things, Tessie Lou." He grinned, crinkling his pale blue eyes. "I think the big kids have got this one." He opened the front door and disappeared down the steps.

"I hate you," Tess said to me. "I really, really hate you." She turned and ran up the long staircase. In a few seconds, her bedroom door slammed.

I stood alone in the foyer, listening to the measured bongs of the grandfather clock, trying to figure out how things had gotten so messed up. If Maddie hadn't run away with Jackson and left the house in such an uproar, I would have packed my things and moved out then. But now that Maddie was on the run, and I had been accused of facilitating her escape, I couldn't leave until I knew she was safe.

A few minutes later, I slid into the Mustang's passenger seat beside Gordon. "Do you think they're at Taylor's Point?"

"Not a chance." Gordon drove through the open gate and started down the mountain. "We're not really looking for them. We're just going through the motions. They're not in any danger. Maddie's eighteen and Jackson's twenty-one. In the eyes of the law, they're adults."

“Not in the eyes of Olivia St. Clair.”

“Jackson's been threatening to leave Bitter Ridge for years. He always said if he had enough money, he'd get Maddie out from under her mother's thumb.” Gordon pulled onto the highway. “Tess said you were looking through your aunts' old papers last night. Find anything interesting?”

“I was in my room with the door closed. How did Tess know what I did?”

“Nothing gets by that girl. She’s raised snooping to an art form.”

“If Maddie and Jackson get married, what will your mother and Olivia do?”

“Oh, they’ll be fine. Once those grandchildren start coming, they’ll have plenty of other things to worry about—like how to run *their* lives.” Gordon pulled into a scenic overlook and parked the car. He cut the motor and turned to me. “Is James buying the Austen property on Crow Mountain from your aunt? I need to know.”

“He says not. But I can’t say for certain.”

“Have you seen the deeds? Do you know how many plats of land she owns up there?”

“I don’t know the exact number, why?”

“I want to know if my parents will have to move off Crow. I can’t see them staying there if they build a ski resort. Especially my father. His health is deteriorating rapidly. Where does your aunt keep the deeds? Do you know? Could you take a look and find out for me?”

“I believe the Austen land runs across the top of Crow Mountain and down the northside. I’ve been told it would be difficult to build anything substantial up there without it. But not impossible.”

"That's why I want to be sure," Gordon said. "Our land runs alongside yours. If your aunt won't sell to Mr. Castril, then our property will be much more valuable to him. This will give us some leverage in negotiations if it comes to that."

"I think you can search North Carolina property records online."

"I'd rather look at the real thing. Just to be certain. Does she keep them somewhere safe? Like in a safety deposit box at the bank maybe?"

"I don't know. I'll ask her. But right now I think we should go look for Maddie and Jackson. I promised Olivia."

"All right." Gordon started the motor. "I can't believe how upset she was that James hadn't returned her calls."

"He's her son. She counts on him."

"James is a grown man. He needs to get a big pair of scissors and cut that apron string. My mother's bad enough, but if I had Olivia St. Clair freaking out every time she lost track of me, I'd push myself off a roof."

We drove around aimlessly for another hour then headed back to the St. Clair house. Gordon insisted on walking me to the door, but the moment he stepped onto the porch, he slid his arm around my waist and gently pushed me against the wooden archway.

"Gordon, don't," I said.

"Aw, Emory, why not? I like you. You like me. You do like me, don't you?"

"Well, sure, but I don't—"

He unfastened the barrette at the nape of my neck. Hair tumbled around my shoulders. "Your hair is wild," he murmured. "Are you as wild and sexy as your hair?"

He threaded his fingers through the tight ringlets and lowered his voice to a whisper. “Come on, Emory, relax.” He leaned forward. “Let me get lost in that wild hair of yours.”

I laughed. “I don’t think so. You’d need a roadmap to find your way out.”

“Maybe next time,” he said.

“Yeah, maybe next time.”

Tess was waiting for me in the foyer.

“Come on, Emory, relax,” Tess said, mocking Gordon. “Let me get lost in that wild ugly hair of yours.”

“Don't you have anything better to do than to spy on people?”

“Not really.” She crossed her arms over her chest. “Are you ever going to leave this house? Everyone around here thinks your welcome has worn a little thin.”

“Any news about Maddie?”

“Nope. But James is back. And he’s not happy.” Tess circled me in the foyer like a jungle cat stalking its prey. “You know, I can understand you going after James—he’s good-looking and will be rich as hell one day. But Gordon Spencer is a loser.” She laughed. “But I guess you’ll go after any man with a heartbeat and a bank account. Maybe I should warn Olivia because you'll be trying for old Doc Turner next.”

“I don’t think I’m his type.”

“Here.” She tossed the hair clip to me. Gordon must have given it to her before he left. “We don't want anyone getting lost in that wild sexy hair of yours. They might never come out alive.”

****

I crossed the foyer and traveled the length of the hall leading to James' suite of rooms. I'd never been to the backside of the house before and I was surprised how isolated and private it was. The hallway curved back into the mountain with a wide panel of windows, giving the daytime illusion of walking into the middle of the forest.

His bedroom door was open, and I stood on the threshold looking inside. I knew I was trespassing, but blatant curiosity outweighed any shame I might have felt. The outer office was impressive. Moss green walls, oversized prints of rare buildings, a stone fireplace flanked on either side by floor-to-ceiling bookshelves. A library table stretching the length of the back wall held his laptop and printer with stacks of old blueprints and architecture books piled high beside them. There were also two buttery leather chairs, a wall-mounted TV, a shelf of video games I'd never heard of, and a bronze bear collection. If the room had been any more masculine, it would have offered testosterone on tap behind the black granite wet bar.

James wandered out of the adjoining room and stopped when he saw me. "Hey, I was just coming to look for you."

Before I could decide if I'd made a mistake, he had closed the gap between us and was pulling me into his arms. He buried his face in the deep hollow of my neck. A quick blast of his warm breath against my chest caused my back to instinctively arch into him, sending a surge of heat rocketing south. *Way* south.

"Oh, no, no, no, no," I said, pulling out of his grasp.

"What's wrong?"

"Maddie," was all I could say.

He pulled his hand away and laughed. "Well, blurting my sister's name is almost as effective as a bucket of cold water."

"Aren't you supposed to be out looking for her?"

"Maddie's fine. She's with Jackson. He won't let anything happen to her."

"And you trust Jackson Spencer?"

"Of course, I trust him. He's a little rough around the edges, and he can come across as kind of aggressive and unfriendly—"

"Kind of?"

"But he's always had Maddie's back. She's only running away with him to assert her independence. She won't do anything stupid."

"But your mother—"

"—will get through this. Maddie's making a point. I doubt if she'll be gone more than twenty-four hours. Look, if I thought my sister was in any real danger, I'd have Will Riley and every cop in the county out searching for her. I'm sure she's all right. If she doesn't want to be found tonight, she won't be." He reached for me and grinned. "Now, where were we?"

I took another step back, dodging his hands.

"What's wrong? I thought we had something zinging between us. You liked kissing me before, didn't you?"

"Yes, I did. And I'm not saying it wouldn't be pleasant to do it again."

"Pleasant," he said dryly. "Just the reaction I was going for."

"Okay, fun. It was fun. And I am attracted to you. I just think this—whatever this is between us—we're still getting to know each other. Still stepping on each other's toes. I can't do anything—*think* about anything—until Kent's murder is solved. You're distracting me. And I need to focus."

"You're working too hard. You need distracting. Let me be your distraction." He ran his finger along the crook of my arm. "I'm really good at it."

"I'm sure you are."

A ringtone that sounded like a bird squawking blasted from the inside of his shirt pocket. He fished out his phone. "It's my mother. She's having cluster migraines. I have to answer it."

"Go ahead."

"I'm here, Mother. Are you all right?" He motioned for me to sit down. "What do you mean some of the deeds for Crow Mountain are missing? I pulled them all. I've got them right here with me." He put his hand on a stack of folders on his desk. "Sure. I'll bring them right up."

After he ended the call I said, "The deeds to Crow Mountain? I thought you didn't own any lots on Crow."

James scooped up a stack of folders. "Not me, personally. But my family still has holdings up there." I had a bad feeling about this. "Some of the lots were accidentally left out of my parents' divorce settlement. They're trying to resolve it. That's all this is."

"And you still have no plans to let Pris sell her land to you?"

"I said I didn't."

"And you're absolutely sure about that?"

He looked at me solemnly. His dark eyes betrayed nothing. Was he telling me what I wanted to hear because I wanted to hear it? Or because it was the truth? "I'm not going to take your home away from you, Emory. Trust me."

Trust me. Two little words that should have been so wonderfully reassuring but were probably the worst words James could have uttered. To me, anyway.

How many times had I heard Kent say those words? Hundreds? Thousands? And I had believed him. Every. Single. Time. *Trust me,* I'm working late. *Trust me,* I'm still attracted to you. *Trust me,* I didn't know the man I'm following on Grindr lives in Asheville. *Trust me,* I wouldn't withdraw all the money in our joint savings account and spend it on a weekend luxury suite at the Grove Park Inn with a barely legal guy who lives two miles from my parents.

"I'd better go," I said.

"This will only take a few minutes. I have to drive to Knoxville this afternoon, and I may end up staying overnight. One of the historic homes down there needs some work, and they want me to take a look at it for them. Don't go yet. Let me give you a proper goodbye."

I didn't answer. I was still trying to fight the feeling that I was walking into a dark cave without a flashlight with only seven minutes of oxygen left. I waited for him to close the door then gulped in air. I was being ridiculous. Suspicious. Irrational. I was the textbook version of every woman who's ever been deceived by a man. And I couldn't help it.

The last rays of sunlight filtered through the trees outside the office window and across his desk. A blue file folder like the ones he'd gathered up to take to Olivia lay on the corner. He must have missed it. I picked it up and started for the door to take it to him.

I glanced down. The name Austen, in neat square printing, was written on the label in black ink. Why would James have a file folder with my family's name on it if he had no intention of buying our property? I opened it and scanned the legal-sized document: *Property Sale Agreement. Crow Mountain. Building improvement. Seller, Priscilla Austen. Buyer, James St. Clair.*

Of course, he was going to buy the Austen estate on Crow Mountain. Why had I ever thought anything different? He had lied to me. He had been lying the whole time.

From day one, he had had every intention of buying my family's land and tearing down the house to build a ski resort. Pris may have begged him to do it, but he sure as hell didn't refuse. We were his Plan B to restore his damaged reputation and make a killing selling it back to Mr. Castril. Then Pris had suffered a stroke and I showed up in Bitter Ridge out of the blue, throwing a huge monkey wrench into his plans. But he had adapted. Quite well, in fact. He'd just been biding his time, waiting for Pris to recover enough to sign the papers, and for me to go back to New York.

My eyes began to swim. My heart felt like someone had wrapped an elastic band around it. But I had nobody to blame but myself. What should I do next? Confront James? Wave the property sale agreement in his face and ask him exactly what he thought the word *trust* meant? Or should I put it back on his desk and pretend I'd never seen it until I had come up with a plan? Either way, I was not going to be upchucking rainbows.

Gordon had been right about James wanting my

aunt's property. He'd also been right about James having a dark side beneath all that good-old-boy southern charm. But at least now, I knew the truth. And I would do well to remember that if James had misrepresented himself once, he would certainly do it again. If there was one thing I'd learned from living with a habitual liar it was that one lie was never enough. Not when two or three would make life that much more interesting.

How could I have been so stupid? I'd gone on and on about my feelings for the Austen house. How much it meant to me. How much I wanted to live there. When all along, James was doing everything in his power to make sure that would never happen. Had he lied to me to placate me? To throw me off track so I wouldn't talk Pris out of selling before it was a done deal? Or did he just want to take a quick, guiltless dive into my pants?

I laid the folder back on the corner of the desk exactly as I'd found it.

Then I walked out and closed the door.

Upstairs, I splashed cold water on my face and grabbed my purse. I would take the envelope Mrs. Shipley had given me back to her for safekeeping. I didn't trust anyone at the St. Clair house, and the sooner I got out of there, the better. I glanced at my drawing pad on the easel. Olivia's dark eyes met mine. "I'll finish you tonight," I said to the portrait. "And then we'll be even." I would finish it before I left and consider my debt to Olivia St. Clair paid in full. Then I could walk out of their lives free and clear and never look back.

On the way to Laurel Haven, I stopped by the Thompson Motor Lodge. Mrs. Shipley had assured me it was timeworn but quite respectable. Mr. Thompson let me check out the room before I rented it, and I was relieved to find it clean and cozy, not the disgusting rattrap Olivia had described. I decided to stay in the main building instead of the small log cabins that sat back from the road. I would feel safer there near the staff. And I could park Narwhal around the corner away from prying eyes.

I gave the Manilla folder to Mrs. Shipley then went back to the hospital wing to have dinner with Pris. Her spirits had lifted, and she seemed to be in a much better place mentally than I had seen her since the stroke. The nurse said the doctor had talked about moving her back to her regular room and letting her continue outpatient physical therapy from there. I didn't bring up James or the property sale or anything that would spoil our time together. It was out of my hands anyway. Maybe I was finally beginning to accept the fact that the Austen house wasn't my home and never really was. Without someone I loved living inside, it was just a house. A shell. A means to an end.

Pris' twinkling blue eyes and sweet, slightly crooked smile warmed my heart like a hearth fire glowing brightly on a snowy mountain night. No matter what happened with the house on Crow Mountain, I would always have a home with her. Aunt Pris was my home. She was my family. My lifeline. It had taken me years—so many years—to figure that out. But I'd finally gotten it.

After Pris fell asleep, I drove back to the St. Clairs' house. I couldn't help feeling relieved that James' Jeep wasn't there. I felt strong and sure of myself but knowing I wouldn't have to run into him took the pressure off. I slipped inside without anyone noticing.

I took a long bath then spent the next few hours packing my things and stacking my luggage beside the bedroom door. Fitting my bags and Portia's framed watercolors into the little Volkswagen would be a challenge, but I was determined to make a clean break and not have to return for a second load. I stripped the bed, cleaned the bathroom, and carried the bags full of my aunts' papers that I didn't deem worth saving to the trash, carefully obliterating all traces that I'd ever been a guest there. It was time to go. Even with the electric fence, I didn't feel safe there anymore.

I stood at the window and gazed out. The brilliant ribbon of outdoor lighting that came on every night at dusk obliterated the view of the mountains. But I knew they were there. Watching over me, crouching in the dark like my own personal guard dragon who never sleeps.

Why had James lied to me?

I'd asked myself the same thing after discovering Kent's dirty little secrets, and I never got an answer. I was tired of trusting the wrong people. Tired of feeling like a victim. I pushed my palm against the center of my chest to stop the ache. None of this was my fault, but *damn.*

Maybe I would skip confronting James about the sales agreement. What would be the point? It would be easier to just leave town. Staying in Bitter Ridge permanently had never been part of the plan, anyway. Once I sold my parents' house in Upstate New York, I would have enough money to move anywhere I wanted. Aunt Pris and I could start a new life together. Somewhere without memories.

I settled into the straight-backed chair in front of the easel I'd constructed. I spread out my pastel sticks and a box of soft, cotton rags I'd found in the utility closet, perfect for keeping the edge of my hands clean while using my fingers to blend colors. I rolled up my sleeves and braided my hair into a long messy plait down my back. In no time, I'd blocked out the world and lost myself in the simple act of creating something. It had always been cathartic for me, as well as soul-satisfying. And it was the only thing I'd ever been good at.

The center of Olivia's face was almost finished; it just needed to be anchored with her dyed black pixie haircut and her signature white starched collar. If I simplified the background by smoothing it out with crosshatch and kept the focus on her brown eyes, which was her best feature, it wouldn't take long to complete. By 3 a.m., I was done and inscribed my signature in the corner—*Emory Austen*. I didn't want to be a Chandler anymore.

I stepped back and studied it. I could have gone into a little more detail, but I was happy with the end result. It was a flattering likeness, which was probably all that mattered to Olivia. Her dark eyes looked kind. Her high cheekbones appeared youthful and taut. The dimple beside her mouth, identical to the one she'd passed down to James, made it appear as if she were ready to break into a smile. I'd been careful to depict the façade she presented to the rest of the world, but I doubted if it even began to scratch the surface of the real Olivia St. Clair.

Too tired to walk downstairs, much less drive a car, I decided it was foolish to leave in the middle of the night. It would be more practical to grab a few hours' sleep and go in the morning. I peeled back the soft quilt and slid between it and the bare mattress, wishing I hadn't been in such a hurry to stash the sheets in the laundry bin. As I was drifting off, a noise outside my bedroom jerked me awake.

The floor in the hallway creaked outside my door. Someone was standing there, waiting to come in.

My first instinct was to catapult out of bed and run to the bathroom. But before I could move, the sound of metal scraping metal as the key turned in the lock stopped me. I silently curled into a fetal position facing the wall and tried to stay calm. Which wasn't easy with every nerve in my body zinging back and forth.

The door clicked open. The pulse in my neck thudded against the pillow. I forced myself to lie still.

Footsteps swished across the thick rug. They paused beside my bed for a few seconds, then turned and moved toward the armoire. Drawers opened and closed. Empty wire hangers scratched along the closet pole. Whoever was in my room wasn't there to harm me. They were looking for something.

The floor creaked again as the intruder moved toward the dresser. The sound of my purse being unzipped made me indignant. I felt powerless listening to the last scrap of my privacy being invaded, and I moaned softly, startling whoever was holding my purse. It dropped into the chair with a thud followed by the sharp jangle of my keys as they hit the floor. Footsteps shuffled to the door then hurried into the hall. The heavy door clicked softly as someone pulled it closed.

I took a deep breath and blew it out, then got out of bed as quietly as I could and carried the desk chair over to the door. I tilted it back and shoved the top slat beneath the doorknob like I'd seen in countless movies and TV shows. I had no idea if that actually kept anyone out who wanted to break in, but it made me feel better doing it.

I slid back in bed and pulled the quilt over my shoulders. At least I'd had the foresight to place my aunt's blackmail letter safely in the hands of Will Riley. Even Tess, with her knack for unearthing secrets, wouldn't be able to find a way to steal it back from the county sheriff.

The next morning, I opened my eyes and groaned, wishing I'd thought to pull the curtain closed the night before. Sun streamed through the tall windows, bright and unrelenting, showering the room and the tilted chair beneath the doorknob with fresh pink light. I glanced at the overturned bag beside the door and smiled, hoping the intruder's shin still felt a few lasting effects from slamming into it. I sat up in bed and spread out my arms in a long stretch.

And then I froze.

Something felt different. *Something felt wrong.*

I touched the back of my neck. Sticky short stubs of hair curled around the elastic hair tie like broken bristles on a styling brush. I glanced at the open door leading out to the patio, then slowly twisted around and looked behind me.

A choking cry exploded from my throat.

My long blonde braid lay coiled across the pillow like a snake. Or the bottom of a severed scalp.

Chapter Eighteen

I threw on my clothes and pulled my Yankee baseball cap down snug on my head. I carried my bags to the car as quickly and quietly as I could. I was running on automatic, putting one foot in front of the other, trying not to think or feel or cry until I got to a safe place. I crammed my belongings into Narwhal, opened the garage door, then stopped.

No, damn it.

Tess wasn't getting away with it. Not this time. Not with me.

I marched up the stairs. Back straight, hands curled into fists, eyes tearing up from the sheer injustice of it all. It was my hair, for God's sake. And I wasn't going to slink away like I'd done something wrong.

I stood in the hall and rapped on Tess' door.

The splintering crash of breaking glass inside her room sent a jolt of fear rocketing through me. *"Tess?* Are you all right?"

I turned the knob and opened her door. As soon as I stepped inside, the stomach-churning, all too familiar smell I remembered from living in a girl's boarding school for nine years assaulted me. I swallowed hard and opened the bathroom door.

Tess was leaning over the toilet wiping flecks of food off her face with one of Olivia's luxurious hand towels. A jar of citrus bath gel lay shattered on the white tile floor. The sickly-sweet aroma of concentrated oranges filled the air.

"What's wrong?" I said, even though I'd known what was wrong the second I opened the door. "Are you sick?"

"Get out!" she hissed. "Get out of here."

"If you're sick, I could call someone. Do you want me to get Olivia?"

"I'm fine." She turned her head toward the wall. "I just ate something that didn't agree with me. Go away."

"No."

She swung her head around and glared at me. "What do you mean, no?"

"I'm not going anywhere until we talk." She flashed daggers at me, but I didn't flinch. I was beyond flinching. I went back to the bedroom to wait. Tess' clothes and shoes were strewn everywhere—across chairs, on the floor, piled high on the bed. Open jars of high-end cosmetics covered a glass tabletop. Stacks of paperback romance novels toppled over on the nightstand beside the bed. I crossed the room and tripped over a can of cashew nuts. Two candy wrappers, a half-eaten hoagie, and an open bag of potato chips lay on the padded window seat. I lifted the eyelet bed skirt—six empty soda cans, a half-eaten jar of Nutella, and an overturned box of Lucky Charms spilling tiny pastel marshmallows across the dusty floor.

Tess wasn't sick. Tess was bulimic.

On my way to her room, I had practiced the harsh words I would fling at her, imagining the stunned look on her face when I finally told her off. But things had taken a dangerous turn. Tess was more fragile than I'd realized, and now I had to choose new words. Words that wouldn't send her careening over the edge without a soft place to fall.

Didn't anyone realize that Tess was binging and purging? All the signs were there: picking at her food during dinner, sneaking leftovers upstairs in the middle of the night, weighing ninety-three pounds soaking wet. Olivia had complained about food disappearing from the kitchen. Hadn't anyone noticed that Tess was in trouble? Did anyone really notice Tess at all?

She came out of the bathroom and winced when she saw me. "I thought I told you to leave."

"You and I have some unfinished business."

"Get out of my room."

"You might as well sit down because I'm not leaving until you hear what I have to say."

She sat on the edge of the bed and stared at me with disgust. She'd been caught doing the unthinkable by the one person who wouldn't cut her any slack. She had no choice but to listen, and she knew it.

"First, there's the little matter of my hair. I know you snuck in through the patio door and cut it, so don't even try to deny it."

"I'm not denying it."

"Good. That's a start. But when I get back to New York, I'm going to the best hair salon in town for the full treatment, and I'm sending your parents the bill. Secondly, you'll be glad to know that I'm moving out."

"It's about damn time."

"Don't get too excited. I'm leaving this house, but I'm not leaving Bitter Ridge. Not yet, anyway. The only family I have is still here, and you're not going to force me out until I'm ready to go." The teardrop clinging to

Tess' bottom eyelash rolled onto her cheek. "I've known girls like you since I was eight years old. Girls who are mean because they don't know how to be anything else. Girls who aren't happy unless they're making everyone around them miserable. Girls who are lost and can't find their way back." I softened my tone. "Tess, you're not stupid. You know you can't keep doing this or you'll die. You need help. And I think you could use a friend right now."

"So, are you volunteering?" She slapped a second tear away with the back of her hand. "That's rich coming from you. You hate me."

"Well, you're not exactly my favorite person in the world at the moment, but you'd be surprised how much we have in common."

She laughed harshly. "You mean, besides James?"

"Tess, you need help."

"I'm fine."

I pulled off my baseball cap. "Look at me. Look what you did to me. Is this something a person would do who is fine? If you keep treating people like this, you're going to end up alone. Just you. And a shitload of food you can't keep down."

Another tear rolled down her cheek. "I hate you," she whispered.

"I know. And if I didn't feel so damned sorry for you, I would hate you right back."

I put on my baseball cap and fished in my jacket pocket for my business card. "Take this. What I saw here today is between you and me. I won't tell anyone. But when you're ready, I'll help any way I can. If you decide you want to talk, call me. If not, Tess—" I shook my head and laughed. "—it's been real."

****

I held it together driving down Gray Top. I held it together stopping for gas on Route 620. I held it together walking then running down the hall toward Mrs. Shipley's room. I was fine until I opened the door and saw her sitting in her wheelchair waiting for me with her arms outstretched. That's when the dam broke. Emotion welled up in my throat until the tears I'd held back couldn't be contained any longer. I knelt in front of her wheelchair, laid my head on the crocheted lap blanket she always kept over her knees, and lost it.

"Emory, honey," she said. "When you called you sounded so upset. What's wrong? What's happened?"

I pulled off my Yankees baseball cap.

"Your hair! Oh, my poor child. Who did this to you?"

"Tess," I said, choking back a sob. "Tess Winslow did this to me."

She patted my back.

"I'm sorry," I sniffed. "You must think I'm the vainest person in the world. I hated my hair. I told it I hated it every day. But it's been on my head for a really long time."

"Don't be silly," she said. "I got a bad permanent wave once and bawled for three days. I looked like the north end of a southbound poodle." She handed me a tissue. "Honey, we need to talk. But first things first. There's a clean washcloth in the bathroom. Run it under cold water and hold it on your eyes while I make a phone call. Pastor Jenkins' wife Connie is in the women's lounge today doing hair for the residents. It's her mission work for the elderly."

When I came out of the bathroom, she said, "Good

news! Connie can take you in twenty minutes." She laughed. "Don't look so scared. I've seen Connie work miracles." She leaned back and folded her gnarled hands in her lap. "Which gives you plenty of time to tell me exactly what has been going on since you came to Bitter Ridge."

I hesitated.

"Let's cut the crap, all right?" Mrs. Shipley's gray eyes met mine. "I'm a strong woman, Emory. Most people forget that because I'm down to a hundred and two pounds and stuck in a wheelchair all day. I've lost my home. I've lived through four wars. I've buried the three people I loved most in the world. And I'm still here. Whatever you're holding inside, I promise I can handle it. Now, start at the beginning and tell me everything."

Which is exactly what I did. Not because I needed another shoulder to lean on—although, that was decidedly a plus—but because I wanted someone I trusted to know the truth. And I knew I could trust Etta Shipley with my life.

When I had finished telling her every sordid, unbelievable detail of the past week, I sat on the edge of her bed.

"Do you think Jackson could have blackmailed Portia?" she asked. "Or somehow found the letter and sent it to your Uncle Edward? You said he works for the Hoskins, didn't you?"

"Yes." I blew my nose. "The Hoskin's kept Portia's trunk in their root cellar. Alpha said Jackson had keys to everything, so he would have had access to it if the letter was hidden there."

"No one's mentioned Maddie. Do you think she

could have snuck back into the house last night and searched your room? Possibly to retrieve the blackmail letter for Jackson?"

"I don't know. I suppose so. Maddie would jump off a cliff if Jackson asked her to."

Mrs. Shipley took off her thick glasses and cleaned them with the corner of her sweater. "What about Olivia? Or that boyfriend of hers, Doc Turner?"

"Boyfriend?" I had to smile. "Seriously?"

"Well, I don't know what else you would call him. When Olivia's husband Carl left her for another woman, you would have thought she was the first woman in the universe to have a man walk out on her. Then I heard she'd been stepping out on Carl at the same time with Doc Turner. After that, I didn't have nearly as much sympathy for her."

"I wonder if James knows about that."

Mrs. Shipley glanced at her watch. "You'd better scoot, dear. Connie will be waiting. But come back for tea when you're done. I've got some thinking to do."

****

Connie Jenkins was one of those large, bountiful women who wore straight denim skirts and carried the bulk of their weight above their waist like a sumo wrestler. She took one look at my hair and whistled through her teeth. "I don't know what happened to your hair, hon, but it looks like you got it caught in a weed whacker."

"That's exactly what happened."

"So, how do you know Mrs. Shipley?" Connie helped me into an old barber's chair then stomped the pedal until she'd raised me up another foot.

"We met here at Laurel Haven," I said. "My aunt is

Priscilla Austen."

"Why, I know Miss Austen. I'm always trying to get her to cut that hair. Was your hair as long as hers before you cut it?"

"Longer."

Connie measured the choppy curls over my ears. "You're not from around here, are you? I can tell by your accent."

"I'm from New York. I've been staying with Olivia St. Clair."

"Oh, Lord," Connie moaned. "Are those people friends of yours?"

"She took me in after the fire at the McAlister."

"Well, I hope you know what you're doing. They're not very nice people. I'm still steaming over that dirty business that son of hers pulled on me and Delbert—Delbert's my husband. We got burned real bad on the Gray Top Mountain deal. It's been almost two years, and I've still got a bad taste in my mouth."

"What happened?" I thought it might be useful to hear her side of the story without mentioning my run-ins with Delbert at the inn and the hospital. My hair looked bad enough without his wife reducing it to rubble.

"James St. Clair promised a lot of things to a lot of people. Back when the lots on Gray Top were going cheap, some of us old-timers bought a bunch of them in case the land ever got developed. Our church—Living Waters Pentecostal—sunk all our savings into it so we could build a youth center up there one day. Then somebody decided they wanted to build a ski resort. And we thought, well, why not? The Lord works in mysterious ways. Maybe this is what He wants for us. If we sold the lots to James St. Clair, we could triple our investment—which is what James swore we'd do—then we'd have enough money to build a brand-new church."

Connie pushed my head down. "Them big ski resorts like Sapphire Valley and Cataloochee do real good. And it don't even matter no more if it snows or not, because they've got these big machines that make snow when you need it. *Poof!* Just like magic. We were hoping that's what was gonna happen with Gray Top. James said it was a sure thing, and we believed him. But when the options to buy our land were nice and neat in his back pocket, he up and said the land couldn't be developed after all. Said he was real sorry."

"That must have been disappointing for you."

"Oh, it was." Connie glanced at her own reflection in the large mirror. "But we've survived. Even though I don't think everybody got reimbursed. My Delbert is a man of God, and he's helped us keep the faith that things would turn around. And, praise the Lord, they finally have. Delbert's begun to make a name for himself. He's risen up and led our church to the mountaintop again—a different mountaintop, of course—but the Pentecostal leaders have taken notice. He's begun to get offers."

"What kind of offers?"

"He's been asked to speak at the Pentecostal World Conference—a very big honor. And one of the producers at Trinity Broadcasting has contacted him about going on TV. Maybe even having his own show. One day, Delbert and I might be as famous as Jim and Tammy Faye Bakker. With better hair, of course."

She whirled me around, still snipping the hair over

my ears.

"James promised us restaurants and construction jobs and tourists by the truckload. But none of us got any of it. That's why this time, we're selling our lots on Crow Mountain to Mr. Castril. I don't know him, but he can't be any more of a crook than James."

"I think he's buying the McAlister Inn, too," I said.

"If that's true, then Gordon Spencer will be happy." Connie clucked her tongue. "When James froze the Spencers out of the resort deal, they owed everybody in town. And Gordon was all set to marry that Hoskin girl."

"Angel Hoskin? She and Gordon were engaged?"

"Oh, yeah. Gordon busted up with her right after James hoodwinked him. Gordon broke that poor girl's heart. And Alpha's, too, I expect. She and Henry ain't been the same since Angel left for Colorado. That girl turned her back on the Lord, though. She threw away a respectable teaching career and started working in a bar."

"I thought she still taught for the university."

"That's what Alpha wants everyone to think. Poor Alpha. She's had a hard life. Those rich Austen sisters treated her like Cinderella—*Do this. Go get that. Bring me my breakfast. Clean the house.* She supported her family. She didn't have any choice but to work for them. No wonder she hated those women so much."

"Alpha hated Pris and Portia?"

"With a vengeance. She told me one time she'd do just about anything to get back at those hags." Connie's eyes widened. "Oh, I forgot all about them being your relatives." She ran the blower back and forth over my short new curls.

"That's all right," I said, filing the information away. I couldn't imagine Aunt Pris treating anyone, much less Alpha Hoskin, without kindness and respect. But I had only the summer memories of a lonely teenage girl to support that belief. I had never really known Portia, but her psychological problems would have made being around her a nightmare.

I glanced in the mirror, not quite recognizing, but not hating the shorthaired girl who stared back at me either. I tipped Connie and made the long trek back to Mrs. Shipley's room.

Was Pris aware that Alpha hated her? Or had Alpha hidden it all those years, working for her and Portia with resentment boiling deep inside, waiting for a chance at revenge. No wonder she hadn't cared what happened to their house. If what Connie said was true, I wasn't sure I would have cared about it either.

No one in Bitter Ridge was who they seemed to be. The more I learned about them, the more I realized they were like the cast of a small-town horror movie where the inhabitants appeared so charming and quirky at first until you found out they'd been secretly gathering in the woods under a full moon to perform rituals involving fresh blood.

Chapter Nineteen

Mrs. Shipley lay propped up in bed with lists and charts scribbled on blue stationery spread across her tray table. Her eyes shone with excitement. “I think I've had a breakthrough.” She painstakingly made a note at the bottom of one of the lists. “By the way, your hair looks darling. I knew Connie would know what to do.”

Her glasses had slipped to the end of her nose. Pencils stuck out of her disheveled hair like chopsticks. She looked like a 1940’s madcap reporter about to break the big story ahead of Cary Grant.

“What’s going on?” I asked.

“I’m solving a mystery.” She finished scrawling the last name. “*Your* mystery” She read the list of suspects she had compiled, “*James St. Clair, Olivia St. Clair, Doc Turner, Tess Winslow, Henry Hoskin, Jackson Spencer, Melvin Owens.* Have I left anyone out?”

“Alpha Hoskin,” I said.

“Motive?”

“Evidently, my aunts treated her very badly. I’m not sure Alpha would have any qualms about extorting payment from Pris or Portia. She may feel like it was money she deserved.”

Mrs. Shipley sighed. “Well, Priscilla was raised in a different time. And—don’t tell her I said this—she can still feel a little…entitled.”

I glanced down. “Melvin Owens? Why is he on the list?”

“I never liked him.”

I laughed. “Mrs. Shipley, you can’t put someone on a list of suspects just because you don’t like them.”

“Of course, I can. *And* I've been asking questions. I’ve seen enough *Murder, She Wrote* episodes to know that if you're old, you can get away with asking the most personal questions and people will just answer them. Anyway, I've found a nurse here at Laurel Haven who used to work at Avery Hospital.”

“You’re kidding.”

“She didn’t know Portia Austen, but she *did* remember a theft in the office from some of the older inactive patient files that were waiting to be uploaded to a computer. The secretary went to work one morning and found that her file keys had been filched from her purse. After further investigation, she discovered that some of the files were also missing, and the young man she had recently begun dating had disappeared.”

“Do you think this man stole Portia's files?”

“I think it's a real possibility. If someone wanted to blackmail Portia, or any of the Austens, stealing her files from a mental hospital would be quite an achievement. I'm sure all the family secrets were there for the taking, although I’m not sure how reliable they were. I called Avery Hospital, but they wouldn't tell me anything. I suppose the sheriff could get the information for you.”

“Who was the boyfriend? Did the nurse give you his name?”

“No, but on TV they never use their real names. The nurse is going to call the secretary today and get a physical description then call me back tonight."

"Maybe we're finally getting somewhere."

"That isn't all." Mrs. Shipley selected another piece of paper and held it to her chest. "Before I show this to you, promise you won't think I've gone completely bonkers."

"All right."

She laid the paper on the table. "It may not mean anything. I was just doodling, trying to get my old swollen fingers loosened up enough to write, and I wrote out the name *St. Clair*. I'm not sure if you know how much I love anagrams, but as you can see, the name *St. Clair* is an anagram for *Castril*."

"Seriously?"

"Isn't Mr. Castril the man who's trying to buy up Crow Mountain? The man no one has ever seen?"

I lowered myself into the chair beside the bed, trusting it would be there when I reached it. "Castril. You don't think—"

"Now, we mustn't jump to conclusions. The anagram could be just a coincidence."

"But you don't think it is."

"No."

"What if James is Mr. Castril? He said he wasn't trying to buy my aunt's estate, but I found a property sale agreement that says he has. So, we know he's told one lie. Could he buy other property under an assumed name?"

"Easily."

"But isn't that illegal? Wouldn't the police find out and—"

"The police can't just look at your bank accounts whenever they want to. They would need to file a subpoena in court and have a judge sign off on it."

"How do you know this?"

Mrs. Shipley smiled. *"Law and Order.* We could call the Registrar of Deeds Office and find out if a Certificate of Assumed Name or DBA form has been filed."

"DBA?"

"Doing Business As."

I shook my head. "Again, how do you know this?"

"Google."

I got up and began to pace. "If the only way James can get people to sell their property to him is to pretend he's someone named Castril, then he's lying to them too. Does that sound like a man trying to regain his good name? Or does it sound like someone who sees a chance to get back at the people who've injured him and his family?"

Mrs. Shipley pulled a pencil from a tuft of gray hair. "If he is masquerading as Mr. Castril—and I'm not saying he is—what kind of funds would he need to buy lots on Crow Mountain? It can't be going cheap. Do the St. Clair's have that kind of money?"

"I don't know. On the surface, they seem well-off. But Olivia said she'd been forced to live more frugally since her husband left. I think she may have taken a financial hit in the divorce."

"Or she wants everyone to think she did."

"I overheard Doc Turner say that Olivia made out like a bandit in the settlement, but I thought he was being sarcastic."

Mrs. Shipley rolled her wheelchair over to the bed and pulled herself to her feet. "Maybe the St. Clairs were never as financially solvent as they let on. James' father, Carl, was one of the developers in competition with James. Did you know that? I think there was some bad blood there."

"No, I didn't. James said he and his father don't get along, but I assumed it was because his father left his mother for another woman."

"Hold my arm, dear, while I climb into this ridiculous bed."

I helped her swivel her matchstick legs around and smoothed the white thermal spread across her knees.

"Fathers and sons," she sighed. "I'd say James wanted to prove something to his father and make him proud. Most sons do. I'm sure when the Gray Top deal fell through, things between them went from bad to worse." She peered at me through her magnified lenses. "When did the blackmailer send Pris' letter to Edward?"

"Almost two years ago. He got it the day he died."

"So the first blackmail letter to Portia could have been sent a few months before that. Which would have been right around the time James was trying to develop Gray Top."

"What are you getting at?"

Mrs. Shipley leancd back. "When that development deal collapsed, and Gray Top was rezoned, people went crazy trying to buy a piece of it. They thought it was going to save them financially, but as it turned out, most people couldn't afford to keep the land they thought they were going to sell at a profit. James ended up owning Gray Top by default. You can imagine how something like that would rankle the residents who had put their trust in him."

"Did they think he let the deal fall through on

purpose? Just so he could own Gray Top at a reduced price?"

"Well, yes. Wouldn't you think that?"

I stared at her. "Do you think James blackmailed Portia to finance Gray Top for himself?"

"I'm only playing devil's advocate."

"But by that time, my aunts had gone through the bulk of their inheritance. The only things they owned of any real value were the house and the land."

"But did James know that? If James blackmailed poor deluded Portia and thought the letter could be traced back to him, he would be desperate to recover it before anyone owning land on Crow Mountain found out. Everything points to him as a suspect. He was at the McAlister the night of the fire. He could have waited in the bar until you went upstairs then finagled his way into the room across the hall to set off the smoke bombs. His sister works there. He could have managed it somehow."

"I think I would know if James grabbed me from behind and tried to steal my purse."

"Would you? You said you kicked your assailant in the shin. Wasn't James limping up the stairs when you talked to him later that night on his deck? Didn't you say he explained his sore leg by saying that some child had kicked him in the shin at the town council meeting?"

"Yes, but—"

"James could have followed you on the highway that night."

"To his own house? But that's crazy. James left the nursing home driving his Jeep Wrangler back to Charlotte. The car behind me was not a Jeep."

"Could he have used someone else's car? His mother's, perhaps?"

"No, Tess was driving Olivia's car. James couldn't possibly have been following me." I wasn't sure why I was defending him so vehemently, but Mrs. Shipley was feeding me worst-case scenarios at warp speed, and I was having a hard time believing any of it. "If James was behind me in someone else's car, what was his plan? To run me off the road then look for the letter? It wasn't even a real blackmail letter. It was only a letter telling Edward he had a child. There was no mention of extortion."

"True," Mrs. Shipley said. "But why tell an eighty-year-old man with a bad heart he had fathered a son if you're not going to gain from it?"

I began pacing again. Back and forth. Like a tiger I'd seen once in a holding pen at the zoo.

"Honey, calm down." Mrs. Shipley slipped her hand beneath the folds of the bedspread and pulled out a box of assorted chocolates. "I've been saving these as a last resort—brainpower." She chose a milk chocolate oval and nibbled the end. "You know, when people lie about one thing, it's a pretty sure bet they've lied about other things as well."

"I believe that, too."

"Don't make me eat this whole box by myself."

I lowered the bed railing and scooted in next to her. I reached for a dark chocolate heart. "Okay, Mrs. Shipley, let's consider suspecting someone other than James for a minute. Like Henry Hoskin."

"We know Alpha hated your aunts, but what would Henry's motive be?"

"Money to move near his daughter, Angel. Alpha

said Henry's world revolved around her, and she's never coming back. She's working in a bar while trying to heal from a broken heart. He'd do anything to live close to her again."

"What about Olivia and Doc Turner? They were at the restaurant that night."

"Olivia said they were going home to see James."

"But if they called first and found out he was here at Laurel Haven with you, they could have waited and followed you in Doc Turner's car. Who else drives a big dark car?"

"I don't know." I licked chocolate off my finger. "The Hoskin's have a—no, that's a truck. It was definitely not a truck behind me." I sat up. "Jackson has a blue—no, that's a truck, too." I leaned back and reached for a dark coconut cream.

"Didn't you say Jackson is a mechanic? He would have access to all kinds of different cars, I imagine."

"Or if he couldn't borrow one, he could steal one."

"And that brother of his—Gordon. What kind of car does he drive?"

"Red Mustang."

"What about his parents?" The hospital room phone rang. "Get that, will you, dear?"

I reached across the tray table to answer it.

"Mrs. Shipley?" the familiar baritone boomed. "This is James St. Clair. I'm looking for Emory."

I swung my legs over the side of the bed. "James, it's me."

"Are you all right?"

"I'm fine."

Or not so fine. If I took a deep breath and pretended I hadn't just heard Mrs. Shipley list eight reasons why James should be moved to the top of the suspect list, I could get through this.

"I just got back from Knoxville," he said.

"Any word about Maddie and Jackson?"

"Maddie finally called to say they were safe. I thought you'd be at the house when I got home, but you'd already left. Please, tell me you're okay."

I hesitated. I didn't want to talk to him. Not now. Not yet.

"Is it true Tess cut your hair?"

"Yes." I reached up and touched the tufts of curls bunched at the back of my neck. "It doesn't matter. I was sick of it anyway."

"Yes, it does matter. Tess told me what happened, and she's sorry."

"Well, that's something, I guess."

"I saw Mother's portrait. It's wonderful, Emory. She cried when she saw it. I knew you were an artist, but you're really gifted. You could set up shop downtown and draw portraits of the tourists during ski season. And in the summer, too. There are always people wandering through the art shops on Main Street. Plenty of artists make a good living doing it in Gatlinburg and Pigeon Forge. Or there's Asheville. It's close by. You could still be near your Aunt Pris. "

I took another breath. "Look, James—"

"I'm coming over there."

"No. Don't. Mrs. Shipley and I are visiting right now, and—"

"I have to see you. I have something to give you. It's important."

I couldn't avoid him forever. Sooner or later, I would have to confront him about finding the property sale agreement for the Austen property and ask him why he'd lied about it. I didn't believe for one minute that he had blackmailed my aunts to get enough cash to build his house on Gray Top, but I needed to hear his side of the story. If I gave him the chance to explain, maybe he could vindicate himself.

I wasn't sure why it mattered so much. But it did.

"I'll talk to you," I said, "but not here. I'm staying at the Thompson Motor Lodge. Room 108."

"You're not in one of the cabins?"

"It felt too isolated. I'm in the main building near the office."

"108. I'll find it. I'm leaving now."

I hung up and turned to Mrs. Shipley. "I agreed to see him."

"I heard." Mrs. Shipley closed the candy box. "Are you sure that's a good idea? I know my imagination tends to run a little wild, but for your own safety, you must consider him a suspect."

"I'll be careful."

"It's not you I'm worried about."

"I know." I leaned down and kissed her withered cheek. "But I'll be fine."

"One hour, Emory. You've got one hour. And if I don't hear from you, I'm calling the sheriff."

Chapter Twenty

The Thompson Motor Lodge was strictly no-frills. But the room was clean and, in some ways, much nicer than the one at the McAlister. The flowered drapes looked like they'd hung there since Nixon was president, but the air conditioner worked, and the bathroom sink didn't take ten minutes to drain.

I stacked my bags in the corner then propped Portia's framed watercolors on the dresser. I switched on the shaded bedside lamp, which made the atmosphere a little too one-night-stand-ish, so I turned it off again and opened the curtains. I tried to tame my short curls into submission the way Connie had done, but my hair marched to the beat of its own drummer. It would take more than water and a few swipes with a styling brush to mold it into something it didn't want to be.

I gave up and stared in the bathroom mirror.

I hated confrontation, and this one was going to sting.

What was I going to say to him? Ask him why he'd hidden his plans for Crow Mountain from me? Demand to know the truth about the blackmail letter? If there even *was* a blackmail letter. It all felt too familiar: The lying. The secrets. Pretending to be something completely different just to save face. One good thing that had come from dealing with another liar was that I seemed to have finally stopped underestimating my ability to cut through the bullshit and ferret out the truth. Or were those two good things?

Mrs. Shipley's imagination was endearing, but her clever discovery of the anagram was spot-on—another thing I dreaded to ask James about. Before I'd learned of the St. Clair/Castril connection, the thought of James blackmailing one of my aunts would have seemed laughable: holed up in his office, banging out blackmail letters on his mother's old college typewriter, squeezing every penny he could out of the Austen family to pay for the lots on Gray Top Mountain and make his father proud.

I honestly didn't believe James was guilty of anything other than trying to regain his reputation with the town, but I had to face facts: I'd only known James for a week. And no matter what my heart believed, or wanted to believe, until the nurse phoned Mrs. Shipley with the description of the man who had stolen Portia's files, I couldn't afford to let down my guard.

Four sharp raps on the metal door snapped me out of my trance.

"Emory?" James said. "It's me."

I slid the chain and opened the door.

He stood off to one side beside a scraggly honeysuckle bush, carrying a leather briefcase in his hand like he was selling door-to-door insurance. His eyes found mine, and he smiled.

"Come in," I said. "There's a chair and a bed. Take your pick."

He stepped inside, filling up the tiny room, and we stood looking at each other uneasily. Like old friends who've changed so much since the last time they saw each other; they are barely recognizable. The little crush I'd had on him since the night he read me the Riot Act in the Laurel Haven parking lot felt spoiled and sad and a million years ago. I was going to miss his face: the dark eyes that could look right through me, the dimples, the cleft in his perennially unshaven chin, the flat, soft lips that had found their way to mine once or twice and made me feel, at least for a short time, desirable again.

"Wow," he said. "Tess really did a job on your hair."

"Connie Jenkins trimmed it for me."

"Well, I hope you gave her a big tip."

"I did. I told her to stay away from Tess."

He glanced at my luggage stacked in the corner then turned his gaze back to me. "I'm sorry you had to leave. I knew Tess had it in for you, but I never thought she would go this far. She's had a lonely life and—"

"Spare me," I held up my hand. "Tess Winslow isn't the only rich kid who's had a hard life. She's an adult. She knew what she was doing."

"Did she hurt you?" he asked hoarsely. "When Tess cut your hair, did she hurt you?"

"I was asleep."

He laid his briefcase on the chair. "Are you still angry with me?"

"Oh, I'm *way* past angry." I stood with my back against the dresser. The last thing I wanted was a mirror forcing me to view the scene that was about to play out in duplicate.

"Are you going to tell me why?"

"I saw the sales agreement for the Austen property." His face never moved. "You know, the one you put together and said never existed? I wasn't snooping. When you took the files to Olivia, you left it behind on your desk. I thought it was a mistake. I was going to bring it to you."

"I can explain."

I laughed. "I'm sure you can."

"Pris insisted I have an SPA drawn up, but—"

"An SPA? What is it with these acronyms?"

"Sales and Purchase Agreement. It isn't binding unless it's signed by both parties."

"How inconvenient her stroke must have been for you, then."

"I didn't want anything to do with the damned thing. Yes, I admit I'd like to buy land on Crow Mountain and develop it. I'd like for the people in this town to trust me again. But I didn't think it was right to—"

"—steal my inheritance?"

"I didn't know you then. I mean, I knew you existed, but…look, I never would have signed it."

"Oh, please. You would have signed that agreement in a heartbeat."

"Emory, you're not hearing me. I'm not trying to develop Crow Mountain." He sat on the side of the bed. "It would be useless to try, anyway. Everyone in Bitter Ridge thinks I'm poison." He looked up. "And I'm not rolling in dough like you think I am. The hit I took on Gray Top has taken me two years to pay back. That deal falling through left me dead broke, and I've worked my ass off to reimburse everyone. My father built the house we live in on Gray Top, not me."

"Oh, boo hoo."

"Boo hoo?"

"If you don't like it here, then leave. You want to stay? Then stop whining about everyone in Bitter Ridge having it in for you and do something decent for them. At least then, they would know your heart's in the right place. You're an educated man. You've got resources. Find a way to help the tobacco farmers whose contracts have dried up. Find a way to help them salvage their lives by planting something worth selling. You may not be rich, but you've got a lucrative career restoring old houses. You've made a name for yourself. Take some of that fame and money and invest it in the farmland surrounding Bitter Ridge instead of lining your own pockets. Help revitalize the struggling artists' community downtown. That's how to get people to forgive you."

He blinked at me. "Anything else?"

"Have you ever met Mr. Castril? The man who's buying all the lots on Crow Mountain that he can get his greedy little hands on?"

"I don't think anyone's met him. Why?"

"Because today, Mrs. Shipley discovered that the name *Castril* is an anagram for *St. Clair*. Don't you find that odd?"

James's eyes narrowed. "And what? You think I'm Mr. Castril? Is that what this is all about?"

"Yes."

"You think I'm buying up Crow Mountain under an assumed name? Trying to trick my friends and my family?" He looked at me as if I were a stranger. "You really believe that, don't you?"

"No, it's just that—"

"Why would I do that? So I can have the pleasure of screwing the town's chances for the good life one more time before I turn forty? Or do you think I can't stand to see anyone else succeed where I've failed?"

The world was sliding out from under my feet. I felt like I'd slipped on a slick spot on the floor. I was desperate to give him the benefit of the doubt. "I should have started at the beginning," I said. "While you were gone, some things happened."

"What things?"

"I think my aunt Portia was being blackmailed. I found an old letter she had intercepted from Pris telling him they had a son. Someone sent it to my Uncle Edward, and I think there's a pretty good chance the shock of reading it gave him a heart attack."

"Keep going."

"The night you left to go back to Charlotte, someone chased me in a car on Route 620. I believe they were after the blackmail letter, which was in a bag in the backseat, although I didn't realize it at the time. Then, someone snuck into my room to look for it while I pretended to be asleep, but I'd hidden it under my pillow. Oh, please, don't look at me like that. I'm saying all this badly, I know, but—"

"You suspect me, don't you? You think I blackmailed two helpless old women for…what? The money?" He laughed harshly. "Well, good work, Detective. If you needed a motive, I've just admitted to you I was dead broke two years ago. When did the blackmail letters start?"

"I'm not sure."

"But your best guess is two years ago right before Edward died, correct? Do you think I chased you up Route 620 in a car? Do you believe I kissed you goodbye in the parking lot at Laurel Haven, told you I was falling in love with you, and—" His voice caught.

"James—" I whispered.

"Well, let me check my calendar." He flipped through the imaginary pages of a datebook. "Ah, here we go: Thursday night. Kiss Emory goodbye, then scare the bejeezus out of her on the way home. Then follow her to—where did I follow you?"

"It wasn't you. It wasn't your car."

"Okay. So, what else do you think I'm capable of? If I could blackmail an eighty-year-old woman, what's a little arson? Do you think I set off the smoke bombs at the McAlister Inn and chased you down the hall? Do you think I drove to Asheville and shot your husband between the eyes while you were at a deli eating a pastrami on rye?"

"*No.* Stop it! I don't think any of those things!"

"If you believe one, you might as well believe them all." He stared at me. "I thought we were friends. I thought you were starting to trust me. But you never will, will you?"

"James, please," I said gently. "I don't believe you're Mr. Castril, but he's got to be somebody. People are angry with you. You're an easy target. Maybe someone is trying to frame you." I stopped. "How did you know I was eating a pastrami on rye when Kent was killed?"

"Because I read it in your file. Detective Logan isn't much of a detective, but he does take pride in his paperwork." He walked to the table and flipped open his briefcase. He pulled a cream-colored folder from the inside pocket. "This is what I wanted to show you."

I looked at it, astonished. "It's Kent's police report. How did you get this?"

“I have an old college buddy from UT who has ties to the District Attorney's office in North Carolina. He pulled some strings and got me this copy.”

“Why did you want to see Kent's police report?”

“I didn’t. But you said if you could just read his file, you might be able to make some sense of his murder. I thought if I got you a copy, you could see that his murder wasn't your fault. Then you could put it all behind you and start fresh. With me.”

“I’m not starting fresh with anybody. Not for a long, long time.” I waved the report at him. “And let’s be honest. You didn't do this for me. You did it to make sure I had an airtight alibi.”

“The only reason I looked at the police report was because I thought I should see it first in case it was too graphic and might upset you.”

“Yeah, right. You're just like the friends I left behind in New York, the ones who turned their backs on me. You’re ninety-nine percent sure I didn't shoot Kent. But, oh, how that one percent does wear you down.”

He snapped his briefcase closed. “So, that's it, then?”

“Pris and I won’t be staying in Bitter Ridge too much longer. I don’t care what happens to the house on Crow Mountain. I’ll talk to Pris and find out if she still wants to sell the Austen property to you or Mr. Castril. If she does, then fine. I’ll let you know.”

He stopped with his hand on the door. “I’m sorry we didn’t meet sooner when the baggage we're carrying around didn't weigh so much.” He flashed me a quick smile. “One day, you’re gonna have to start trusting somebody, Emory. I just wish it could have been me.”

I closed the door behind him and pressed my forehead against it.

If James wasn't Mr. Castril, then who was? Doc Turner? James' father, Carl? Could either of those people even *afford* to be Mr. Castril?

I cracked open a bottle of water and kicked off my shoes. I sat cross-legged on the bed and opened the police report, steeling myself against the memories of that terrible day. It wasn't as bad as I'd feared. Most of it was typed and sounded like the plot of an unoriginal murder mystery. And the cold, impersonalized details scribbled in Detective Logan's handwriting made it easier to take. All the facts were just as I remembered. There wasn't anything new to learn.

I pulled Kent's phone out of my purse and powered it to ON.

I winced when his boyfriend's face came up as the screensaver: Dark straight hair, impish brown eyes, long black lashes, skin smoother than mine—the exact opposite of me. Go figure. I had met him briefly at Kent's funeral and decided that part of the attraction, besides being blessed with a few key body parts I didn't own, was his laid back personality. He seemed like the kind of person who would never sweat the small stuff, or think to question Kent's choices, or let his temper flare over the cold, wet discovery of a raised toilet seat in the middle of the night.

I scrolled through Kent's app list, refraining from revisiting the gay hookup sites out of self-defense, and stopped at an intriguing app I hadn't noticed before called Private Photos. I held my breath and clicked on it then quickly scrolled through the first three albums. There were selfies of Kent and his new boyfriend everywhere—in the park, on the Coney Island Ferris wheel, at a gay bar with flashing lights and dancing men dressed in outrageous party wear. *Flip. Flip. Flip.* What was I looking for? I didn't have a clue. But I knew the faster I ripped through these photos, the faster I would never have to do it again. *Flip. Flip. What?*

I backed up.

In the center of a group of stunningly beautiful drag queens, standing directly behind Kent with a full martini glass in his hand and a black leather vest framing his bare, beefy, biker-chained chest was Delbert Jenkins, beloved pastor, and moral compass of the Living Waters Pentecostal Church.

"Well, I'll be damned." I dabbed at the damp spot on the bed where I'd unceremoniously spit my water across the room.

Delbert Jenkins?

Delbert-holier-than-thou-Jenkins was cavorting at Club XYZ in Knoxville, Tennessee, less than two hours away from his loving, clueless wife, and a church full of evangelical parishioners who, I was pretty sure, would not approve of his alternate lifestyle.

Had Delbert known Kent? Had he seen Kent taking a selfie that he knew he was in, freaked out, and realized he was in danger of being outed by someone at the club? Or maybe Delbert hadn't freaked out at all. Maybe he had asked around until he found out Kent's name, then looked him up online—Kent was an open book online—then set about figuring out how to get the incriminating evidence deleted from Kent's phone. First, he would have to find Kent's phone. Which meant he would have to track down Kent. Or, since Kent had already moved out of our apartment, he would have to track down Kent's soon-to-be-ex-wife—me.

If the photo I couldn't stop staring at ever surfaced, Pastor Delbert Jenkins' life, and everything he'd worked for, would explode in his face. He would lose it all: his wife, his church, a television career, the most promising future he'd ever dared dream for himself. *Pfft.* Gone. Just like that. How far would Delbert go to make sure his secret life remained secret? Would he break a commandment and kill someone? Would he go to New York and follow them to their estranged wife's apartment and shoot them in the face?

My cell phone rang in my pocket, shattering the quiet.

I hoped it was Sheriff Riley calling with some news about the fingerprinted letter or Mrs. Shipley with the description of the man who'd stolen Portia's Avery Hospital files. But this was a number I didn't recognize. "Hello?" I glanced at the door to make sure I'd secured the safety chain.

"Emory? It's Tess."

"Hey, Tess. Look, I know I told you to call if you needed me, but this is really a bad time."

"Don't hang up, Emory—*please*. I'm here with Maddie."

"Where? At the St. Clair house?"

"No, I'm calling from Maddie's phone. She wants to know if she and Jackson can stay at your aunt's place tonight."

"On Crow Mountain?"

"They don't know where to go, and they're out of money. They just need to stay there for one night until Jackson picks up his check at the garage tomorrow."

"Tess, the house is a wreck. There's no electricity

or running water. It's not fit for anyone to spend the night in. Let me talk to Maddie."

"She's out in the car. Please, Emory. They've been driving all day, and they're really tired. Can't we all go to your aunt's house and figure things out? We'll meet you there after dark. Maddie doesn't want anyone to see us."

"That's not a good idea. Tess? *Tess!*"

Tess had ended the call before I could tell her no. I tried calling back, but it went straight to voicemail.

Why was Tess running interference for Maddie? Tess would be the last person Maddie would ask for help. Why didn't Maddie call James? She must know he would help her. Why did they want to go all the way out to the Austen house of all places to figure things out? Jackson's house was just over the crest on Holly Berry Road. If they were hiding out, why would they risk his family seeing them?

Nothing Tess had said sounded logical.

It did sound romantic, though. In a teen angst/young-love-will-prevail kind of way. Kids on the run hiding from the powers that be and their parents who, in their minds, had forgotten what love and passion felt like. Someone had to make them realize the only way to solve their problems was to go back home and face them head-on. Someone had to talk some sense into them. And it looked like that someone was me.

For Maddie's sake, I had to tell James where she was. I hadn't put his number in my phone, trying to make our budding friendship remain casual and loose, but I had filed his business card in my wallet. I pulled it out and read the Old English printing, elegantly embossed in black and gold.

James St. Clair, Architect.

Specializing in the Restoration, Conservation, and Preservation of Historic Buildings.

No job too small. No person too short.

I laughed softly, then keyed the number into my phone contact list. I called him and left a message saying I was going to talk to Maddie. I didn't divulge her whereabouts; that would have been a huge breach of trust. I would tell him where she was later, after I'd met with her.

Convincing Maddie to go back home would be something I could do for him. A goodbye thing. A friendship that wasn't meant to be thing. The last thing.

I wanted to do it for Maddie, too, even though I knew she would hate me for it. Life was too short to have it derailed at the tender age of eighteen.

I wanted to do this. And I had to do it alone.

Chapter Twenty-One

It never occurred to me not to go.

Maddie was a sweet girl, and I wanted the best for her. If I chose my words carefully and didn't try to convince her that her feelings for Jackson weren't real or justified, she might listen to me. It was worth a shot, anyway.

I wasn't too keen on having to deal with Jackson. Although it did occur to me that showing up at a house with a suspected killer without any kind of protection might not be the smartest thing I'd ever done. But I didn't have any kind of protection to take. Unless you counted the lug wrench in Narwhal's trunk and the cylinder of three-year-old pepper spray I carried in my purse.

I had to trust that Jackson wasn't the loose cannon I feared he was. I was reasonably sure he wouldn't harm me in front of the woman he loved. Not if he wanted her to marry him. And I had believed him when said he loved Maddie. It was the one thing about him I was sure of.

It was almost dark when I drove up Crow Mountain.

There weren't any crows out at this time of night. They didn't hang around much after dark, cawing and clicking in the trees, flying in circles across the meadow. I missed them. Not everyone loved the shiny black birds that flew around their namesake mountain. Some people considered them a harbinger of death, but I thought they were intelligent and soulful. I'd read once that they could recognize human faces, and when one of their own died, the others gathered around the dead crow to stand silently and pay their respects. And then, of course, there was the fact that three or more of them was called a murder. A murder of crows. How could anyone not love that?

Light from a fat crescent moon shimmered through the tall trees, slashing across the rushing waters of Stoney Creek like a spotlight. I topped the hill on Holly Berry Road. A pale wispy glow emanated eerily from the front room of my aunt's house. I'd found several oil lamps stored in the pantry the day I'd searched it, and I guessed Maddie and Jackson had made good use of them. But how had they gotten inside the house with the new lock in place? If they had busted it, I'd have to buy another one.

Maddie's Jeep sat in the driveway alone. Tess must have met them with Maddie's car then driven them to my aunt's house. Jackson and Maddie had taken precautions to remain undetected, but their logic left a lot to be desired. Other than mine, any car parked in front of the Austen house would look suspicious.

I drove to the corner of the porch and cut the engine. Narwhal rattled back and forth like a jalopy before it sputtered and stopped. I loved the quirky little car, but if I planned to keep it, I would need to get it worked on. And de-unicorned. And de-stickered. Maybe Jackson could do it if he were still speaking to me after I persuaded Maddie to go home.

I dug out the pepper spray, just in case, and

climbed the front steps.

The brittle wood around the doorknob had been splintered. No surprise there. But what was Jackson thinking? Why would he smash the door open when he knew I was on my way with the key? Was he showing off his Taekwondo moves for Maddie and Tess? Or was the guy one beer short of a six-pack?

I slid past the tattered screen door and stepped into the foyer. The parlor was bathed in the soft rosy glow of the oil lamps and still reeked of mildew.

Things didn't feel right.

Why hadn't anyone come out to greet me? Hadn't they heard my car pull up? Didn't they know I was there?

I peered through the open archway and tried to get my bearings in the flickering light. Geometric shadows crisscrossed the watermarks on the walls like stained glass. Tess sat on the brick hearth with her arms wrapped around her knees like a little girl. Even from across the room, I could tell she'd been crying.

Damn that Jackson. How hard was it to be civilized? Tess had a smart mouth and made no bones about how unappealing she thought he was, but that was no reason to make her cry. I took a deep breath and walked into the parlor. I didn't want to challenge him in front of Maddie, but enough was enough.

"Emory," Tess sobbed. "He made me drive him here!"

"Come on in, Emory," a man said from behind the high-backed sofa. "We've been waiting for you."

At first, I couldn't place the voice, and I half-expected to see Delbert Jenkins, sans leatherwear, waiting for me with a Bible in one hand and a gun in the other.

"He's got a gun!" Tess wailed, reading my mind. She jumped up and ran to me, almost knocking me over.

Gordon snapped his fingers and pointed to the hearth. "Sit." His pale blue eyes flickered with amusement. "I'm glad you're here, Emory. Maybe you can convince this brat to shut her pie hole. She's driving me up the wall."

"It's all right, Tess. He's not going to hurt us."

I didn't believe it for a second. We were in serious trouble, and from the look on Tess' face, she knew it, too.

"What's in your hand?" Gordon grabbed my arm and twisted it. The pink plastic cylinder fell to the ground, and he scooped it up. "Pepper spray? Seriously?" He laughed. "Did you carry this with you in New York?" He lobbed the pepper spray into the dining room. "What a waste."

Gordon let go of me, and I hustled Tess back to the hearth. The sweet, moldy odor permeating the room made my stomach churn. Gordon's face glistened with sweat. He took my purse from me then motioned with the revolver for the two of us to sit. It occurred to me that having him shoot us might be the least of our worries. While Gordon went through my purse, I put my arm around Tess' thin shoulders. She leaned into me, trembling.

He tossed my purse on the far end of the sofa. "Where is it?"

I gazed into Gordon's pale blue eyes—Kent's eyes—and forced myself to smile. "So it was you. All this time? You?"

"Yep."

"Where are Maddie and Jackson? Are they here?"

"Nope. That was just our little trick to get you up here. Tess is a mighty fine actress on the phone, aren't you, doll? Then she started bawling the minute she hung up and hasn't stopped since. Never took her for a crybaby."

I tried to keep my voice steady. "What are you looking for in my purse? Cab fare?"

He looked up. "Well, first, I want to know what the hell happened to your hair?"

"I got it caught in a weed whacker."

Gordon laughed. "I like you, Emory. I really do. I'm just sorry we didn't get to know each other better."

"Yeah, that's a real shame," I said.

"You were smarter than I'd counted on." He swiped the back of his hand across his damp forehead. "Most of the blondes I know are as dumb as a box of rocks. But not you."

"I'm going to take that as a compliment," I said.

"Now, if you'll just tell me where it is, we can all pack up and go home."

"Where is what?" I asked.

Gordon's eyes turned cold and dead. The sheen on his face flushed crimson. "The letter, Emory. Where's the goddamned letter?"

"I gave it to Sheriff Riley."

Gordon waved the gun in the air like he was swatting a mosquito. His eyes narrowed until they were icy blue slits. "And why did you do that?"

"I don't know," I said. "Isn't that what you're supposed to do with blackmail letters? What should I have done with it? Bought a nice frame and hung it over the mantel?"

Gordon jumped up, and I thought he was coming for us. Tess cringed against me with a whimper.

"You think I'm talking about a blackmail letter?" he said.

"Aren't you?"

"I don't give a damn about the blackmail letter. I was careful. It can't be traced. Why would I want it back?" He took a step toward us. "I'm talking about the letter my father gave to your Uncle Edward signing over the inn to him. Except now that your uncle is dead, and your aunt is in a nursing home with broccoli for brains, it goes to you." He leaned over the sofa. "I want it back, Emory. I'm selling the McAlister Inn. I'm not giving that up to you or anyone else."

"The McAlister Inn?"

"Is there an echo in here? My father lost it to your uncle in a poker game. My father got drunk, and—" He stopped. "My father hadn't had a drink in seven months when Edward Gilmore blew into town. What a piece of work he was—strutting around like he was better than everybody else, pouring on that English accent until I wanted to puke. He took advantage of my father, which is why I pawned your aunts' things. I thought it was only fair."

I glared at him. "Was it fair to blackmail a helpless old woman? Edward dropped dead after reading one of those letters. How fair was that?"

"How was I supposed to know the old guy had a bad heart? I just wanted the letter back. I found Portia's diary in her trunk. It said she hid the letter he signed with Edward's treasure. I've torn this house apart looking for it. Now, where is it?"

"Why do you think I have it?" I said.

"Because, honey, you're the sole Austen heir. When you started searching this house, I figured I could just sit back and let you find it for me. According to Miss Ditz here, you already had."

Gordon had killed Kent. I was sure of it. I wanted to make him confess, but I didn't have the courage. Blackmail was one thing, but if Gordon admitted to murder, he would have no choice but to kill us both.

"Why do you think destroying this letter is going to change anything?" I asked. "Weren't there witnesses at the poker game?"

"Of course, there were witnesses. Doesn't matter, though. They're both dead now."

I gasped, and Gordon laughed.

"Don't worry," he said. "I didn't kill them. They died of natural causes. They were both old as the hills. I didn't know this letter existed until Mr. Castril approached me about buying the inn. Then Dad had to tell me what he'd done."

"Why did he wait so long?" I said, trying to stall him.

"My father was a blackout alcoholic. He didn't know what he was doing when he bet the inn. Edward Gilmore knew that."

"Oh, my, Gordon." Tess sat up. "I guess it would be a little awkward to try to sell a hotel you don't actually own. A property like that has to be free and clear of any claims, and you can't sell it until it is."

"You're not as dumb as you look, are you, Tess?" Gordon said.

"I know an asshole when I see one."

"Shut up!" Gordon shouted.

"Bite me!" Tess screamed.

Gordon pointed the gun at my face. "Make her shut up, Emory." His hand shook as he fought to steady his arm. "You do not want to make me mad."

I squeezed Tess' shoulder to silence her.

At least the old Tess had emerged from her state of shock with her wits intact. If we had to make a run for it, I wouldn't have to carry her.

"So, you're the one who stole my aunts' papers from the cellar?" I said. "That was you?"

Gordon lowered the gun. "Little Miss Sneak here said James was going to put a lock on the door, so I had to move fast. I'd already searched through the papers, but I was afraid I'd missed something. I took what I could carry with me and looked through them again. But there wasn't anything there. There never was."

"That's where I found the blackmail letter," I said.

"In the basement?" Gordon said. "I don't believe you. I'd already searched through the trunks. There wasn't anything—"

"That's because I put it there," Henry Hoskin said quietly.

My head swung around. Henry stood in the arched doorway with his old straw hat pulled low on his forehead and the barrel of his hunting rifle aimed directly at Gordon's back.

****

"You girls all right?" Henry asked.

"Fine," I said.

"Put the gun down, son," Henry said. "You aren't gonna shoot anybody today."

Gordon let the gun drop onto the sofa.

I grabbed Tess' wrist and gently led her to the

window seat behind Henry. I wasn't about to make any sudden moves with two loaded guns in the room.

Henry stepped forward and pulled the hammer back. "Put your hands where I can see them, son. Then turn around and look at me."

Gordon raised both hands and slowly turned. His gaze never left Henry's gun. The four of us stood face to face in the flickering glow of the oil lamps.

"You gave Emory one of the blackmail letters?" Gordon asked.

"That's right," Henry said. "I slid it into one of the bags we'd filled. Right on top, where she'd be sure to find it. I knew Emory would flush you out, Gordon. Knew it the minute I met her. I just thought I'd speed things along."

Gordon lowered his hands a few inches.

"You've been sending those rotten letters to people for years," Henry said. "Bleeding this town as dry as a sack of cornmeal. You've ruined lives. You've torn families apart. And for what? Just so you could get a little cash to keep the hotel going and pay off your daddy's gambling debts? Trouble was, he just kept piling on more debts, didn't he, son? He just kept drinking and gambling with no end in sight.

"Then I saw you stealing Portia's trunk out of our root cellar. I'd already removed most of her letters, but I left a few as bait. Ever since you broke my little girl's heart, I've been biding my time, waiting to give you what you deserve."

"This is because of Angel?" Gordon asked.

"You didn't have the guts to end it with her like a gentleman. You fixed it so she'd walk in on you and that tramp from Taylor's Point. You tore her heart out, and you're gonna pay for it. I didn't know about your daddy signing over the inn to Mr. Gilmore, but I'm damned glad he did. If there's anything I can do to help Emory find that paper and screw you to the wall, I'll do it."

Gordon's leg flew up and kicked Henry's rifle. The gun fired through the ceiling as it sailed through the air. Tess screamed. She tried to cover her face, but I grabbed her hand and dragged her out the front door. We ran down the crumbling porch steps to the Volkswagen. Only then did I realize Gordon still had my purse.

"Tess, I don't have my keys. Give me yours. We'll have to take the Jeep." The Jeep would be better anyway. I knew firsthand the power it wielded.

"I don't have them!" Tess cried. "Gordon took them from me when we first got here."

The sounds of scuffling feet thundered onto the porch, followed by the sudden peal of shattered glass. Aunt Pris' piecrust table crashed through the front window like a drunk tossed out of the bar on a Saturday night.

Henry was a strong man, but he was old. I didn't know how long he could hold off Gordon. We were on our own. And we needed to move fast.

"Come on." I pointed to the open meadow below the house. "We'll have to run for it."

It was our only choice. If we kept to the road, Gordon would find us before we topped the hill. If we ran in the opposite direction, we'd end up on the other side of Crow Mountain at Gordon's house. If we ran toward the Hoskin's pasture, we would have to cross the wide part of Stoney Creek.

None of these thoughts flying through my head made any difference because Tess and I were already running for our lives toward the dark woods. We sprinted side by side down the hill past the cherry orchard. As we bent to climb through the rusted pasture gate, the jarring crack of a gunshot split the night. For one terrifying instant, our gazes met.

"*Go,*" I yelled.

We ducked under the metal slats and tore across the meadow then cut through the field to the bottom of the hill. Tall scrubby weeds stung our hands and arms. We both had on long jeans, but nothing could save my bare ankles from being shredded. Tess ran like a trained athlete while I struggled to keep up.

Stumbling through the tall weeds, more than waist-high in places and full of ragweed and thistles, my soft athletic shoes slid across the damp grass. My lungs were burning. I ached to stop, just for a few seconds, but I forced myself to keep going. We were close to the edge of the meadow. If we could make it through this last patch of land, the forest would hide us.

Clouds drifted across the moon, darkening the sky. I strained to see where I was going. I parted the long sticky canes with my hands and tried not to think about deer ticks and chiggers and snakes. We neared the trees, and I was grateful for the fat sliver of moon that reflected Tess' white sleeveless shirt and made it easier for me to see her. Both of us grunted and yelped as we slashed our way through the deadly weeds.

The forest loomed in front of us, an endless black wall. We grabbed each other's hand and leaped over a rocky ditch, then plowed through the thick line of Carolina pine trees. The inside of the forest was open and cavernous, like a huge cathedral that seemed to go on forever. Feathery white pines and scruffy hemlocks towered above us. Rhododendron grew in sparse thickets along the ground. The shuddering cry of an owl shrieked through the trees.

We stopped to get our bearings and, for the first time, I looked behind us. I strained my eyes searching the countryside for a flashlight, a movement, any indication that Gordon was following us. I had a bad feeling about that. Gordon wouldn't just clock Henry Hoskin, give up, and go home. Gordon would find us and finish what he had started come hell or high water.

Tess leaned against a tree, gasping for breath. "Do you see him?"

"I can't see anything. I don't think he's back there yet."

"I can't run anymore. My legs are cramping."

"Mine, too. But we've got to get farther into the woods before we can stop."

"Emory, what happened back there? Do you think Gordon killed that old man?"

"I don't know." While we'd thrashed through the weeds, I had tried to dispel the thought of Henry lying dead on the parlor floor. But Henry's image kept getting mixed up with Kent's until I couldn't separate the two.

"Do you think Gordon is coming after us?"

"Oh, yeah," I said. "He's coming after us."

"Oh, God, Emory. I'm so scared."

"Let's find some cover."

We picked our way around broken tree limbs and over slabs of jagged rock. After trekking through the thistles, it was a relief to feel the soft crunch of leaves beneath my feet. The dark enveloped us and twice I walked into a tree, slamming my shoulder and face against the rough bark.

“Let's stop over there.” I pointed to a recessed alcove in the rocks sheltered by a moss-covered overhang.

“My legs hurt.” Tess leaned against the rock and massaged her calves through her thick jeans. “And my ankles are bleeding. Are yours?”

“I’m numb.” I closed my eyes.

I was anything but numb. I was used to tromping the flat concrete sidewalks of Manhattan, not the gopher holed hills of North Carolina. The scrapes on my arms and ankles stung. The cuts on my hands throbbed with each beat of my heart.

“Do you know where we're going?” Tess asked.

“Stoney Creek runs all the way through the forest. If we can find it, we can follow it back to the main road. Alpha's farm is just below the bridge. There are other farms sprinkled around. We're bound to run into one of them eventually.”

“Alpha Hoskin—that was her husband Gordon shot tonight, wasn't it?”

“We don't know that. The gun might have fired accidentally. Or maybe Henry shot Gordon and we're doing all this running for nothing.”

Tess started to cry. “This is all my fault.” Her silky hair hung in damp strings around her face. An uneven scratch sliced the skin above her left eye.

“Let's sit down for a minute,” I said gently. “We need to rest. And don't cry. This isn't your fault. It's Gordon's fault.”

“You don't understand. Gordon was so desperate; I knew he would do something crazy. I should have warned you." Tess wiped her nose with the back of her hand. "I was with him the night he chased you up Gray Top in Olivia's car."

"That was Gordon? But how did you—"

"I scrunched down in the front seat, so you wouldn't see me. He said he was just doing it to scare you, and I hated you so much, I wanted him to. Gordon had hidden his Mustang at the bottom beside the St. Clair's road. I was sure you'd see it after you made the turn."

"I didn't."

"When we got across the highway, he jumped out. I took the wheel and followed you up the mountain."

"I didn't believe your story about going to the pharmacy."

"I know. You'd think I'd be a better liar by now."

"Did you sneak into my room to look for the letter giving the inn to my uncle?"

"A couple of times. Gordon was sure you didn't know it was him scaring you, but after he followed you to the sheriff station yesterday, he was convinced you'd seen him. He's so paranoid."

"How did you know where to find me tonight?"

"Gordon followed you to the motel. He follows you all the time. I asked him if you ever noticed him behind you, and he said you were too busy running over curbs to notice."

"Well, that's true." I shivered from the cold and wrapped my arms around my waist.

"Gordon said if he had that paper, he could keep James from ruining him. I didn't understand what it was all about, but I wanted to hurt you so badly I went along with it. Ever since I saw James kissing you, I've wanted to hurt you both. I knew I didn't have a chance with James, but he was the only thing that made staying at that house every summer bearable. Maddie and Olivia couldn't stand me, but James made me feel like part of the family."

"And you loved him for it."

"This year, I thought he would notice that I had grown up and stop treating me like a kid. But that didn't happen. Nothing happened. And then you showed up."

"The houseguest from hell."

"I was so jealous, I wanted to scratch your eyes out."

"Or scalp me."

Tess nodded. "I'm sorry about your hair. That's why I cut it. Because James liked it so much. Can you ever forgive me?"

"I'm gonna try."

Deer rustled near us, snorting at each other like ponies. I had seen them at the edge of the meadow before we disappeared into the sanctuary of the thick trees. I closed my eyes and listened for the sound of rushing water, or frogs, or anything that would direct us toward Stoney Creek.

"Did they ever take you with them?" Tess asked.

"Who?"

"Your parents. Did they ever let you go with them on trips?"

"I went with them to China once before I started college."

"That's cool."

"Turns out, I'm not much of a traveler. They'd always said I could go with them when I got older, but when I finally went, I was miserable. I tripped over a fishing net the first day and had to have six stitches in my knee. I got food poisoning in Nan-Ching, sun poisoning in Suchow, and no matter what province I was in, I never learned enough Chinese to find the bathroom. Which, nine times out of ten, was a very small hole in the floor."

The sound of distant barking brought us scrambling to our feet.

"What was that?" Tess whispered anxiously.

"It sounded like a dog. Or an owl."

We stood clutching each other's arms, listening.

I heard it again. Two short barks and a long wailing howl.

"That's Daisy," I said.

"Who?"

"The Hoskin's hunting dog. The one we saw on the road."

"Do you think Mrs. Hoskin is out looking for us?"

"I don't know. I don't think there's been enough time for anyone to know where we are. If Henry's alive, he might've gone back to their house to get help."

"What about Gordon? Couldn't he have gone back to Henry's house and gotten the dog? You said he didn't follow us."

"It's dark. You saw what we ran through. He could've been six feet behind me, and I wouldn't have seen him."

"But what about the dog?"

"*Shhh.* The dog is coming from the other direction. She can't be tracking us."

"Why not? Isn't that what hunting dogs do?"

My heart sped up. Adrenaline trickled through my bloodstream, begging me to shove Tess aside and run for my life. I stepped back and clutched the stone wall with my bleeding fingers, pressing hard against the rock formation, wishing I could disappear into the mountain.

"You're right," I said. "Gordon takes Daisy hunting. The dog knows him. I've got a sweater in my car. Gordon could have used it to give Daisy my scent. We have to run in the other direction before she tracks us."

Without another word, we took off, running deeper into the forest. We dodged pine trees, leaped over stumps, tripped over rocks that suddenly jutted out of the ground like sinking ships. I could hear Daisy's bark in the distance. The low timbre of her howl echoed through the trees, reverberating up and down until I couldn't tell where she was.

Tess took the lead as we entered a dense grove of perfectly spaced fir trees. Were we on the Joyner's Christmas tree farm? The scent of pine was intoxicating.

Suddenly, the terrain changed again, and I was standing ankle-deep in a patch of long, coarse grass. The sharp blades licked at my ankles, stinging them unmercifully. I bit my lip to keep from crying out.

And then I heard Tess scream.

Her voice ripped through the night, shattering the still air, shoving my heart into my throat. My feet slid out from under me as I tumbled down the hill. I landed on my stomach in a streambed with my chin squished into the mud and Pris' silver locket mashed into my right nostril. I scrambled to my feet and looked behind me. Tess lay in the middle of the cold rushing water clinging to a rock.

"Tess!" I screamed. *"Tess!"*

Stoney Creek, swollen from the recent rain, was strewn with huge brown river stones. I held onto one and slid into the freezing water, sinking to my waist. When I reached Tess, her arms were ice cold. I slid my hand beneath her head. The warm ooze of blood seeped through my fingers.

"Keep still," I said. "I'm holding your head out of the water."

"Don't let go."

"I've got you."

"My head hurts." She started to cry.

I helped her to the top of the slick incline, one slippery step at a time, and flipped her over onto the grass. My shoes couldn't get any traction and began the long slide back down the bank. I grabbed for the edge, but nothing could save me. Pain shot up my left arm, sending me sprawling. I stumbled to my feet then slowly pulled myself to the top of the bank with one hand. I fell onto the grass beside Tess.

"Emory, what happened? Are you crying? Did you get hurt?"

"I think I broke my wrist." I rocked back and forth, cradling my arm in my lap. "Something tells me I'm not cut out for this."

"I don't hear the dog anymore, do you?"

"No, Daisy must have gone in another direction. But we can't stay here. We have to get you to a hospital. Your head's stopped bleeding, but I think you might have a concussion."

A twig cracked beside them.

"I hate to keep spoiling your fun." Gordon stepped out of the shadows. "But you girls aren't going anywhere."

Chapter Twenty-Two

I stared at Gordon for what seemed like an eternity, then something extraordinary happened. An eerie calm wrapped around me like soft Irish wool. My wrist stopped throbbing. My cuts no longer stung. It was as if my mind had stepped back from reality for an instant to let me watch myself from another plane. I knew my fate was sealed. Whatever happened was going to happen. And with that simple revelation, Gordon Spencer lost his power over me.

"Well, look who's here," I said.

"What rock did you crawl out from under?" Tess said.

"Shut up, Tess." Gordon towered above us. "I saw you running toward the woods, so I circled around and came up through the Joyner's farm. I figured you'd try to follow the creek out." He glanced at their wet clothes. "Did you cross the creek here? There's a shallow spot just around the bend. How stupid are you girls?"

"Not stupid enough to lose our hotel in a poker game," Tess said.

"I said *shut up,*" Gordon yelled.

"You're disgusting," Tess said. "What would your mother say if she knew you were holding two injured women hostage?"

In a flash, Gordon vaulted behind me and curled

his left hand around my shoulder. He jerked me back hard. The edge of his gun touched my forehead. I reached out my good hand to Tess and felt her cold fingers close around it.

"Shut her up, Emory." Gordon nudged the gun against my skull. "Shut her up, or I swear, I'll—"

"—blow my brains into next week?"

"That's right."

"If I thought you had the guts to do it, Gordon, I might consider it. But I'm not scared of you anymore. You want to kill me, then let me turn around. That way, you can shoot me in the face like you did my husband."

Tess gasped and squeezed my hand.

"I didn't shoot your husband," Gordon said.

"Oh, I think you did," I said. "And Sheriff Riley thinks so, too."

"Sheriff Riley doesn't know anything."

"Of course, he does," I lied. "A witness saw you leave my apartment building in Asheville. The police are just waiting for a positive identification before they pick you up. That's why Sheriff Riley has been following me. To protect me from you. Didn't you see him when you were behind my car today?"

"You're making this up," Gordon said.

"Sheriff Riley thinks you killed my husband, Kent Chandler. And so do I."

"You're lying." The gun bobbled against my head then fell away. Gordon stumbled to his feet.

"Emory wouldn't lie," Tess said, picking up her cue as if she'd rehearsed it. "Even I know what you did."

He shuffled around to face me, and I knew I had him. "No one could've seen my face. I was careful. There was no evidence. No trace—"

"Of course not," I said smoothly. "Because you thought of everything, Gordon. Everything except a little boy hiding in the stairwell." My lies sounded so convincing, I almost believed them myself.

"What boy? It's been four months. Why is he just now coming forward?"

"He was afraid," I said. "The detective went back and talked to the neighbors again. That's when the little boy said he saw you."

"Then why isn't Sheriff Riley here now? Why didn't he follow you to your aunt's house?"

"Because I asked him not to. Tess said Maddie and Jackson didn't want anyone to know where they were. That's what you told her to say, remember?"

"Yes, but—"

"Riley said he'd give me a half an hour before he came looking for me. And he *will* come looking for me."

"I don't believe you," Gordon said. "You're lying."

I was on a roll. My words had taken on a life of their own, crashing and reeling down the mountainside with no obstacle too large to stop them.

"You must be a crack shot," I said. "You put a bullet right between Kent's eyes."

"Well, that was the damnedest thing," Gordon said. "I went to your apartment looking for the paper my father signed handing over the inn to your damned family. It wasn't hard breaking in. I've busted locks on gym lockers that were stronger than that. Then your husband showed up. He reached for his phone to call the police, and I couldn't let that happen. I was just gonna wing him, lay him flat until I could get out of the apartment. I told him to turn around and face the wall, but he wouldn't. He raised his head and looked at me. We just stood there staring at each other. It was like looking into a mirror. Then I pulled the trigger."

I kept going. For Kent's sake, I had to finish it.

"You killed Kent. You stole my Aunt Portia's files and blackmailed her. Then, when she wouldn't pay up, you sent the letter she'd intercepted to my Uncle Edward and killed him. Tess is right. You *are* disgusting. You'd make anybody's skin crawl."

"You know what, Emory? I don't think I like you anymore." He waved the gun in front of him. "Now turn around."

Daisy's howl ripped through the night like a siren.

Gordon jumped back. His face twisted into a mask so depraved, I wondered how I'd ever thought he looked like Kent. The air swirled around my face. Time decelerated to a comfortable crawl. I held Tess' hand and looked up at the sky. The moon, pale and crescent-shaped, hung suspended between the tops of two Carolina pines.

I opened my mouth, relying purely on whatever instinct I had left, and began to shout. "*Daisy! Daisy! Come on, girl! We're over here! Daisy!*"

"*Stop it,*" Gordon cried. "I'll shoot you. I swear, I will."

"*Daisy!*" Tess joined in. "*We're here! We're here! Daisy! Daisy!*"

"I'll kill you both."

"*Daisy! Daisy! Daisy!*"

The dog barked louder, barreling toward us through the woods, seconds away from finding the source of the scent she'd been tracking.

"Emory! Where are you?" James called. "*Emory!*"

Gordon pointed the gun toward the woods and fired—*one, two, three.*

I flattened Tess to the ground. A scream ripped from my throat. I looked up.

Gordon stood behind me with the gun pointed toward the trees. He cocked his head to one side and listened, trying to identify the direction of the sound and take aim.

I rolled over, pulling both feet up until my knees were under my chin. Then I shot them forward, slamming them into the backs of Gordon's thighs.

He went down like a bowling pin. The gun flew out of his hands. He clawed at the ground, clambering to his feet and cursing.

"You'd better run, Gordon," I said. "They're coming for you."

He limped into the woods, thrashing through the brush like one of the wild animals he was so fond of hunting.

The arc and sweep of a flashlight bounced off the trees. Daisy and James seem to materialize out of thin air. Daisy, head down, strained at her leash while James ran behind her, fighting to keep up. He let go of the rope. Daisy ran to me, whining and snuffling against my neck, covering me with slobber, licking my face until I couldn't breathe.

"Where is he?" James said. "Where is the bastard?"

"He ran away after Emory knocked him down," Tess said. "I saw him drop his gun over there."

James shone his flashlight on us. "Are you all right?" He stood for a second then burst out laughing. "You both look…terrible."

"Well, thanks, James," I said.

"Yeah, thanks, James." Tess petted Daisy, who, after being praised so lavishly for a job well done had decided to lay on her back and roll in the grass.

James helped me to my feet then put his arms around me. Through his thick denim shirt, I could feel him shaking.

"Thank God, you and Tess are safe. Not knowing where you were, I—" His voice caught. "I might have gone just a little crazy."

"How did you know to come looking for us?" I asked.

"Tess left a note stuck to the bathroom mirror saying she was going to the Austen house with Gordon."

"Smart girl," I said.

"Which tipped me off," James said. "Because he hates Tess."

"Gordon really is an idiot," Tess said. "He kidnapped me then let me go to the bathroom before we left the house."

"I had almost made it up Holly Berry Road when Mrs. Shipley called," James said. "She was worried you weren't answering your phone. She wanted to tell you that the nurse's description of the man who stole Portia's files was a dead ringer for Gordon. When I saw the Jeep and the Volkswagen parked out front, I knew it was time to call the sheriff."

"Is Henry okay?" I asked. "Did he make it back to the house?"

"They don't come much tougher than Henry Hoskin," James said. "It'll take more than a bullet in the shoulder to slow him down. Alpha let Daisy smell the sweater I found in your car. She took out after you the second we got the leash on her."

Daisy bounded over to me, alternately whining and howling with unbridled joy. She planted her huge paws on my lap and licked me again soundly on the face. "Good girl," I whispered, laughing. I was never so glad to see any living creature as much in my life. I hugged her to me and nuzzled my face in her velvet fur.

"Daisy and I had a lot of false starts out there in the woods," James said. "For a while, she had me zigzagging all over the place. But she wouldn't give up on you." He grinned at me. "And neither will I."

****

Olivia St. Clair was waiting for us outside the emergency room entrance.

She looked a little rough around the edges. Her usually perfect windswept bangs stuck out from her head like they'd been caught in a gale storm. The blue-gray tint beneath her eyes told me her migraine was still hovering beneath the surface. Her thick black eyeliner looked as if she'd slept face down on a pillow.

"I was beside myself with worry," she cried, wringing her hands like Lady Macbeth.

"We're all okay." I was used to voicing what everyone else expected me to say after a crisis, whether it was true or not. I wasn't sure any of us would ever really be okay.

James had called his mother after the sheriff and his deputies got Tess and me out of the woods on the coolest all-terrain vehicle I had ever seen. The ATV had booked it through the forest, which was something I suspected Sheriff Will Riley lived for, terrifying every nocturnal animal in sight. Its roaring engine and white spotlights bounced off the trees like the lasers at a Lady

Gaga concert.

“Are you sure you’re all right?” Olivia asked. They had already X-rayed my wrist, and I had been parked in an empty hallway waiting for someone to take me to the casting room.

“I’m fine,” I said wearily.

“James told me what happened—the blackmail letter, Frank Spencer losing the McAlister to your uncle in a poker game, Gordon Spencer killing your husband. It boggles the mind, doesn’t it?”

I nodded. “That it does.”

I was so tired of answering questions. Filling in the blanks. Pretending I was a lot braver than I felt.

Olivia sat opposite me and straightened the fringe on her long silk wrap. “If Gordon can’t find the paper agreeing to use the inn as collateral for his father’s poker bet, what will happen?”

“I guess nothing. There were a couple of witnesses, but they’re both dead. And Mr. Spencer had been drinking, so I’m not sure his testimony would hold up in court. If the paper still exists, it would be the only proof. But no one’s found it yet. And believe me, they’ve tried.”

Olivia’s eyebrows pulled together in a single black line. “What if Gordon sells the inn to Mr. Castril and *then* someone finds the paper? Would the sale be reversed, or would it still be binding? Would Gordon legally have to give the money back to the buyer, or would the buyer have to sue him?” She shook her head. “I guess a lawyer could tell us.”

Even through the comforting fog of whatever pain meds the ER nurse had shot into my bloodstream, I could tell Olivia was asking some interesting questions.

Too interesting.

Everything about Olivia St. Clair suddenly made sense: Her determination to buy back the Crow Mountain lots from her ex-husband. Hiding the fact that she'd wrangled a huge settlement by not contesting their divorce. Desperately needing to repair her son's reputation in order to reinstate her standing in a community she once ruled.

"It's you, isn't it?" I said.

"What?" Olivia's eyes widened.

"You're Mr. Castril."

"I…I…." She glanced up. Her gaze shot past my shoulder, then upward. Panic washed over her face. "James," she whispered. "I didn't see you there."

I twisted around in my chair. James had been standing in a little alcove beside the water fountain, listening to us.

"I'm waiting for your answer, Mother. And this time, I want the truth."

****

James unlocked the door at Thompson's Motor Lodge and helped me into the room. He slid the safety chain behind us. "Wouldn't you be more comfortable coming back to our house? Since they're keeping Tess at the hospital overnight, there's no one there but Maddie and Jackson."

"What happened to Olivia? I saw her leave."

"She stormed off to Doc Turner's. That's where she always goes after a big argument."

"I heard the two of you yelling in the waiting room while they were casting my wrist."

"Are you kidding? They heard us yelling on the other side of Old Baldy Mountain."

“Can you help me…”

“Sure.” He painstakingly unbuttoned my cardigan then helped maneuver the thick plaster cast through the armhole.

“Are you sure you’re okay?” he said, staring at my bruised arms. “You look like you’ve gone three rounds with a Smoky Mountain Black Bear.”

“Yeah, too bad Halloween is six months away.”

It had taken over an hour for the nurse to get me out of my muddy clothes and bandage the cuts on my hands and ankles. I would be forced to deal with a plaster cast from my wrist to my elbow for five weeks, but at least the purplish mark on the side of my face had stopped swelling. And at least old right-handed me had broken my left wrist and could still paint. Not sure about steering Narwhal, though. That might take a miracle.

“I'm sleeping in the sweatpants and shirt Alpha brought to me at the hospital.” I threaded my arms into the red flannel plaid shirt I was sure belonged to Henry. “I like this shirt. It makes me feel like a lumberjack.” James laughed. “Tell me what Olivia said after I went into the cast room. Did she admit to posing as Mr. Castril?”

“Oh, yes.” He leaned against the bathroom sink counter while I brushed my teeth. “And would you like to know why she decided to become Mr. Castril? Because I think you’re going to be surprised. Revenge.”

“What?”

“Doc Turner and my mother have been posing as Mr. Castril together. They wanted to buy lots on Crow Mountain to redeem my reputation, but they pretended they wanted to buy the McAlister Inn to get back at

Gordon."

"For what? Being mean to you?"

"No, sweetheart. Gordon was blackmailing my mother, too."

James swirled a capful of my mouthwash in his mouth then spit it into the sink. "Gordon made her pay through the nose to keep her affair with Doc Turner secret from my father."

"But your father was having an affair, too."

"Yes, but if my father had discovered what my mother was doing before the divorce, he never would have been so generous with the settlement. God knows how Gordon found out about Mother and Doc Turner, but he did. And he blackmailed them for months until her divorce was final. All this has kind of blown me away."

"What's going to happen to the lots Mr. Castril bought on Crow Mountain? Isn't what your mother did illegal?"

"Not really. She had the money. She offered to buy them in good faith, even if it was under an assumed name. But I hope she opts out. I don't want her wasting her resources restoring my reputation. You were right when you said there are other ways to win back the respect of the community. I'd like to take your advice and try to help the artists and farmers. I hope Mother will buy the Hoskins' farm, though. They've wanted to go live with their daughter for so long, I'd like to help make that dream come true."

"Are you staying here tonight?" I laughed softly. "Rewind...*will* you stay here tonight? At least until I go to sleep?"

"Absolutely."

James turned down the bed and waited for me to crawl between the sheets. He pulled off his Timberland boots, peeled off his socks, and stretched out on top of the bedspread beside me. I nestled into the crook of his shoulder and rested my plaster cast on his stomach.

"I'd try to kiss you again," he said. "But my beard is too rough."

"It might remind me of a Fraser fir I had a close encounter with tonight."

"Never thought I'd be jealous of a tree."

I smiled. He was still wearing his mud-stained jeans and torn brown shirt. The same nurse who had bathed me and left my short hair caked with sandy grit, had bandaged his rope burned hand with thick strips of white gauze. He promised he would help me figure out a way to wash my hair in the morning with only two good hands between us.

I pressed my ear into the side of his chest and listened to the strong, steady beat of his heart. My eyelids felt like lead. "James?"

"Hmm?"

"Don't you wish you could've seen Gordon hopping from trunk to trunk on the Joyner's Christmas tree farm? Sheriff Riley said he looked like Yosemite Sam. He couldn't stop laughing about it."

"I'm just glad the bastard's in custody."

He adjusted the pillow and propped his head against the wooden headboard.

"Emory?"

"Hmm?"

"I was just noticing Portia's paintings lined up across the dresser—the watercolors she did of the Austen house. Have you looked at them closely? The house is shown from different angles, but each painting points to the same place in the yard. Out by the side near the old grape arbor."

"Only an architect would think of that."

"I think there's a wisteria bush planted there now."

I closed my eyes. Sleep began to pull me down into its thick billowy softness.

"Emory?" James' deep baritone rumbled against my ear. "I think I know where your Aunt Portia stashed her treasure."

Chapter Twenty-Three

I stood on Aunt Pris' porch and watched Will Riley remove two shovels from the trunk of the Haywood County Sheriff's car.

The piecrust table still sat upside down where it had come sailing through the window the night before. Inside the house, bloodstains from Henry's wounded shoulder streaked across the floor, the oak hall tree lay on its side like a coffin, and one of the oil lamps had been shattered. Everyone said it was a miracle the place hadn't caught fire.

I wrapped my good arm around the wooden porch post and gazed across the meadow at the brilliant azure sky. One lone crow soared overhead. A harbinger of death or a good luck sign? Its glossy black feathers reflected off the sun. The bird dipped across the horizon, leading with its sharp pointed beak, riding the breeze up and down before disappearing behind the woods I had run for my life in the night before. In the morning light, the deadly thistles were invisible, blending in with the tall grass to cunningly disguise their razor-sharp leaves.

James climbed the steps and stood beside me. "Are you ready for this?"

"As I'll ever be."

I raked my fingers through my short curls, the same curls he had washed so carefully in the sink at the

Thompson Motor Lodge. He held out his bandaged hand, blistered to the bone from holding Daisy's rope, and I took it.

Sheriff Riley rounded the corner of the house. “We've found something.”

James and I followed him up the hill to the arbor. A freshly dug hole gaped beneath a thick tangle of chopped wisteria vines. An old, rusted paint box, the kind that held brushes and little glass bottles for turpentine and water, sat on the mound of weeds and dirt.

“It's locked,” Sheriff Riley said. “Hand me one of those shovels, McBride.”

“No, wait,” I said. “I think I have the key.”

I pulled the silver chain from under my plaid shirt and dangled the key in front of James. He held up his bandaged hand helplessly.

“I’ll do it.” Riley unfastened the locket from around my neck, then opened it and shook out the little brass key. The key caught in the lock on the first try, but the box wouldn’t open. Deputy McBride, clearly the muscle in the department, banged it with his shovel a couple of times to loosen the rusted lid.

McBride opened the box and crossed himself. “Sweet Mary, Mother of God.”

For a moment, the only sound was the low whisper of the wind as it blew down the mountain and through Aunt Pris’ pear trees.

“It's the baby, Emory,” James said. “You don't have to look if you don't want to.”

“Yes. I have to look.”

“There's not much to see,” Sheriff Riley said.

I went to stand beside the little casket. The tiny

bones of Pris' son were drawn into a fetal position, barely filling half the box. Short strands of matted hair lay near the skull. A thatch of rotted fibers wound around one of the leg bones.

"What are those gray strings?" I asked.

"Probably a blanket," Riley said. "I'm surprised there's anything left after all this time. Not much of a treasure, if you ask me."

My eyes filled with tears. "Oh, but it is. This is what Portia stole from the man she loved. It's not her treasure. It's Edward's treasure."

Sheriff Riley pulled on a pair of latex gloves and extracted a zip-locked bag tucked beside the skeleton. He opened it and shook out a folded piece of paper.

"What is it, Will?" James said.

"It's a paper that says Frank Spencer turns over the McAlister Inn to Edward Gilmore as payment for all debts past or present. It's even been signed by two witnesses. Can't get more legal than that. Looks like Gordon was right. The McAlister Inn belongs to your family, Emory. How long has this paper been missing?"

"Since before Uncle Edward's death," I said. "At least two years."

Sheriff Riley shook his head. "Your aunt must've dug up this box and put it there for safekeeping. I never heard of such a thing."

"What happens now?" James asked. "Will there be an investigation into the baby's death?"

"There'll be an autopsy, of course. Then we'll take a DNA sample and check it with Emory or her aunt to make sure it's the Austen baby. After that, it's just a matter of signing a few affidavits. And burying the body."

"It's really over then?" I asked.

"We've got a confession from Gordon for your husband's death," Sheriff Riley said. "And we've found what he was after. So, yes. I would say it's over."

I stepped carefully over the mound of cut wisteria, then turned to James standing beside the trellised arch of the grape arbor. He smiled, and I thought of my parents. Preston and Alexandra Austen had smiled at each other, then mouthed the words *I love you* no matter where they'd been: from opposite ends of the table during a boring dinner party, in the middle of a concert at Albert Hall, on a crowded bus in the mountains of Peru. That's the kind of love I wanted. The kind that transcends time and space. The kind that would never betray me. From someone who could look at me and make me feel like I had turned a corner in an unfamiliar place and suddenly realized I was home.

James walked me to the front of the house. "What are you going to do now? Wait until Pris recovers then sell the inn and go back to New York?"

"I don't think I'm going anywhere," I said softly. "At least, not for a while."

"I'm glad," James said.

"You're going to think I'm crazy, but I'd like to convince Pris to give the inn to Jackson. I feel like I've misjudged him, even though he's got a lot of growing up to do. My uncle took unfair advantage of his father. The inn should stay in their family, but I don't want Gordon to have it. Maybe I'll put a condition in the agreement that Jackson has to finish school first. Then if he and Maddie get married, they can do whatever they want with it."

James laughed. "Mr. Castril will have a fit. But it's

a good idea."

We climbed the porch and gazed at the string of mountains stretching lazily across the horizon. They were my mountains now. As much a part of me as Aunt Pris and the people of Bitter Ridge I'd grown to know and love.

"I still haven't taken you hiking on the other side of Crow Mountain," James said.

"Maybe I'll paint you there one day. In your plaid shirt and your Timberland boots, sitting on a rock with a rhododendron blossom behind one ear."

"How about an eye patch and a parrot on my shoulder?"

"It might suit you. Not everyone can wear that sort of thing and get away with it."

"Could you give me a tattoo? I've always wanted a tattoo, and I'm too chicken to get one."

"How about *Love Sucks*?"

"Perfect."

"Anything else?"

"Biceps." He laughed, threading his bandaged arm through mine. "Could you give me some really big biceps?"

A word about the author…

Rebecca lives with her husband and a dog named Wilbur in the beautiful, misty mountains of East Tennessee, where the people are charming, soulful, and just a little bit crazy. She's been everything from a tax collector to a stay-at-home-mom to a professional actor and director. She loves to travel the world because it makes coming home so sweet. Her Southern roots and the affectionate appreciation she has for the rural towns she lives near inspire the settings and characters she writes about. www.rebeccaleesmith.com

Thank you for purchasing
this publication of The Wild Rose Press, Inc.

For questions or more information
contact us at
info@thewildrosepress.com.

The Wild Rose Press, Inc.
www.thewildrosepress.com

www.ingramcontent.com/pod-product-compliance
Lightning Source LLC
La Vergne TN
LVHW020536100826
845148LV00010B/1483